Praise for
Bone Harvest

"The most satisfying story yet from Logue."
—Minneapolis *Star Tribune*

"Fine writing, a charming setting and an attractive and intelligent heroine add up to a satisfying and pleasurable read."
—*Publishers Weekly*

"Logue's characters are likable, down-to-earth types. [*Bone Harvest*] is filled with suspense, and she takes readers back to the old crime in a creepily effective way. The ending shocks and saddens. This is the third in a series that keeps getting stronger. If only Logue would write faster."
—*Romantic Times*

"Ample suspense and swift turnings to keep readers up well past bedtime. For larger collections and fans of down-to-earth regional mystery writers, such as Jance, Barr, or Pickard."
—*Booklist*

Also by Mary Logue

POISON HEART

BONE HARVEST

A Claire Watkins Mystery

Mary Logue

FAWCETT

BALLANTINE BOOKS • NEW YORK

Bone Harvest is a work of fiction. Names, characters, places, and incidents are the products of the author's imagination or are used fictitiously. Any resemblance to actual events, locales, or persons, living or dead, is entirely coincidental.

2005 Fawcett Books Mass Market Edition

Copyright © 2004 by Mary Logue
Excerpt from *Poison Heart* copyright © 2005 by Mary Logue

Published in the United States by Fawcett Books, an imprint of The Random House Publishing Group, a division of Random House, Inc., New York.

Fawcett is a registered trademark and the Fawcett colophon is a trademark of Random House, Inc.

Originally published in hardcover in the United States by Ballantine Books, an imprint of The Random House Publishing Group, a division of Random House, Inc., in 2004.

This edition contains an excerpt from the forthcoming book *Poison Heart* by Mary Logue. This excerpt has been set for this edition only and may not reflect the final content of the forthcoming edition.

ISBN 0-345-46223-8

Cover illustration: Don Sipley

Printed in the United States of America

www.ballantinebooks.com

OPM 9 8 7 6 5 4 3 2 1

For Elizabeth Gunn,
a woman of wonderful courage and energy,
a great writer, and a not-half-bad talker

Therefore the land mourns,
and all who dwell in it languish,
and also the beasts of the field,
and the birds of the air;
and even the fish of the sea are taken away.
—HOSEA 4:3

July 7, 1952

It was a warm day in Pepin County, Wisconsin, so warm it was hard to tell where your skin ended and the air began. Although it was late in the afternoon, the sun was still high above the treetops. The clouds curled in the sky as if they could grab the blue of it.

On the Schuler farm, the chickens circled the trees in the front yard, scratching for seed. Cicadas cracked out their gentle, grinding song, the undertone of all summer nights. A soft wind stirred the sheets on the line.

The farm was located four miles from Fort St. Antoine and seven miles from Plum City, up on the edge of the bluffs. Standing at a high point in the fields, you could see Lake Pepin stretched out far below, shimmering in the sun.

For dinner there would be a pot roast, new potatoes creamed with sweet peas, radishes fresh from the garden, salad, and, of course, German chocolate cake for Arlette's first birthday. She was the youngest of the five Schuler children. Denny was ten, Louise eight, Schubert six, and Elisabeth three.

The table had been set by the children. Bertha Schuler was finishing up in the kitchen, the baby underfoot. The rest of the children were scattered around the farmhouse, reading or playing. Except for Denny. He was out in the barn with his father, helping with the milking.

Then the quiet was broken. The baby reached up a hand and jerked at the tablecloth. A spoon hit her on the head and she started to cry. Bertha stuck her head out the door and called that dinner was ready. The clock in the hallway struck the half hour.

And the first shot was fired.

CHAPTER 1

———+———

Rich fingered the small package in his pocket as he walked down the hill with Claire to the farmer's market in the park—his mother's diamond engagement ring. His mother had given it to him a few days ago with her blessings.

Meg ran ahead of them, skipping and leaping over imaginary boulders in the road. Her legs looked as long as the rest of her body. She was shooting up. Eleven years old. Not the little girl he had first met almost three years ago.

Claire held his other hand and carried a big colorful plastic satchel that she claimed was her shopping bag. At the bottom of the bag was her cell phone. Claire was on call to the sheriff's department this weekend.

Meg was going to a friend's house for a sleepover tonight—and Rich had invited Claire to his house for a romantic dinner. He had it all planned out. He would ask her tonight.

He was slightly nervous because they hadn't really discussed marriage. But, he assured himself, their lives were intermingling as easily as the St. Croix flowed into the Mississippi, twenty miles to the north. They had been seeing each other for long enough. He knew he wanted to live with Claire.

He squeezed her hand. She turned and smiled at him.

She had let her dark hair grow and today was wearing it loosely braided. A thread or two of silver hinted at her age. She was wearing cutoff jeans, yellow flip-flops, and a big T-shirt that she and Meg had tie-dyed yellow and blue. He wanted to be connected to her in a tangible way. He never wanted to lose her.

The farmer's market was held in the park every Saturday morning during the summer months. It was organized by a few of the local farmers who grew transitional or totally organic crops. Ted Wallis brought his honey to sell. Penny Swenson and her husband Louie brought their brick-oven-baked bread. Other farmers showed up occasionally with strawberries, or asparagus, or morels when they were in season.

The mainstay of the market was the produce from the Daniels farm. They were a couple in their late thirties who had immigrated to Pepin County from the Twin Cities about ten years ago. They had moved down to start an organic farm. At first they just sold produce from a stand. But they were now bringing vegetables into Red Wing to sell at an organic outlet, and they had also been instrumental in setting up the farmer's market.

As he approached the stands, Rich saw a flash of red. Nine months he had been waiting. A pile of red fruits. The first of the tomatoes. He walked right to them and picked up a couple. If he had a salt shaker he would have stood right there and eaten one. His mouth watered just thinking about the first bite. His mother used to tell him that his grandfather had called them love apples and had eaten them with sugar and cream.

A plate of sliced tomatoes with a little salt and pepper, oil and vinegar, and freshly cut basil would be the perfect side dish to his meal tonight. A good sign of what the evening might bring.

"Two per customer," Celia Daniels told him. "We're

trying to spread them out so everyone can take a couple home."

"Sounds fair. How do you manage to get ripe tomatoes this early?"

"The greenhouse makes it all possible. This is the earliest I've ever had them. July first. Well before the Fourth of July. Can you imagine?"

He carefully selected the most perfect two he could find. Round, ripe, and red. Claire was busy picking through the large selections of greens and lettuces. Meg had run off with the two Daniels kids to play on the swings.

Then he heard a distressing sound. If he hadn't known what it was, he might have thought it was a mother bird fending off an attack on its young. But he recognized the strident beep. Claire's phone was ringing. She glanced over at him and reluctantly reached into her bag.

"Watkins," she said, and then turned her back to him and listened.

His hands shook lightly on the steering wheel, but he just repeated the phrase over and over again: *First step done, first step done.*

He parked down the old field road that no one used anymore. Most people didn't even know it was there. He drove the road ten times a year in order to keep it from growing over completely—once in April, once in May, twice the next three months, then back to once in September, and once in October. Then the snow came and he didn't have to worry about the road until the next year.

This was the start of his plan. So far it was working. He didn't feel too nervous. Just a little excited. It was so inevitable. It had to be done. He had thought it through for many years and he was ready. What he had done

today was the first step. There would be many more. He
hoped they would all go as smoothly as this one.

And in the end, he might get what he wanted.

He got out of his truck, went around to the back, and
opened the topper. He reached into the bed of the truck
and grabbed the two-gallon jug. He put that into the
backpack he had brought with him. Then he wrapped
his arms around the two boxes. It was a lot to carry, but
he didn't want to make two trips. He had been away
from home for too long already. He wanted to get this
stuff safely stowed away.

He knew the number of steps it took to get to the hiding place. He counted them as he went. Each step had a
number, and if he thought that number he would get
there. It was a way of holding on to the world.

The world was out of balance. It had been so for
nearly fifty years. Only he could see it. Only he could
change it. He had lived with this knowledge most of his
life. It was time to rectify it.

He walked down the hill and into the shade of an old
oak. He stopped for a few moments to catch his breath
and to cool off. The day was a hot one. But he didn't
relinquish his burden. He couldn't put it down until he
got to where he would store it. It was the way it had to
be. When you decided on a plan, you had to keep to it.
There was only one way to do most things.

Not far now. The steps counted off in his mind as he
came up to the indentation in the earth. He wondered if
anyone in the county even knew this was here anymore.
Gone out of use many years ago. A wooden cover over
what looked to be an old pump. He knew what it was.
He had been there when it had been dug.

Now he could set the boxes down. He put them right
next to where his feet would go. He bent over and lifted

the hasp on a slanted wooden door. He raised it up and propped it open with a stick.

When he looked down into the hole, he saw a long, thick bull snake slither across the rock wall of the hole. Just so it wasn't a rattler, he didn't care. Regular snakes didn't bother him. He liked to see them around. They ate other critters. He had only seen one rattler this year, three bull snakes, and fourteen garter snakes. Slow year.

The ladder was in place. He grabbed the boxes and carefully stepped down the ladder into the damp coolness. He had put a plastic tarp on the floor of the hole for the boxes. He set them down and then took off his backpack and put the jug on top of the boxes.

His supplies. He had what he needed. He knew how it would happen. Step by step. They all had a number. But what he didn't know, what he couldn't control, was how many people would be dead at the end.

It was inconvenient for Claire, living in Fort St. Antoine and working for the sheriff's department located in the county seat of Durand, that they were as far apart as two towns could be and still be in Pepin County. She drove the thirty miles at a consistent five miles per hour over the speed limit. All Sheriff Talbert had said on the phone was that there had been a burglary. He hadn't said where, or what had been stolen, but by the tone of his voice she knew it was important.

The minimum staff was working this Saturday morning. Judy was manning the phones. She looked up from the magazine she was reading and said, "Everyone's back in the sheriff's office. They're waiting on you."

Claire walked into his office and found two men sitting in chairs across from the sheriff. She didn't recognize either of them.

The sheriff looked as if he had been pulled from the

golf course. He was wearing canary-yellow pants with a blue-and-white-striped polo shirt. "Claire, I'd like you to meet Ron Sorenson and Petey Hauer. They are the president and vice president of the Farmer's Cooperative. Claire is a deputy with my office and acting as chief investigator."

The only investigator, Claire thought as she proffered her hand. The two men stood up and shook hands with Claire. She smiled and said hello. She noticed that they didn't smile back.

She guessed Ron Sorenson to be close to sixty: thinning white-blond hair, sunburned face, and soft blue eyes. Not handsome, but appealing. He had the look of a minister even though he was dressed in jeans and a button-down shirt. Petey—probably not much older than thirty—was chunky, short, dark-haired with deep brown eyes. Reminded her of a chipmunk.

There wasn't a fourth chair in the room, so she stepped around the men until she was next to the sheriff's desk and perched on a filing cabinet. The two men took their seats again after she had settled.

"I'm not sure I know what the Farmer's Cooperative is," Claire admitted. She had found out early in her career that it never did any good to pretend to know something she didn't. It always caught up with her in the end.

"We sell farm equipment, feed, fertilizer, and weed control to all our member farmers in the area."

"The area is?"

"Mainly Pierce and Pepin counties."

Claire turned and looked at the sheriff.

"I called you in, Claire, because they had a break-in last night at the warehouse. Behind their main office. You've seen it. It's that big cream-colored pole barn just about a half a mile east of Durand on Twenty-five."

"Past the Dairy Queen?" she asked.

All the men nodded.

"What was taken?"

The sheriff waved at Sorenson. "Why don't you explain it to Claire?"

"He took two boxes of Parazone and a two-gallon jug of Caridon," he said gravely.

Claire didn't recognize these names. "They are . . . ?"

"Sorry. Pesticides. Parazone is an herbicide and Caridon is an insecticide. Fairly common pesticides that we stock regularly."

Claire didn't know what to say. It didn't sound like much of a haul to her. Certainly not enough to generate the tension she felt in the room. All the men were looking at her. What did she not understand?

The sheriff jumped in. "Tell her how much you figure the whole haul was worth, Ron."

Sorenson cleared his throat as if he hated to talk about such things. "Between sixty and seventy thousand dollars."

Claire tried not to let the surprise show on her face. Not your ordinary pesticides, she figured. That amount probably equaled what the two men earned in a year. A loss like that could really hurt a small business, especially a cooperative.

"What exactly happened?" she asked.

"We don't know much," Sorenson answered. He appeared to be both the president and the man in charge. "If the lock off the back storeroom hadn't been busted we might not even have noticed that anything was gone until we did inventory. No one saw anything that I've been able to find out."

"Nothing else was taken?" This puzzled Claire.

"Nope. Just those two pesticides. It's surprising, since we've got a lot of valuable equipment on the floor that he could have hauled out of there."

"I'm guessing these pesticides aren't something I'd be able to pick up at the Home Depot?" she asked.

"Right," Sorenson said, looking her in the eyes, then added, "You need to know what you're doing to handle these products. If the wrong person got hold of them, someone could get hurt."

CHAPTER 2

Sorenson opened the passenger-side door to his pickup truck and watched Watkins climb in. Nice-looking woman. His wife had once been as handsome. After all but one of the kids had left home, she had continued cooking for a big family and then ate most of it herself. She had filled out well past what could be seen as attractive. He still loved her, but he didn't like looking at her as much as he once had.

As he walked around the truck and climbed in his side, he thought about what the neighbors would think if they saw him driving through town with a strange woman. Part of him liked the idea. But it made him nervous that he had to be working with a woman on this problem. He was used to the company of men.

"How long have you been president of the cooperative?" Watkins asked him once they were settled in the truck and he had turned onto the main street.

"A year. We take turns."

"At being president?"

"Yup. Nobody really wants to do it. It just means more work. Take today. I should be out in the fields. Here I am dicking around with this burglary business." He needed to watch himself. "Excuse my language."

The woman deputy laughed. It was a nice, solid laugh, no pretense. It came from her stomach but had a little sweetness in it. "Hey, don't worry. I was a cop in Minneapolis. I've heard everything."

He felt a smile tug at his lips. "I bet."

They rode for a few moments in silence. Sorenson debated whether he should turn the air-conditioning on. He tried to use it as little as possible. Cost him in gas and he wasn't sure it was good for his health. When it was hot, he thought it was better if you stayed one temperature. But he worried that maybe the deputy was uncomfortable.

"Cool enough for you?" he asked.

"I'm fine. After that winter, I'll take all the warm days we can get."

"The corn is sure liking it."

"More than knee-high, isn't it?" she commented.

"Mine's up to my thigh," he told her with pride. Most of his field was in feed corn, but he had planted a few rows of sweet corn close to the house. He could hardly wait until they could start eating it. Super Sweet, it was called, and the name was accurate.

"Tell me about these pesticides," she said.

"Well, like I said, one's an insecticide and one's an herbicide. Both of them are pretty common. Caridon is used mainly against grasshoppers and some weevils. We've had a few this year. Doesn't look like they should be too bad. Parazone is used as a general herbicide; controls weeds and grasses. It's usually applied to the fields a few weeks before planting, when the weeds are about half a foot high."

"Is it too late in the season to use it now?"

"I'd say."

"Do you have any ideas about who did this?"

"I'd hate to say off the top of my head." Sorenson kept his eyes on the road. The cooperative building was coming right up. He was wondering who was working today. He tried not to think about Ray, his seventeen-year-old son. He had been getting in trouble lately. What made Sorenson nervous was that he didn't know where the kid had been last night. He hoped Ray was just hanging out with his friends. Although that could be what was getting him in trouble—his friends. He wanted to talk to his son before he accused him of anything.

The truck bumped over the ruts in the dirt parking lot. He pulled right up to the building, trying to park the vehicle as close to the wall as possible and as far out of the sun. If he planned it right, he wouldn't need to turn the air-conditioning on when he drove the deputy back to the sheriff's office.

"The cooperative is open today?" she asked.

"Yeah, this is a busy time for us right now. Farmers working nonstop in the fields. We cut hours way back in the winter."

He hopped out of the truck. Before he could walk around to open the door for the deputy she had climbed down. He guessed he should treat her like a cop and not like a woman. She followed him into the store.

At the entrance, she stopped and looked around the warehouse. He looked around it too, trying to see it the way she might. Nothing fancy about the place. They had opened the back sliding door and a nice breeze was moving through the space. Riding lawn mowers were lined up face-out from along the far side of the warehouse. They were having a sale on picnic tables and there were a couple set up near the cash register. A sweet dusty smell, a mixture of birdseed and various ground meal products, filled the air.

He glanced over at the register. Tim was ringing up a pile of items for Kate Thompson and her bevy of six kids. He remembered that his son wasn't working today.

Watkins turned and looked at him. "Where are the pesticides kept?"

"We keep them locked in the back."

"Sounds like a good idea."

"A precaution that didn't exactly work."

"Have you ever had anything stolen before?" she asked.

"The occasional item, like any retailer. Small hand tools such as wire cutters or hammers, things that fit into pockets. A few years back, some guy tried to walk off with a lawn mower. We caught him halfway down the next block, pushing the thing as fast as he could go. That's about it."

"Would it be possible to resell these pesticides?"

"Maybe. I don't know who'd buy them. It's not like there's a black market for pesticides. But it's possible."

"So do you think someone stole them for use on a farm?"

"More likely, but it's an odd time of year to use either one. Not so much the Caridon, but certainly the Parazone."

"How did the burglar get into the warehouse?"

"I think he must have had a key. There was no sign of forced entry into the building."

He walked her back to the storage area. "However, he didn't have a key to the storage area, so he pounded the lock right off the door." He pointed at the fastener hanging by its hinges, the door bashed in like it had been hammered on. A chair was pushed up to the door to keep it closed. He pulled the chair away.

"How did he do that?"

"One of our mauls. We found it lying right on the floor by the door. Don't worry. We didn't touch it. I put it in a big bag and set it in my office."

"Who all has a key to the warehouse?"

"Petey and I. Our manager, Cliff Snowden. Any one of our past employees might have a key. Who knows how many are floating around." He stopped for a moment and then added, "And the two young guys who sometimes open up. Tim Loch and Ray Sorenson."

"Is Ray any relation?"

"He's my son." That was the second reason he had a bad feeling.

She looked at him and nodded, not saying anything.

"There's one more thing you have to see. He left something for us. We haven't touched them. Only Petey and I know about this. We've kept it quiet." He ushered her into the storage room and pointed at the shelf where the pesticides had been.

There, sitting on the shelf in a row, were seven oddly shaped cream-colored pellets, all about an inch long.

In midwinter, when cold froze everything out of the air, Rich forgot what a July night could smell like. In order to store it up, he closed his eyes to take in the scents more fully. The smells rode the humid air as if they had been simmering all the warm day—a frothy stew of sweet wild roses, soft grasses, even a hint of the earth's dankness. A potent brew.

When Rich opened his eyes, he saw that the soft blue was falling from the sky, the lake was turning a darker teal, and the bluffs on the far side of the river had gone somber green like the underside of pine boughs. He sat on his side porch, watching the sun set. So close to the summer solstice, it was past nine o'clock when it finally went down.

He was waiting for Claire.

Claire had called twenty minutes ago and said she was on her way.

He wasn't going to get mad. That did no good. And he

certainly understood, because, from time to time, his pheasant business called for long hours with little regard to his personal life.

But he didn't feel he was in the right mood to ask her to marry him.

He had to work up to it. He wanted her to be in the right place. He wanted it to be a moment they could both remember with pleasure in the long years to come. So he had tucked the ring into the top drawer of his dresser. It would come out again soon. He didn't want to put it off for long.

Claire's patrol car pulled into the driveway. She jumped out and rushed up the steps. Because of her haste, he worried that she needed to check back into the department, that she wouldn't be able to stay. But then she kissed him and swung around to stare in the direction he had been looking. The last glint of the sun lay across the horizon like a thin red thread.

"I didn't completely miss the sunset," she said, leaning into him. His arms automatically went around her waist.

"Nope."

She turned in his arms and kissed him again, more slowly, with more feeling. He felt as if he had been waiting for her for a long time. Somehow they fit together.

Then she pulled back and smiled up at him. "I haven't completely missed our date, either, have I?"

"Doesn't look like it."

"Are there still things to eat? I'm famished."

"I waited for you."

"You are the best guy. What have I done to deserve you?"

"Existed." He could tell that she was pumped up about whatever had taken her away the whole day long. When she got her teeth into something, she seemed more full of energy, as if her whole life had been elevated a notch or two.

He enjoyed watching her dig into what she was doing, but he did worry sometimes about the toll it might be taking on her. Then he laughed at himself. Doctors, lawyers, and stockbrokers probably all had more stress in their lives. Serious crime didn't happen very often in Pepin County, the smallest county in the state of Wisconsin.

The table was set for two. The ice had melted in the water glasses, but that didn't matter.

"I'm going to go change," she told him.

She ran off to his bedroom, where she kept a few pairs of pants and some shirts. He had given Claire her own drawer.

Earlier in the afternoon, when he realized she might not be on time for dinner, he had modified the menu. Boiled potatoes became cold potato salad. He had made a pheasant ragout that could be reheated rather than the grilled pheasant he had planned on.

He turned the heat on under the ragout. He brought out the fresh loaf of bread he had bought at the farmer's market that morning, and then the plate of thick-sliced tomatoes.

She appeared in a tight white T-shirt and a pair of jeans. Her hair was loose. She looked lovely.

"Wine?" he asked.

"You bet."

He poured them both a glass and they clinked them together. After taking a sip, he started serving their food. She looked at him over the rim of her glass and smiled. "This looks wonderful."

"What went on today?" he asked. He could tell she was dying to talk about it.

She launched right in. "Somebody stole two kinds of pesticides from the Farmer's Cooperative. Do you do any business with them?"

"Once in a while I get some feed from the co-op. Who's in charge over there this year? Sorenson?"

She nodded, then added, "He's pretty upset."

"He's a very conscientious guy."

"Yeah, I guess you're right. I think he feels responsible. And these are no lightweight pesticides we're talking about here. He gave me the warning labels off both the products. I looked them over before I left the office tonight. Both of them are fatal if you mishandle them. You probably know all this, country boy that you are." She lifted her fork and took a bite of the ragout. "This is beyond good."

"Any ideas who did it? Someone got a grudge against the cooperative, against Sorenson?" he asked.

"Could be. We'll start out by checking anyone who has a connection to it, including former employees. One of the kids who works there is Sorenson's son."

"Awkward."

"I've got a lot of people to talk to tomorrow. We fingerprinted the place, but I'll be surprised if we find anything. Unless it was some kids doing it for a prank. Anyone serious would make sure they didn't leave any prints."

"I don't like the idea of some kid running around with those products. Thank God school isn't on. Can you imagine what could happen if a kid decided to fumigate the school?"

"I don't think that's what's going on. Somehow pesticides don't seem glamorous enough for a kid to use. Probably someone who decided they'd been paying high prices for all these products long enough. We'll check on

all the farmers who have bought these products in the
past. Someone down on their luck? Who knows?"

"Well, if anyone can find out what's going on, you
can."

"I hope so. If some farmer decided to steal them and
then just use them on their fields, we might never know."

Claire was holding something in. He could tell.

She took a sip of wine and then looked up at him and
said, "Whoever did it left us a little memento to think
on." Claire paused as she swirled the wine around in her
glass. He saw fear in her eyes as she said, "Bones."

It was exactly twelve o'clock. The second of July. Time
for step two. It had to be done the way it had to be done.
He sat in the truck and waited until it was three minutes
after midnight.

He had mixed the spray carefully. He had read the
sheets on it a couple times over. One fluid ounce for
three gallons of water. He poured it into the pump that
he had used to spray fertilizer on his lawn. It was all
loaded into the back of the truck. He had an old tarp
wrapped around it so it wouldn't tip over.

You had to be very careful with this stuff. He knew
that. It was like handling dynamite. Never get too cocky.
It would come back on you. He was wearing a long-
sleeved shirt and long pants even though it was still close
to eighty degrees out. He had his waterproof gloves in
the truck. And he had brought an old pair of sunglasses,
even though the sun had already gone down. Might
look funny, but he didn't think anyone would notice.

He didn't think anyone would be around.

The town died at night. A few bars had a scattering of
cars around them, but there wasn't much to do in Durand anymore after dark, not like it had been when he

was a kid. Then there had been restaurants and movie theaters. Friday night had been the night everyone went to town. Didn't happen anymore.

He checked his watch again. Time to get in place to do the next step. This was step two. He had thought about it and this needed to be the second step. Everyone would understand when they knew the truth. It would all make sense.

He drove the truck up the hill on the west side of town, away from the Chippewa River. No one even passed him on the road. He drove past the sheriff's department, kept going up the hill, then pulled over on the shoulder for two minutes. There were three cars parked in front of the building. He would have to risk it. It would only take him one minute. He had practiced.

He drove back to the sheriff's department and parked right in front. That way if someone drove by, they would think he was there on business. For this run he was driving an old truck he had put in storage and he had rubbed mud on the license plates so it would be hard to read. Better to be cautious.

After taking the pump out of the back of the truck, he put on his gloves and sunglasses. He kept the pump hidden in the brown-paper grocery bag with just the nozzle sticking out. He walked around the side of the building and came to the front stairs.

In front of the building, next to the stairs leading up to the doors, was a big flower garden. He knew the names of all the flowers because of his mother: petunias, roses, snapdragons, pansies. Allysum encircled the others. He loved the smell of that small white flower. Intoxicatingly sweet.

He had to be careful not to breathe.

He looked at his watch: 12:07.

He took a deep breath, then held it. Seven passes over the garden, a thick mist coming out of the end of the nozzle.

There had been seven of them. He wanted no one to forget that.

CHAPTER 3

Had there been a frost last night? Debby Lowe wondered as she stared at the remains of the flower bed. For a moment she could think of no other explanation for what was in front of her eyes. She was standing outside the Pepin County office building that included the sheriff's department, where she worked as a receptionist.

Friday afternoon, when she had left work, the flowers had looked fine—the allysum mounding up nicely, the snapdragons taller than she had ever seen, the marigolds full of bright orange flowers and many buds. She had been using Miracle-Gro and it was doing the trick. She watered them religiously, checking on them often.

Debby had planted all the flowers herself after consulting with the design person at the garden center. The sheriff had let her take on the job of planting the garden as part of her normal workload. She couldn't believe her luck that she was going to get paid to garden. She loved it more than anything else in the world and dreamed that someday she might be able to take classes and go into landscape design.

Debby remembered her last glance at the flowers—they had filled the bed with their bright colors. This morning they looked blasted. Dried, shriveled, straw-colored growths. Had they been through some sort of small nuclear winter?

What could have happened to her flowers?

Had someone done something to them? Sprayed them with weed killer? Why would anyone do such a mean thing? She felt like sitting down on the sidewalk and howling; then she got mad.

She ran up the steps with determination. She would not let someone get away with this awful act of vandalism. The deputy sheriffs weren't the only ones who could solve a crime.

She walked up to her desk and stopped only long enough to drop her purse on top of all her work. Judy gave her a look, but Debby didn't want to talk to her. She was going to take it right to the top. She strode through the department and knocked on the door to the sheriff's office.

His voice boomed through the door, "Come on in."

When she pushed into the room, she was surprised to see four faces turn her way: the sheriff's, two deputies, and an older man she had seen before around town, but whose name she didn't remember.

Debby felt her lips quiver. She wasn't accustomed to all this attention. But the flower bed was her responsibility. Gathering herself together, she thought of what her bed of flowers looked like now—not even good enough for compost. All her work for the last two months destroyed.

"Debby?" The sheriff rose from behind his desk as he said her name. His face was full of concern for her. Everyone in the room seemed to be staring at her.

She tried to say something, but the words stuck in her throat. They were all waiting for her to speak.

Such a horrible little act, killing the flowers in the bed in front of the sheriff's office. It worried Claire. It felt big-

ger than how it appeared. She sensed a terrible anger behind the devastation.

A group of people gathered around in front of the
flower bed as if standing at a funeral. Debby sobbed and
Judy tried to comfort her. As soon as they could determine that the bed wasn't still lethal, they should pull up
all the plants so Debby wouldn't have to look at them
anymore.

Claire wondered how long it would be before the
ground could be planted again.

Ron Sorenson crouched, examining the destroyed flowers. "It could be our guy. Hard to tell by looking. But the
desiccation is consistent with Parazone. I don't know
what else would work this fast or this effectively."

"If it is Parazone, is it still dangerous?" she asked, not
knowing if that was the right term to use.

"Well, this product has an REI of at least twelve
hours. Do we know what time this happened?"

"All I can tell you for sure is it happened after dark
and before morning. What do you mean, REI?"

"Sorry. Restricted-entry interval. Depending on how
heavy it was sprayed, people should stay away from it
for twelve to twenty-four hours."

"So should we all be standing here?" she asked him.

"Probably not."

Claire relayed the information to the sheriff and he
shooed everyone back into the building, except Claire
and Sorenson. They stepped back from the garden and
continued to look at it.

"What can you tell me?" Claire asked.

Sorenson pulled on his nose and stared at the devas-
tated flower bed. "Whoever it was knew what he was
doing. He covered the whole bed and he did it pretty
evenly. The desiccation is thorough and complete. That's
how Parazone works. It dries up all the green plant tis-

sue. I figure he used a pump sprayer to do such a small area and to get such an even application. He didn't get much on the lawn. The grass around the bed doesn't look bad at all. He was very careful."

Claire was amazed, as she often was, by what an expert could tell you about a subject you knew nothing about. She would have noticed little of what Sorenson had seen. "So he knows what he's doing."

Sorenson nodded.

"I'm not sure that makes me feel better," said Claire. She handed him a pair of plastic gloves. "I thought we both might need these."

"I'll pick a plant and give it to our agronomist. He should be able to tell for sure what pesticide was applied to this bed."

After pulling on her plastic gloves, Claire reached into her pocket for a plastic bag. "I'll be doing the same with the crime bureau."

Sorenson looked over at her. "A word of warning— when you get near the plants, try not to breathe."

"Okay." She pulled on her gloves, inhaled deeply, and went in for a plant. She tugged at a large marigold that was right in the middle of the patch. It must have had roots that went down to China. She was almost ready to give up on it when it came loose from the soil and she landed on her butt.

That was when she saw the hint of white in the flower bed. She needed to breathe, so she stuffed the plant into her bag, stood up, and backed off again.

Sorenson had his plant in a bag and he appeared ready to leave.

"Wait a minute. I think I see something." Claire pulled another plastic bag out of her pocket and, again, took a deep breath. She walked in toward the flower bed, ducked her head down so she was on the level she had been when she was sitting, and examined the white object again. She inched up to it, put her gloved hand in the bed, and came out with a white bone the length of a matchstick.

No way of knowing if it was human or not until the lab reported on the bones she had already sent in to them.

She looked over at Sorenson and held up the bone. "I think it's our guy."

Harold Peabody loved coming in to work on Sundays. It was so quiet in the newspaper office. He had worshiped at his typewriter for many years. The town shut down and his office on Main Street was his private sanctum. Neither of his two reporters ever bothered to show their faces on Sundays. They were young and probably off gallivanting.

The missus understood. She never bothered anymore to ask him if he wanted to go to church. He went on Easter and on Christmas. If the choir was putting on a special performance, he might go. He liked singing the hymns, the old hymns. God and he had an understanding: God could watch over the world and Harold Peabody would watch over Pepin County.

Harold had been working on the *Durand Daily* for fifty-one years. It had truly been a daily when he first started writing as a cub reporter in 1950. Old Mr. Lundberg owned it then. Harold had bought it from him in 1970. After ten years, he stopped publishing the Saturday and Sunday editions. They had changed from Linotype to offset press shortly after that. Saved a lot of money, but he missed the smell of the hot type being spit out by the machine, and reading the paper upside down on its metal bed.

He didn't figure he'd be at it much longer. He wondered if he put the paper up for sale if anyone would even buy it. Revenues weren't high, but he had his steady customers who advertised every week. The community counted on his paper to tell them who was getting married, who had died, and who was having a rummage sale. In this rural community an announcement for a wedding was often made in the paper rather than the couple sending out individual invitations, since everyone in town was usually invited.

Maybe he'd retire in the next year or two and start to work on his memoirs. That Frank McCourt had done so well with *his* memoirs. Americans found terrible Irish childhoods so romantic and exotic. Would they feel the same about a tough Wisconsin childhood? He remembered his family trying to make it through the Depression years. Many nights they ate beans. Some nights they didn't eat. Harder to look at your own poor. Nothing romantic about that. But he didn't think the young people of today realized how tough it had been during those years. It might be worth trying to write about it so that the Depression wasn't completely forgotten.

He had been one of the lucky ones. He had been sickly, so he couldn't help out that much in the fields. And he had been bright. His mother had fought for him and kept him going to school, years after most children quit. He had been the first child in his family to graduate from college at the University of Wisconsin at Madison.

He was working on his usual Sunday-afternoon project—the column called "Fifty Years Ago Today." It was his excuse to spend hours looking through the archives, remembering the past, studying it. *How little we seem to learn from it,* he thought. And yet, there had been no big world wars for nearly sixty years now. That was something to be thankful for.

Agnes and he were childless. After they found out they

couldn't have children, they talked about adopting, but they just never got around to it. To be truthful, he figured they liked their lives the way they were. But sometimes, on his Sunday afternoons, when he was paging through a century's worth of news, he wondered about the future. He felt oddly adrift from it. Because he had no progeny, he felt he didn't really care what happened to the world. He heard so many people go on about the sacredness of human life, and yet every day some small creature, the end of a species, was dying. No one did too much about that. He thought the world might be just as well off without any humans. Such egotistical critters. Who knew what wonderful being might come to take their place?

This was one of the reasons he didn't go to church. Everyone there seemed to want to believe that God, the so-called higher power, was a kind of father. Harold didn't buy it. He did believe in a power, but it was beyond words. In the day, he would stare into the blueness of the sky and dive into it. At night, he fell into the stars. Both movements of falling gave him the same feeling he had when he tried to imagine the vast extent of this power. *So beyond us. Yet we try to reach it with our minds.* Harold figured it was good exercise and did it often, but felt like most religions tried to bring God so close to humans that the word lost everything it might mean.

The clock on the wall struck the hour and his mind came back to the office. Every wall lined with bookshelves, every bookshelf filled to the point of collapse. Agnes didn't dare set foot in the place. She was afraid that a pile of books might fall and bury her.

More and more often he felt himself leaving the world around him to dwell in the landscape of his mind. At least he had seen no evidence of Alzheimer's. He just tended to drift off frequently.

He didn't believe one could think too much. As he got older, he felt his mind enlarge. Not the real shape of it, but its ability to sense how large everything was and take it in. He loved this feeling. The universe was bigger than human beings. That was all there was to it. They could come or they could go, but the universe would endure forever. That was as close to religion as he got.

He pulled himself back to the task at hand. He needed to get the column done. What had gone on fifty years ago this week? The Korean conflict was just heating up. McCarthy was beginning to make his presence felt, and wasn't it a shame he was one of the senators from Wisconsin. Even though he hadn't voted for him, Harold had always felt bad that his home state had inflicted that madman on the country.

Harold pulled out a stack of papers and started reading through the ones from the first week in July 1952. One article jumped out at him. He leaned closer and read it through. It had been the biggest crime that had ever taken place in the county. He remembered the incident well. Reporters had descended upon Durand from all over the country to get the news. It had horrified the state for many months. It had never been solved.

CHAPTER 4

The boy was growing out of his body. Claire watched him come into the sheriff's department and then stood to let him know she saw him. Ray Sorenson. He was his father's son—taller than his father, over six feet, hair like dried wheat, big hands, sunburned nose. Not a handsome kid, but one with potential. He just wasn't put together right yet. Time would tell.

As he walked toward her, he hunched his shoulders and dragged his feet. If he stood up straight and tall, he would be closer to being a man, Claire thought. Maybe he wasn't ready for that yet.

"My dad said you wanted to talk to me." His eyes were on the floor.

"Thanks for coming by, Ray. I'm a deputy sheriff for the county. Claire Watkins, but you can just call me Claire. I assume you know what happened at the cooperative?"

He nodded, standing with his weight on one side of his body and then shifting it to the other side. His cutoff jeans hung loose and low on him; she imagined them caught on his hipbones. A big black T-shirt covered the top of the jeans so nothing inappropriate showed. Nike tennis shoes with the shoelaces trailing and the tongues hanging out completed the ensemble. But he looked clean.

"Sit down." She pushed a chair his way. "Can I get you a Coke?"

Ray raised his head at the suggestion and she saw that his eyes were like his father's—light blue, like cornflowers. A Scandinavian blue. They seemed to draw light to his face. "Yeah, a Coke would be great."

"Hot out there, isn't it?"

She walked to the vending machine and got them both Cokes. She didn't usually drink colas, but decided to make an exception on this hot summer day. Also, it would be good to join him in a drink—he might talk easier.

She handed him the Coke and he popped the tab and drank half the can in one swallow. "Thirsty?" she asked.

"Yeah, I just got up," he told her. "Didn't have time to eat anything. This is breakfast."

"Ray, please sit down. I need to ask you some questions."

He folded himself into the chair next to her desk.

"Where were you Friday night?"

She could see his face fall in on itself. "Just out."

"I'm not your parents. You don't need to worry about what you tell me. I'm not going to give you a scolding. This is serious. I do need to know where you were and what you were doing. Were you with your friends?"

"Yeah."

"All night?"

"Yeah."

"Can you give me their names?"

He lifted his head and looked out from under straw-colored eyebrows. "Do I have to?"

"Is there any reason you wouldn't want to?" she asked him, surprised at his reticence. She was just looking for an alibi.

His face tinged red. "Well, one of them might get in trouble."

Claire thought she knew what was going on. "You have a girlfriend?"

Ray looked at her like she had just guessed the right answer on a quiz show, mouth slightly ajar. She would wait him out on this question.

She took a sip of her Coke. Not a bad drink, but a little too sweet for her. It needed ice and a lemon slice floating in it.

"Are you going to have to talk to her?" he asked.

"How late were you out together?"

He ducked his head and then came up for air. "Her parents don't know. They don't know she was out with me Friday night."

"Where do they think she was?"

"At a friend's."

"But she was with you?"

He nodded.

"All night long?"

He slumped in his chair, not denying the statement.

"Where did you hang out?"

"There's an old deserted church up on Double N. You can get in through one of the windows. We spent part of the night there."

Claire knew the church. They must be in love to put up with that place for a night. She would have thought an open field would be better, but the mosquitoes could be bad. "Does your father know?"

Ray shook his head.

"You might want to tell him."

"Are you going to talk to her?" he asked.

"What's her name?" Claire asked back.

"Tiffany. Tiffany Black."

Claire thought, *I should have guessed.* Half the girls in the county were named Tiffany. "I will talk to her, but I don't need to say anything to her parents."

"Cool," he said.

"I hope you're being careful." She was surprised when the words came out of her mouth. She couldn't help it. She was a mother.

Ray stared at her, then finished the Coke in another swallow. This time he looked right at Claire. "Thanks for the Coke."

Charles Folger was glad that Sorenson had warned him that the deputy was a woman. He had heard about this one from the big city. Too big for her britches—and she was wearing britches. Getting ahead of men who had been working for the sheriff for years. She had made some enemies.

Deputy Sheriff Claire Watkins was sitting across the desk from him. He was ready for her.

"So you are the agronomist for the cooperative, Mr. Folger?" she said, referring to a notebook she opened.

She probably didn't even know what that meant. Folger had his spiel down pat. "I am a specialist in the art and science of crop production."

She smiled at him and wrote something down. She had good teeth, he noticed. Large and white. She looked like a very healthy woman. But he did not approve of women working as police officers or deputies or whatever name you wanted to give them in law enforcement.

"How long have you been working for the cooperative?"

"Why? Do you want to know how old I am?"

She looked at him and raised an eyebrow. "Have you been working here since you were born?"

So she thought she could be funny. "I'm seventy-one years old. No mandatory retirement. I've been working here since I was twenty-seven. That's probably longer than you've been around."

"I'll take that as a compliment." She gave him a look and then continued, "Have you had a chance to examine the plant that Ron Sorenson took from the garden that was destroyed in front of the sheriff's department?"

"Yes," he answered. Make her work.

"And what did you find?"

"It was, as suspected, Parazone."

"Is there anything else you can tell me?"

He would do his job. Just because she was a woman didn't mean he would thwart the investigation. It was not his way. "Yes. Whoever did this has probably used this product before."

"Why do you say that?"

"He added a nonionic surfactant to the spray."

She stared at him, waiting for him to continue. He said nothing more.

"And what is that, please?"

"It is an agent we recommend adding to Parazone because it gives it a better spread. In layman's terms, or in this case laywoman's, it makes the Parazone stick to the plants better. It makes the pesticide much more effective."

Watkins wrote some more things down in her notebook. She took her time about her work. He assumed she was thorough. He understood because he was very thorough. He often did his tests two or three times just to make sure they gave the same results each time. He never guessed about anything. As much as possible he believed in taking the guesswork out of his job. He was a scientist, not an artist.

"That is very helpful. So what I gather from what you're telling me is that we are probably looking for a farmer?"

"I would venture to say that, but let us assume that it

is someone who has used these pesticides before, or who has watched them be used."

"Do you know how many farmers there are in Pepin County?"

"Out of a total population of close to eight thousand, I think the last census showed that less than a quarter of the adult men were farmers. Since there are around two thousand adult men, I think that puts the number of farmers at around five hundred."

"Narrows down the search slightly—assuming that our guy lives in Pepin County." She tapped her pencil on her front teeth, a disturbing habit. "What I need to understand here, Mr. Folger, is how dangerous these products are. I've read the labels. I understand that they are both restricted-use pesticides. But what precisely does that mean?"

"It means that both products have the ability to injure people."

She sighed and then said slowly, "Yes, I understand that. But how do they do it and how much does it take? Is it easily accomplished or does it require a megadose? Let's say, rolling in the product, bathing in it, swallowing a gallon of it."

"Let's not get carried away, Mrs. Watkins."

"You can just call me Deputy Watkins."

"Are you not a Mrs.? My mistake."

She let his comment pass. He was sure that he had heard that she had been married and had kept her married name. Apparently she didn't want to be known by that name. Another strike against her.

"Let us start here. Is one more dangerous to humans than the other?"

"Between Caridon and Parazone?"

"Yes."

"That's hard to say."

"Give it a go."

"Which would you think?" he asked her. Let's see what she'd do with this. Would she even give it a try?

Deputy Watkins thought for a moment, then ventured, "I guess I'd say Caridon, since it's an insecticide. We're closer to bugs than to plants. That would be my guess."

"And you would be wrong." It felt good to be able to say that to this cocky woman who thought she knew everything. "Parazone is deadly if swallowed or inhaled, and can be extremely injurious if it is absorbed through the skin. Caridon is most dangerous when inhaled. This effect only lasts a short time after the product has been sprayed on the fields."

"How does it work?"

"Caridon causes cholinesterase inhibition. Parazone causes mucosal damage. Again, more simply: Caridon will knock you out; Parazone will cause you great pain. Either way you will die if you have ingested enough of the product."

"Have you ever heard of this happening?"

"Only once in all my years of work here have I known anyone to run into trouble with one of these products. A young boy was working with his father and stayed in the field too long after it had been sprayed. He had some serious nosebleeds, but he recovered."

Her head came up. "Who was that?"

"Why?"

"I might like to speak with him."

"This was years ago."

"His name?"

Reluctantly, Charles gave her the farmer's name: Hal Swenson. He couldn't think of any good reason not to. Then he snapped, "Why are you asking me all these questions? What do you imagine is going to happen?"

Deputy Watkins put down her notebook and pen and leaned toward him. She then began to talk slowly and clearly. "It is my job to be prepared for what could happen. I need to understand the destructive potential of these two agents. I protect the welfare of the people of Pepin County. Any help you can give us will be appreciated both by the sheriff and by the county."

"Just don't go getting huffy and hysterical on us," he advised her, even though she looked like she would do neither.

She stood up and looked down at him. "I'll do my job. You do yours. We'll get along."

"How's Rachel?" Leaning back in her chair in the quiet office, Claire asked the required question. After first calling the pharmacy where Bridget worked, she had then tracked her sister down at home.

Claire had found in talking to Bridget these days that she might as well make an immediate inquiry about her niece and get it out of the way. Otherwise Bridget would find some way to mention Rachel in the first minute or two. Not that hearing updates on Rachel was a hardship. Bridget's enthusiasm for her young daughter was infectious, although sometimes Claire worried that Bridget's vocabulary was suffering since she was spending so much time with Rachel. "She's fine. I think she's starting to talk."

Claire had recognized early on that this child of her sister's was going to be a genius. At least if she believed half of what Bridget told her. And for the most part she went along with it all. But there were times when Claire had to object.

"I don't think that's possible, Bridget. She's only nine months old."

"You should hear her. She's hardly ever quiet."

"That's called babbling. She's practicing talking. It's not the same thing. She is saying sounds to say sounds, not to communicate."

"Well, when she does start to talk, she's going to be a master at it."

"I've no doubt. Hey, I'd love to chat, but I'm actually at work. I have some questions for you about pesticides."

"Pesticides. Not exactly my area of expertise."

"I'd like to understand better what they can do to a human if ingested or inhaled." Claire explained the theft at the cooperative and the massacre of the flower garden. She concluded with the thought that was uppermost in her mind. "It wouldn't have taken very much of the pesticides to kill the flower garden. This guy probably still has a lot of the stuff left."

"You sound worried. Do you really think he's going to do more with the pesticides? Like what?"

"That's where you come in. I need to understand what kind of harm could be rendered with these substances. I talked to the agronomist who works at the cooperative and he was barely helpful. Made me feel like an idiot because I didn't know what cholinesterase inhibition was."

Bridget giggled. "Well, at least you can say it. Do you understand what it is now?"

"Not really."

"I doubt the agronomist did either. I'm not sure *I* remember completely. Pharmacy school was a few years ago. But basically what it means is the body stops functioning."

"That sounds bad."

"Yeah, deadly. Arsenic acts by causing this inhibition. The body slowly starts to shut down. Or it can happen fast. Depending on the dosing."

"Okay, that helps. I know it's your day off, Bridget,

but I really do need help with this. We need to be ready in case this guy gets crazy on us."

"What do you need?"

"Could you look up what Caridon and Parazone can do, what amounts are needed, and what the antidotes are? I need all the particulars. The agronomist acted as if it were some state secret and I was a KGB agent. I want to disseminate this information to all the deputies by tomorrow so we can be prepared. I don't want to be taken by surprise."

"Sure, I can help out. I was going to go into town anyway. I'll look through my books here and then I'll check at the pharmacy. Rachel has been saying she wants to go for a ride today."

Claire felt relieved that Bridget would be on the case. "Buy the kid an ice-cream cone for me."

Two hours later, Bridget called her back. "I've got what you need. Rachel and I shared an ice-cream cone."

"Vanilla?"

"Of course. She's too young for chocolate. I've written down all the specifics on the pesticides and I can fax that to you."

"You've included the antidotes?"

"Yes, but let me just tell you. For Caridon atropine sulfate is antidotal. For Parazone it would be a little more difficult. It would have to be done in a hospital because they would use charcoal or clay to bind the material in the stomach, removing the main ingredient, paraquat, from the blood by cleaning out the blood. Because it can burn tissues, you wouldn't want the person to throw up."

"It sounds like either way, get the victim to the hospital as quickly as possible."

"That would be my recommendation."

CHAPTER 5

Meg climbed out of the bathtub, rubbed her body dry, and stepped into her new summer pajamas. Her mother had bought them for her—shorty pajamas with bunnies on them and a pink ribbon at the neck. Meg wished she could go stay at someone's house for a sleepover just so she could show them off. Maybe she should visit Aunt Bridget and her cousin, Rachel.

It was only a little after nine o'clock and Mom was letting her stay up later in the summer, but she didn't even care tonight. Meg was tired. Since her mom had worked most of the day, Meg had gone over to the Daniels farm and played with their kids. She had helped them get the eggs away from the chickens. There was one chicken that tried to attack them, but they had managed to escape her sharp claws.

They let Meg bring a dozen eggs home with her. The eggs were not the normal white, but soft brown, as if they had been dusted with dirt. They seemed more real to her; they looked like they actually came from the earth. When Mom fried them, the yolk was a bright orange color.

"Mom, I'm going to bed," Meg shouted at her mother, who was sprawled on a wicker chair on the front porch, reading.

"You going to read for a while?" Claire asked.

"Maybe. I'm kinda tired."

"I'll be up in a few minutes to tuck you in."

Meg stood on the middle stair and yelled down, "Is Rich coming over?"

"I think so. We left it a little vague."

"He should just live here, he sleeps over so much."

Her mother didn't say anything for a moment, almost as if she hadn't heard Meg; then she yelled back, "Everything in its time."

"What does that mean?"

Her mom lifted her head from her book, turned, and gave Meg a look. "When we get good and ready."

"I'm ready right now."

"Noted." Her head dropped back down to her book.

Meg walked the rest of the way up the stairs. She knew her mom was working on another case. It didn't sound that exciting to her. Someone had stolen weed killer out of a store in Durand. What a weird thing to steal. It just sounded like shoplifting. Kids did it all the time. What was the big deal?

Meg climbed into her bed. Clean sheets. She loved the feeling of clean sheets. In the summer Mom hung them out on the line and they carried some of the outdoor smell in with them. She smoothed her hands over the sheets and remembered the one time she had shoplifted.

It had been at the grocery store in Pepin. She had slipped a candy bar into her pocket when she was shopping with her mom. Then she had to wait while her mom had gone through the checkout line. She had almost thrown up, she was so sure that Peggy, the lady who ran the cash register, would catch her. When she got home, she had run upstairs and eaten half the candy bar and then thrown the rest of it away. It hadn't tasted as good as she had expected. She had decided then and there that a life of crime was not for her. Probably just as well with a mom as a deputy sheriff.

But then Mom had told her tonight at dinner that someone had ruined all the flowers in front of the sheriff's department. Meg had only seen them once a few weeks ago, but she thought they had looked real nice. She didn't get why someone would do that. Was it a message to the sheriff? To her mom? She didn't want to have to start worrying about her mother again.

She was glad Rich was in their life. He was almost as good as a dad. Maybe he would be her dad one day. She wondered if he and her mom were ever going to get married. They had been going out forever. She was already too old to be a flower girl. Maybe her mom would let her be a maid of honor. That would be totally cool.

Her eyes were closing. She could hear her mother's footsteps coming up the stairs, but her eyelids were too heavy to lift up again. Her breathing had gone into the deep zone, slow and even. Her mother patted the sheets and then leaned down and kissed her on the forehead.

Meg floated away on top of smooth white water.

Claire looked up from the book she was reading, a new Irish novel called *My Dream of You*—very romantic and with a heroine who was turning fifty. How refreshing to read about an older woman who was still sexual. She thought she had heard something outside the window, but when she checked, she didn't see anything.

When she had talked to Rich earlier, he hadn't been sure when he would come over. He was playing poker with the guys, but they didn't usually go too late. These were older guys who had responsibilities in the morning. She thought of getting undressed and climbing into the bed to wait for him, but it was so pleasant out on the front porch. She had all the windows open and the night air flowed in the house, humid and soft. All the sounds of summer surrounded her.

Claire was a little worried about her relationship with Rich. She had been getting the feeling that he wanted to change it. She suspected that he was going to want to get more serious, and she wanted to head him off.

Suddenly the headlights of his truck bounced down the driveway. Earlier than she expected. How nice. She heard the engine being turned off. She set her book down.

As she stepped outside to greet Rich, the gentleness of the air hit her. Balmy nights were rare enough in Wisconsin that she felt like staying up and enjoying it. She walked up to the truck.

Rich opened the door and swung down. "Hey, good-looking," he said.

"You sound lucky. You bring me any money?"

"You bet. I'm the big winner."

"How much?"

"Twenty-four dollars."

She stepped in closer and they kissed. She could tell from his kiss that he was feeling good about himself.

They broke apart for a moment and looked up at the sky together. Other than the porch light, it was dark outside. The moon wasn't out and the sky was sprayed with the Milky Way, but it gave off little light. She put an arm around his neck and pulled his face to hers again. They kissed a longer kiss—deep and thrilling.

She could feel that he wanted her. The way he was pressed up against her left little to the imagination. He started to lead her toward the house.

"Let's stay outside," she whispered in his ear.

He pulled back enough so he could see her face. "Really? Outside?"

She could feel his resistance. Rich liked everything in

its place, and she knew he thought the place for love-
making was in the privacy of one of their bedrooms.
Usually she agreed with that. But not tonight. She felt as
if the idea had been under her thoughts all night long,
that the warm summer air had been seducing her—and
now lucky Rich had walked right into it. "We could do
it behind the roses."

He looked around, checking to see if anyone was
walking down the road. There were no lights on in the
closest neighbor's house. The town was quiet and dark.

"No one will see us. Everyone's sleeping," she reassured him. "Besides, it's not against the law."

"Indecent exposure?"

"We'll be hidden."

"Let me get a blanket out of the truck."

She patted his butt as he turned back to the truck.
"You must have been a good Boy Scout. Always prepared."

She watched as he grabbed the blanket from the back-
seat. He turned and wrapped an arm around her shoulders and they walked to the other side of the wild
rosebushes. Thank goodness the neighbors weren't close
enough to see anything, even if they had been looking,
even if there had been some light to see by.

He spread out the blanket and settled her down on
it, pushing her back so she was stretched out on the
blanket.

Claire closed her eyes and smelled the wild roses' sweet
nutmeg aroma. The blooms lasted for only a week or so,
and all the rest of the year the bushes were scroungy-
looking, but she loved them for what they gave her this
one week: delicate pink blossoms and gorgeous per-
fume.

Rich knelt down beside her and unbuttoned her blouse.
He spread it open, leaving it loose on her shoulders. He

ran a hand down between her breasts from her neck to
her waist. Then he dipped his head down to her right
breast and kissed it.

She thought of bees; she thought of nectar. She felt
herself opening, blooming inside. She wanted him in her.
She loved what he was doing. She wanted to rush it. She
wanted it to last forever. All of it. She wanted all of it.

She ran a hand up his thigh and then unzipped his
jeans. But there was no hurrying him. Rich knew how to
take his time. She let him set the pace. The waiting made
it sweeter. When he finally came into her, she exploded
immediately. He laughed and moved slowly through her.

The stars were in her eyes. Then they fell into her.

Later, after they had rolled back into their clothes and
laughed their way into the house, Rich went back outside. When she was curled up in bed, he brought her a
rosebud that he had picked and put in a little vase. He
set it on her bedside table, right under the lamp. She
could smell the whiff of nutmeg it gave off.

Then he crawled in next to her, kissed her gently,
curled into her, and fell asleep. Sometimes she thought
he barely got his eyes closed before he was gone.

Claire loved to watch him fall asleep while reading.
His breath would slow and she would glance over and
notice that his mouth was slightly open, the book listing,
and suddenly his eyes would be shut. She often watched
until the book fell and jolted him awake.

She rested her arm over his waist. Rich was a nice man
to sleep with. He didn't hog the covers; he gave her
enough room.

It wasn't that she didn't want to marry him, she thought
as she held him in her arms. She wasn't crazy to get married again. Didn't think the institution offered much to
women. She had never cared for the term *wife*, implying
as it did the biblical *helpmeet*. The last thing she wanted

to be was a helpmeet—ever since she had read the term in the Bible as a child, she had wanted to avoid that designation. Even so, she would marry if that was what Rich wanted. She loved him.

But she didn't want to do it soon. There was something so sweet about the slightly illicit nature of their romance—the coming over after poker games, the stopping by for a coffee and a quick moment of love. She didn't want all that to end just yet. Once they married, they would never retrieve that carefree element.

She hoped the love they would grow into would be deeper, more committed; but what she wanted now was the wild roses that only bloomed for a moment.

He stood in the dark next to the truck.

Dark as the inside of a closet.

The wind moved around him. He could hear the sounds of the night, sounds he had grown up with: crickets, frogs, the occasional howl of a wild animal.

He didn't like everything he had to do. There were moments when he wanted to stop. But it was clear to him that this was the path he had to follow. It had been laid out for him.

The lights were off in the farmhouse. He knew the family had no dog. He knew their habits. He had been watching them. This was the old Schuler place.

He had learned to move quietly over the land. It was his way. He never made much noise. Often when he was a child, he had crept down the stairs at night and startled his mother while she was reading a book. She always got mad at him, asking him why he had to sneak up on her. He didn't mean to. He just didn't like to make noise. And he found that he learned a lot by being quiet.

He had been up to this farm recently to buy vegetables and eggs. He knew where all the outbuildings were. He knew that this family was trying not to use any pesticides. He thought that wasn't a bad idea. But he had to go ahead with his plan.

It would happen quickly, while they slept. It would be over before they would wake, he hoped.

He had made the mixture himself. Grain and some Parazone.

He turned on his special flashlight. A very strong but narrow beam of light cut through the darkness. He held it like a sword in front of him and began to walk. These steps were new for him, but, as always, he counted them. When he got to the door of the building, the number was 107. The right number. He felt like someone had patted him on the back.

The feeder was right in the middle of the yard. He poured his mixture into it. He went back to the door of the building and shone his light around the inside. The birds slept with their heads tucked into their wings. Some of them lifted up and looked at him, jerking their heads and making a low clucking noise.

"You are the next step," he whispered to them.

He left them to their sleep and carefully walked out the way he came. He hoped it would happen quickly and was glad that he would not be there to see it.

CHAPTER 6

———+———

Whirling chicken, whirling chicken. Jilly Daniels stood in front of the chicken coop with the egg basket in her hand and watched the fluffy chicken they called Lupita whirl in front of her. The brown-striped chicken kept turning as if she were trying to look at something behind her.

Two other chickens were sleeping by the door. Usually they went into the coop to sleep. Jilly walked up to one and touched it with the toe of her shoe. It didn't move. So tired. She walked around it and went into the dark chicken coop. She used to be scared to go in alone, but now she was used to it: the dusty smell, the dark, small room, the hay all over.

She made the rounds of where the chickens left their eggs and didn't find very many. Only seven. Maybe the chickens were too tired today to lay eggs. Usually she found between fifteen and twenty. She was only six, but she knew how to count up to a thousand.

She went back out into the sun and looked at Lupita. The chicken had stopped whirling but was still walking funny. Tilted to one side.

It reminded Jilly of how she felt when she had the flu last winter. Like her head was on crooked. Maybe the chickens were sick. The two by the door hadn't moved at all. They should be out pecking at the ground.

What was the matter with them? The chickens were mainly her responsibility. That was what Dad told her when they came and they were only little fluff balls. She had begged him to let her have chickens and he had made her promise that she would take care of them. That meant she had to feed and water and gather their eggs every day. Sometimes when she was reaching under the hens to get the eggs, they pecked her, but it didn't really hurt. She had learned a lot about chickens, but she had never seen them behave like this before.

Lupita went head-down into the dirt. Now look at what had happened. Her chickens were falling over.

Maybe she'd better tell someone, Jilly thought.

Her mother was out in the backyard, hanging up the sheets.

"Mom," she hollered.

Her mother looked over and waved.

"Mom, the chickens are acting funny."

Her mother didn't seem to hear her. Maybe she was too far away. Maybe it wasn't important.

Jilly looked back at the chickens. Lupita rolled onto her back and started to shake. Jilly had never seen a chicken do anything like that before. It reminded her of Henny Penny, the little chicken who thought the sky was falling. Maybe Lupita was scared and that was why she was shaking.

"Mom!" Jilly heard her voice rise up high in the sky, a scream.

Her mother's head lifted at the sound. She dropped the sheet she was stretching out on the line and came running.

Rich had driven to the Daniels farm a few times before. They lived up the bluff from Fort St. Antoine, on the rolling farmland that surrounded the lake. As he approached the farm today, he felt the sky open above him. He sometimes drove up near their farm just to watch the weather. It was so much easier to see when a storm was coming out of the basin of the bluffs.

Rich had bought eggs from the Danielses, but he didn't know them very well. Having moved to the area about ten years ago, they were relative newcomers. Meg played with their children, so Claire knew them better.

Rich had been surprised when Celia Daniels had phoned him this morning—surprised that she even knew who he was. As he drove up the bluff, he remembered her call.

She had been terribly upset, her voice high and shrill. "Our chickens are dying. The vet is out on call. I didn't know who else to try. Because of your pheasants, I thought you might know something."

He wasn't sure he could do anything, but at a time like this it often helped to have someone else there. She had mentioned that her husband had gone to the Fleet Farm in Menomonie and wouldn't be back until late afternoon. Rich had a sack of clothes sitting next to him on the seat. He would change his before he went back home. If the poultry at the Daniels farm were carrying anything, he didn't want to bring it back home to his pheasant flock.

Rich pulled into the long driveway that curved around the farmhouse and headed toward the barn. He stayed on it until he saw the family gathered at the other side of an outbuilding. He stopped the car and got out. A lanky boy of about ten ran out to greet him.

"Four have died so far," the boy announced.

"Are you Thomas?" Rich asked, hoping he had remembered correctly.

"Yeah." The boy pointed at the little girl standing next to her mother. "That's Jilly. She's the one who found the chickens. They're kinda hers. Dad bought them for her. She takes care of them."

On the drive up, Rich had been searching his mind for any disease that could come on this fast and be this fatal. The one that occurred to him was Newcastle disease. He knew that the Danielses were into back-to-the-land living, eschewing pesticides and chemical fertilizers; he wondered if they believed in inoculating their animals. If they didn't, that might be the problem.

As he walked up to Celia Daniels, he could see that she and her daughter had been crying. The little girl's face was streaked with dirt and tears. She was holding an egg in each hand. Her head was leaning against her mother's thigh.

"I don't know what to do about them," Celia Daniels told him. "I don't know what's wrong. They're dying."

Looking over the flock, Rich saw that they were all Barred Rock chickens, handsome chickens with brown and white stripes and small combs. His uncle used to have a flock of them.

As he recalled, Barred Rocks did well in the cold weather of the upper Midwest. His uncle kept them because they were a good dual-purpose chicken for a small farm. They laid nice brown eggs and then when their productive time was over, they could be dressed into good broilers, too.

Rich bent down and looked at the chicken that was flopped on the ground in front of him. No spittle at the beak, no nasal discharge. He touched the small bird, not so long dead that warmth didn't hang in its feathers, and wondered what had happened in its body that it had failed.

"How long has this been going on? Did you notice anything wrong with them last night?" he asked.

Celia reached down and tipped up Jilly's face. "How did the chickens seem last night?"

"Normal."

"What does that mean?" Rich asked.

The little girl looked up at him. "I found a bunch of eggs. They were going to sleep. None of them were dancing or anything. Just normal."

"How many eggs did you find today?"

"Only seven."

"What's usual for them?"

"More like over twenty."

"Are the chickens coughing or sneezing?" he asked.

Jilly thought before she answered. "No. Just spinning around and then lying down and dying."

Rich stood back up. He had some questions for Celia. "Have you vaccinated your birds?"

She stared at him, then reluctantly shook her head.

"Have they been in contact with any other poultry? Did you introduce any new birds to the flock recently?"

"No."

"Has anyone who raises chickens come and had contact with your birds?"

"No. Not that I'm aware of."

"Let me look at their food and water."

Jilly took him over to the feeder that was out in the yard. He bent down and examined the mash that was in it. He could see some hard, granular shapes. Didn't look like any feed he had ever used. "What is this?" He held up a piece for Jilly and her mother to see.

"I've never noticed that before," Mrs. Daniels told him.

"Jilly, bring me a cup of your feed."

The child dutifully ran and got him some feed in a coffee can. No dark, granular shapes were in it.

"It looks like someone might have put something in your chicken feed."

Celia Daniels looked at him with fear in her dark brown eyes. "Will all the chickens die?"

"I can't tell you that. I hope not. Let's get a paper bag for what's in here and I'll take it with me. Then wash out the feeder and put new feed in it."

Thomas ran into the house, happy to help.

His mother yelled at him as he went, "Grab a couple of plastic garbage bags, too."

Rich looked at her and she answered his question without its being asked. "For the chickens. I suppose we should preserve them."

"I'll take them with me, too."

Thomas came back with a brown paper bag on his head. Jilly laughed. Rich found it a pleasant sound. They dumped the contaminated feed into the bag and he rolled the top up so it wouldn't spill over in his car.

Then he reached down to pick up the closest of the dead chickens. First he was surprised by the depth of the bird's feathers. His hands sank in until he found the small body hiding under all that down. Then he wondered at the lightness of the bird. Fluffier than the pheasants he was accustomed to. And lighter still because it was so quiet. No struggling against him as he lifted it. He wondered if the soul of a chicken were a measurable weight.

After he had filled the bag with the four chickens, he looked at Celia.

She shrugged her shoulders as if to say, *What can we do?*

He answered her gesture. "You'll just have to wait and see on the others. I'll bring this feed in to be tested, and if there's an antidote, someone will bring it out."

"What do you think was put in the feed?" She looked at him with swollen eyes. "Why would anyone do this to us?"

"I don't know. I'd hate to try to guess. Someone from the sheriff's office will contact you about this."

Jilly, who had been standing quietly next to her mother, suddenly held up something for him to see. "Lookit what I found."

Rich looked down and saw a small white bone gleaming in her hand. "Where did you find that?"

"In the chicken coop. In with the eggs."

Rich took the bone and studied it. He remembered what Claire had said about the culprit leaving a memento. "I think I need to make a call from your house."

"A story about chickens dying?" Sarah Briding asked him with disappointment and disbelief deep in her voice. Harold knew she had not graduated from journalism school in order to write about chickens. But it was the news of the day. And they needed it quickly, as the paper was about to go to bed.

"Go up to the sheriff's department and talk to the deputy on the case. I think it's Watkins. Dig. There might be more to this than you think." He would see what she found. As he watched her leave the press office, he noted that all of her was in slight disrepair: her handbag dangling from her drooping shoulder, her blond hair pulling out of a loose ponytail, and the hem of her light summer dress falling down in back.

This was a bad business. Sitting at his desk, Harold Peabody worked his forehead with his fingers. He had made a list and he didn't like the looks of it at all. His role as editor was not to scare the public, but rather to give them the news, warn them if necessary. So he wouldn't connect it all together for his readership. At least, not yet.

Chickens twirling and dying. Pesticide in their feed. This was the second incident since the break-in at the Farmer's Cooperative. The destruction of the garden in front of the sheriff's department, he had decided, could go on the third page. This piece he would put on the front page, but below the fold.

Glancing at the clock on the wall, he saw it was after five. Agnes knew that he was often late for dinner on weekdays. She was in the habit of cooking something that could be held indefinitely in a warm oven or a cold refrigerator. In winter it would be some mishmash of noodles and ground beef and cream of mushroom soup. Summers she often made a cold salad of macaroni noodles, canned shrimp, and peas. Suited him fine.

Tomorrow was the Fourth of July. Middle of the summer. The air conditioner in the back window droned on. Nearly ninety out and very soupy. For the holiday, he planned on grilling a chicken; Agnes would make her potato salad and strawberry shortcake. When it started to get dark, they would drive to the river and watch the fireworks.

Harold heard the door to the front office open. He thought of getting up and talking to whoever had entered, but he wanted to finish this last piece before interrupting his work. When the door opened and closed again, he figured his visitor had come in to buy a paper.

A pile of papers was always left on the counter, and a box sat next to them for quarters. The honor system worked pretty well in these parts. Once or twice they had even come out ahead on the money. Maybe he wasn't charging enough for his paper—although circulation was not where the money came from; the money was all in advertising. With two more businesses closing on Main Street, he'd be losing some other reliable clients soon.

Sighing a deep sigh, Harold pushed himself out of his chair. He needed to get up and walk around from time to time. Otherwise his legs bothered him. It was time to lock the front door. He walked out to the front desk and turned the dead bolt.

He waved at Harriette Pinkerton as she passed on the street. She'd be a pretty woman if she didn't pull her hair back so tight and if she put on a little lipstick. Women walked around these days looking more informal than his mother would have ever allowed herself to be seen out of the bedroom: skimpy T-shirts, slippers on their feet, and their bra straps showing on purpose. But he was certainly glad that he didn't have to wear a suit to work every day. Or a hat for that matter.

When he turned to walk back to his desk, he saw an envelope sitting on the counter with his name on it. MR. HAROLD PEABODY, it was labeled, then underneath, PUT IN THE PAPER, PLEASE. Assuming it was a letter to the editor, he wondered who was ranting about what this week.

Curious, he opened the envelope and pulled out a single piece of paper. Not much writing on it. He peered down through the bottom half of his glasses. At the top of the paper was written a series of numbers:

7, 7, 7, 52.

Offhand, he couldn't make them mean anything. Then he read the body of the note:

The killer has gone free for far too long. The truth must be told. Or more will die. The flowers and the birds were only the beginning. The murdered are

*crying out for revenge. I have listened to them for
half a century.
It is enough.
Wrath of God*

Wrath of God. Harold read it again and felt the seri-
ousness of the situation sinking into him. The bad business had just gotten worse. Half a century ago—that
was when the Schuler murders took place. Somehow
what was happening with the pesticides was connected
with them. He saw that the last three numbers at the top
of the note were the date of the massacre. The first number, seven, was how many people had died that day.

His hand holding the letter shook. He needed to sit
down. But first he needed to call the police. He wondered if they would let him put the letter in the paper. He
knew he had to do that. His motto in life had always
been: The truth must be told. Now he knew that someone else felt the same way.

July 7, 1952

Bertha Schuler didn't think much about it when she heard the gunshot, a not uncommon sound around the farm. Otto had probably caught sight of the weasel that was stealing eggs out of their chicken coop. She hoped he got the darn thing.

She picked up the crying child and rocked her in her arms. Arlette. Her last baby, she prayed. Nearly forty, her body had had a harder time carrying this one. She had almost given birth on the farm, but Otto had scooted her to town in time. Arlette had been her smallest baby, barely five pounds, the size of a bag of flour.

Otto wouldn't even hold Arlette for the first month, said they should be done with that. He tried to stay away from Bertha, tried to keep his hands off her, but then, in the middle of the night, he would take her feverishly and they would both wait to see if her blood came when it should.

Bertha had years to go yet before she'd be done with the chance of having another baby. What would they do? She had tried to get Otto to go buy protection, but he couldn't bring himself to do it in Durand. Maybe when they went to Eau Claire.

But her sweet Arlette was a prize. Always sunny, smiling. Now, with her tiny fist, she rubbed her head and gave a little weak cry and then smiled at her mother.

Bertha kissed the girl on her head where the spoon had hit her.

Bertha set the baby in her high chair and gave her a hard cookie to suck on. Footsteps running above her head told her the children were still playing. She should calm them down. Picking up the platter with the roast, she set it next to Otto's plate for him to carve and serve.

When she heard the door push open, she turned to see who it was. The gun was what she saw. The gun coming into her kitchen.

She wiped her hands on her apron and turned to pick up her baby. Her last thought was how she had wanted to see them all grow up, her children, her angels on earth.

CHAPTER 7

"I'm an agronomist. Plants I can tell you about. Crops I can tell you about. Chickens, you got the wrong man." Charles Folger's voice came over the phone like a blast of cold air. "What am I supposed to do with this chicken? I don't know nothing about chickens."

Claire held the phone away from her ear for a moment and wished she didn't have to deal with this cranky old guy, but it was her job. She contemplated correcting his double negative but didn't think their relationship would stand up to the complexities of grammar. She needed this man. If he chose to cooperate, he could be a big help. She had sent the other two chickens to the crime lab, but it might be days before she'd hear back. She needed answers soon.

Claire had just received a call from Celia Daniels. Another chicken had died. The distress in the woman's voice had been alarming.

"We'll never be able to use these chickens again," she had said to Claire. "We raise everything organic, and they've been poisoned. No eggs, no meat. I don't know what we'll do with the ones that survive. We'll have to start over next year. Who could have done this?"

Trying to be reassuring, Claire had promised answers— even though she wasn't sure they would be easy to get.

She needed Folger's cooperation. She imagined him

sitting there with a dead chicken on his desk, and a smile lit up her face. Someone had once told her that smiling made the voice sound sweeter. She tried again.

"What I'm really hoping is that you can analyze the feed. I sent you one of the chickens just in case it might help you out."

She heard Folger grumbling at the other end of the line and imagined his digging through the papers on his desk as if he would find an answer there.

Just then Chief Deputy Sheriff Stewart Swanson squatted down in her line of vision and held his hands in the T position—time out—his signal that he needed her now. He had played football in high school. Claire was sure it had been the best time of his life. Even though he was in his early sixties he could still recite some of his plays.

She needed to wrap up this phone call. "I know you'll do the best you can. I'll call you back later today." Without waiting for an answer she disconnected.

"Yeah?" She looked up at Stewy. He motioned her into his office.

Unlike him to be so secretive about anything, she mused. Following him, she was struck by how broad his back was. Lot of good meat loaf and pie went into maintaining that physique, she was sure. Mrs. Swanson was an acclaimed baker. Even at his age, she wouldn't want to run into his sheer mass on a football field—or down a dark alley.

He held open the door to his office for her and then closed it behind them. "Claire, just got a call from the newspaper."

She nodded.

"Harold Peabody. You know him?"

"I know who he is."

"He just found a note on his counter. A threatening note. He thinks it's related to the stolen pesticides."

Claire hoped this editor wouldn't leave his marks all over the note. "Is it from our guy?"

"I think so." The sheriff looked at her. "You better go talk to him. He wants to run it in the paper tomorrow."

The first thing Harold Peabody did after he called the sheriff was to make a copy of the note and put the copy safely away inside a volume of the Oxford English Dictionary on the page that included the definition for murder. He had bought the set in 1970 at a used bookstore for a hundred dollars. The dictionary was published in the 1950s, but he didn't figure words went out of style.

He spent the rest of his time waiting for the deputy, clearing off his desk. The condition of his desk was an apt metaphor for the state of his mind: mildly organized chaos.

When Deputy Claire Watkins showed up, he ushered her to the back room and held out a chair for her. The chair, too, had been recently cleared of a stack of papers.

Then he sat down opposite her in his rolling chair and looked this deputy over. She was an attractive woman. Harold found that she resembled her name—there was something clear and open about the way she looked at him. She had the start of good lines in her face, and terrific eyes. She was growing outwardly into who she was inwardly—what one did in one's forties. For better or worse.

"You're the new investigator," Harold commented. "I don't think the sheriff's department ever had one before."

"No, this is a new position."

"Good idea." He had folded a piece of paper in two and placed it around the note so he could hold it without disturbing the surface. "Here it is."

She pulled on a pair of latex gloves. First she read the

note; then she turned it over and examined the backside of it carefully. She looked in the envelope, then put it in a plastic bag, and the note in another plastic bag. She placed the plastic-covered note on the desk in front of her so she could see it easily. When she was finished, she looked up at him. "Any idea what the numbers mean?"

"I think so. I think it's a date. The date an entire family was murdered on their farm. The Schulers. Otto and Bertha Schuler and their five kids. Slaughtered on their farm on the seventh of July, 1952. The case was never solved."

"But what about the first seven?"

"The number of people killed."

Claire's hand rose to her mouth and she closed her eyes for a moment. Harold could tell she was visualizing the scene. She knew murder scenes; she knew farms. She was putting them together in her mind.

"What happened?" she asked.

"Someone came and shot the whole family. A neighbor, who happened to be a deputy sheriff, went over to return something and he found them. But they could never figure out who did it or why. Had the whole county stirred up for months."

"I can imagine." Claire shook her head and then asked, "What do you think?"

He wouldn't bite on such an open-ended question. "About what?"

"About the note. About the man who's doing this."

"Sure it's a man?"

"About ninety-five percent sure."

"That's quite a bit. I happen to agree with you."

Claire didn't say anything more. She waited for him to continue. Good interviewing technique. Harold was pleased with this woman deputy. She knew her stuff. She took her time. Especially in this new age of technology, you needed to know how to take your own time.

Harold gathered his thoughts. He had thought of little else since he had read the note. "What do I think about him? I'll tell you what I've figured out from his note. He's slightly obsessive-compulsive. That's shown by the numbers at the top of the note. He's polite. He was raised well. And I'm sure that he's an older man. He'd have to be if he's been around for at least the last fifty years." He paused.

Claire had been following his words closely. She gave one brief nod and said, "Right."

Harold continued. "For other reasons, he's got to be an older man. He addressed me as Mr. Harold Peabody. Anyone under forty wouldn't do that. Titles have just about disappeared from daily life. Also, he asked that I put it in the paper—*please*. Again a nicety that shows he's generally a civil man. But something's got him horridly riled up. He's religious. He reads his Bible. Might be the only book he reads. He has a mission. He thinks that God is backing him on this one. He might do anything."

"Wow," Claire said.

He was both pleased and surprised at her exclamation. It was to the point, but he wanted her to react more to all his work. He pressed his hands down on his desk and said, "That's what I think."

"You could be a profiler."

At first Harold didn't know what she was talking about. The first thing that popped into his mind were those old black cameo paper cutouts that were done of someone's profile. Then he remembered that he had seen a TV show called *Profiler*. A woman solved crimes by studying the criminals' behavior. He chuckled.

"I'm serious. Criminal profilers look at exactly the

things you analyzed. I studied it a bit at the police academy. Let me ask you a few more questions. Do you think he's a farmer?"

Harold scratched his thinning pate. "Could be. Probably if he's lived in this area for fifty years. Seems like everyone used to be a farmer. If he's not, he'd know quite a bit about it. Enough to be able to know how to use those pesticides."

"Do you think he's dangerous?"

"I'm afraid I do. As I've said, he's riled up. He's been on simmer about this happening for fifty years, and it looks like he's about to blow."

"What do you think he'll do next?"

Harold leaned forward. Now they were getting to the heart of the matter. "Talk about the man all you want, but what you must do is outguess him, know where he's going to be, know what he's going to do before he does it." He listed the acts thus far. "First he stole the pesticide. Then he destroyed the flowers. Next he killed the birds."

He paused. Claire waited.

"I'm afraid it's escalating," Harold said. "I'm afraid he'll move on to something bigger. It could be cows; it could be horses." Then he forced himself to say what he was really afraid of. "It could be people."

"Yup." Claire tapped her pencil on the front of his desk. "That's what I've been thinking, too. Imagining the things he might do makes me sick. We are all so vulnerable. This is a place where people leave their keys in their car in case someone needs to borrow it. Doors are unlocked. People are used to being friendly."

"It's worse than that," Harold told her. "This man is one of us. He knows our ways. He knows where to get us."

"Want to venture a guess who it might be?"

Harold had been afraid she would ask him that. He had a couple thoughts, but wasn't sure he was ready to tell her. "Let me think on it. This is serious business. I hate to run my mouth off about people and get them in trouble. It was obviously someone affected by the Schuler murders."

"Do you think it's the killer?"

Harold puffed out his lips. "More than likely. If he's still alive, he'd be an old man like me."

"Well, if you have any more ideas, let me know, the sooner the better. This guy is on a timetable."

"Where will you be tomorrow?"

"With my daughter. Watching the fireworks. But you can always reach me on my cell phone. If the bluffs don't interfere." Claire gave him her number. "Also, any information you can give me on the Schuler murders would be appreciated. I'll go to the cold cases and pick up the file on that."

"I'll put together articles from the time it happened."

"Thanks, Mr. Peabody."

"Harold."

She stood. "After I've talked to the sheriff, I'll let you know what you can put in the paper."

Harold came around his desk to walk her to the door. This was the only false step she had made in their meeting.

"That won't be necessary." The deputy turned to look at him. He continued: "It's running. The note is running. Consider it a courtesy that I let you know about it before you read it in the paper."

Meg heard about the chickens from her friend Katlyn, who lived near the Danielses. Katlyn said that everyone said that maybe Rich's pheasants would be next to be killed. Meg said that Rich had a huge security fence and that no one could get in to hurt his pheasants. When she hung up the phone, she was surprised that she had lied. It was not like her.

Meg walked over to the refrigerator, opened the freezer, and pulled out a lime Popsicle. Then she went onto the porch and sat on the floor under the fan. The thermometer out back said ninety degrees, but the guy on the radio today had been talking about something called a heat index and he said it would feel like one hundred. Hot enough to make her have to eat her Popsicle fast before it dripped down onto her hand.

She wondered what it was like for kids who had sisters and brothers. She found it hard sometimes not to have anyone to talk to about all the things that worried her. It was a big responsibility to be an only child. And it only made it worse when her dad died. Now her mother was totally her concern.

She decided to call Rich. He would understand. Knowing Rich, he might even be able to help.

He answered the phone. "Haggard's Pheasants."

She said, "Knock, knock."

"Who's there?"

"Pop."

"Pop who?"

"Popsicle."

There was silence for a moment; then he asked, "Did you make that one up, Megsly?"

"Yup. Just for you."

"I'm honored."

"Mom's not home yet."

"Another long day?"

"Yeah, she called and said she'd be home soon. She said I could come home and let myself in and wait for her." Meg was done with her Popsicle. She stretched out flat on the cool stone floor of the porch. She stared up at the overhead fan, which was a blur above her head.

"Good."

"I heard about the chickens."

"News travels fast around here."

"What are you doing to protect your pheasants?"

"Staying put."

"But what about tomorrow—the Fourth of July? What about our barbecue and the fireworks?"

"No one would do anything on a holiday."

"Bad guys take days off?" she asked. "Are you kidding me?"

"I am kidding you. But I'm serious when I say that I'm not too worried about my birds. I don't think this guy is after me. I don't think he's after all the poultry in the county. I think he's got something else in mind."

"What?"

"I'm not sure, but whatever it is, your mom will figure it out."

Meg thought for a moment. "My mom is really smart, but she doesn't know everything. She makes mistakes, too."

"Of course she does. But I think this guy wants to be stopped."

"Why?"

"Because he's leaving clues."

Meg liked the idea of the clues. It made it more like a Nancy Drew mystery, something that could be solved and then everything would fall into place.

"You know that I'm going to my grandparents this summer."

"Yeah, when?"

"Not sure, but, I just want to be sure that you'll keep an eye on Mom. I didn't want her to know that I'm worried, but I am."

Rich didn't say anything for a moment; then he cleared his throat. "I will keep an eye on her. You know you can count on me. But I know she wants you to have a good time on your trip and not to worry about her."

"I'll try." Meg was glad she had said it. But once was enough. You didn't need to repeat things with Rich. He got them the first time. "I think it's going to be hot tomorrow. It's hot today."

"It's supposed to be hot on the Fourth of July. With plenty of mosquitoes and maybe even a thunderstorm thrown in."

"No thunderstorms. Just fireworks. That's enough."

CHAPTER 8

Often Earl Lowman dreamed of lakes—deep, clear, sweet-sprung lakes. But when he woke, as he did on this hot July day, he was still in Tucson, Arizona—108 degrees at midday—where the one river that had once flowed through the town, the Santa Cruz, had dried up long ago, and the water table was dropping inches a year, causing the ground below his house to sink.

He turned his head on his pillow and read his alarm clock—5:07 A.M.—noting that it would go off in eight minutes. If he wanted to take a walk, he had to get up. Once the sun rose at six, it rapidly got too hot to be outside. He threw the sheet off his legs.

But the dream of the lake held him in bed for another few minutes. He thought of wading up to his waist in Lake Pepin; he remembered jumping off the old oak tree that bent over the Rush River and plunging into the spring-fed waters. He would love to swim again in fresh water.

Most afternoons Earl wandered down to the community pool and swam a few laps, but it was not the same. The water was chlorinated and way too warm. No one else even bothered to swim in the pool. They stood in the water and gabbed. The heads of other old people bobbed around in the pool like idling ducks on a dirty pond. Earl Lowman wondered what had happened to his life.

After thirty years as a deputy sheriff for Pepin County, he had retired down in Tucson with his wife, Florence. Three months after they had moved into their new town home, Florence had died. Stroke. That was ten years ago. His one daughter was living in Seattle and his son still lived in Durand, Wisconsin. Earl and his son, Andy, hadn't spoken in ten years—since Florence's death. She was the one who had stayed in touch with Andy. Earl had no reason to go back to Wisconsin, but he missed it.

He pulled on a pair of gym shorts that weren't too dirty and dug out an old T-shirt. Wandering into the kitchen, he hit the button on the coffeemaker. He set it up the night before so all he had to do was start it brewing in the morning. He pulled open the front door and found the *Arizona Daily Star* on his doorstep. After pouring himself a cup of coffee and adding artificial sweetener to it, he set the paper and the coffee on the table on the back patio and went in to make breakfast.

He ate the same thing every day. It made life easy. He took out a frozen waffle and put it in the toaster. He poured some maple syrup into a jug and heated it in the microwave. When the syrup and the waffle were ready, he put them on a plate and took them out to the table on the patio.

He ate because he knew he should, not because he was hungry. He didn't seem to be hungry for anything anymore. Fresh sweet corn and ripe tomatoes sounded good to him, but were hard to get in Tucson. Tomatoes didn't grow well down in the Southwest. All the tomatoes he got at the store were from Mexico, and who knew what they put on them down there.

Earl looked at the date of his paper—July the fourth. He had seen in the community bulletin that there would be a potluck at the center tonight. Maybe he'd go. Maybe he wouldn't. There were a lot of older women who gave him the eye, but he wasn't having any of that anymore. He felt too old.

After Florence died, he had dated a nice woman who lived two blocks away. She had even stayed over one night, but they hadn't really done anything except kiss. But she moved back to Atlanta to be closer to her daughter. He understood. Family became important when you got older.

He stabbed at his waffle a couple of times, then let it be. Maybe he wouldn't walk today. It was a holiday, after all. He felt tired. Maybe he'd just crawl back in bed and sleep and then start the day all over again.

Carrying his dishes into the kitchen, he felt exhausted by all he didn't have to do. No lawn to mow, no gutters to clean, no one to worry about.

He sat down at the dining room table and buried his head in his hands. He was a lonely old man and he had no one to blame but himself.

Maybe he should call one of his kids. Maybe he'd catch Andy if he tried now. He wouldn't be out in the fields yet.

Before he could change his mind, Earl picked up the phone and dialed his son's number. Marie, his wife, answered. "Lowman's."

"Hey, Marie. It's Earl."

There was silence on the other end of the line. Then her voice came across strong, worry lacing it. "Earl. My goodness, but it's been a long time since we heard from you. Are you okay? Is everything all right?"

"I'm fine. Just thought of calling, holiday and all." Might as well get right to the point. "Is Andy there?"

Again there was a pause. Earl knew what was happening. Andy was sitting right there drinking his coffee and shaking his head at Marie, telling his wife to say he was gone. "I'm sorry, Earl. You just missed him." She stopped for a moment, then asked in a cheery voice, "Are you doing anything for the Fourth?"

"Not much to do down here. What about you?"

"Oh, just having hot dogs. Then we'll take the kids down to see the fireworks. Down to Fort St. Antoine. They've got the best, as far as I'm concerned."

"That should be fun."

"Yeah, we enjoy it." She cleared her throat. "Warm down there?"

"Plenty warm. I suppose you're getting a little warm weather up there, too?"

"Oh, yeah. It's summer, you know. Hot and muggy. But a nice breeze today. That makes a difference." Her voice ran down and then she said, "There was a strange letter in the paper today. Andy figured it was about the Schuler murders. Something about finding out the truth. Had the date—July seventh, 1952. Were you working for the sheriff when that happened?"

"Oh, yeah. I remember it well." The Schuler murders— that sure came out of the dark to ambush him. He tried as hard as he could never to think of that time in his life. "I was low man on the totem pole in those days. Didn't have much to do with it."

"Not much else going on." Marie gave an embarrassed cluck. "Nice to hear from you, Earl."

"Well, thanks, Marie. Say hi to the kids and tell Andy I called."

"I'll do that, Earl. You try again."

He hated this sham and decided to speak his mind. "Do you really think I should bother?"

"Yeah, I do. I think you should. Who knows? Glad you called. 'Bye now."

When he hung up the phone, he stared down at his hands.

He remembered driving to the Schulers' farm to return the saw he had borrowed from Otto.

He remembered what he had found there.

This was another reason he didn't want to go back to Pepin County.

He remembered the fingers. He would never forget the pile of fingers.

Arlene Rendquist had been born on the Fourth of July. Fifty years ago this day. Named after her little cousin, who had died a few days later: Arlette. Her mother had been brokenhearted, wanting the two cousins to grow up together. Bertha, her sister and Arlette's mother, had been killed too. Terrible tragedy, her mother had always said. Every year her mother would be reminded of it on Arlene's birthday.

Arlene wondered what her husband, Larry, would get her for her birthday. She wondered if he had even remembered. He hadn't mentioned a thing, and she decided she wasn't going to bring it up.

Larry worked for the railroad. It was a good, steady job, but dirty. He was sleeping in today, since it was his day off. He had gone out and tied one on with the boys last night. She didn't mind so long as he didn't come home all soused up and wake her up, hoping to party a little more. She was getting too old for that kind of behavior. He was too. He was more apt to sit quietly at home, nursing a six-pack these days, than go out with his buddies.

Arlene finished folding the laundry and decided she had done enough work around the house to have earned the right to a little rest and another cup of coffee. She walked out to the mailbox to pick up the paper. Even though it was a holiday, the *Durand Daily* would be there.

The day was perfect. Eighty degrees. Fluffy clouds in the sky. She wondered if her dad would stop by today. He lived a half mile down the road, and even though he was eighty, he was still farming. He had over five hundred acres of land. Larry said that when her father died, they could sell his land and retire to Florida. But Arlene knew that her dad might well live to be a hundred. She wouldn't put it past him to outlive them all. Dad was made of tough stuff.

She pulled the newspaper out of the box and walked up the driveway. Dad would probably show up about suppertime, wondering what they were eating for the Fourth. She thought she'd make hamburgers. No big deal. Taste as good as anything.

When she got into the kitchen, she could smell the coffee—a burnt odor that she didn't find altogether unpleasant. Last cup in the bottom of the coffeemaker. She poured it into her favorite mug, the one labeled SHE WHO MUST BE OBEYED, that Larry had given her for Christmas a few years ago. She had gotten such a charge out of it.

She went out and sat on the front steps. Such a day as this should be enjoyed. Reading the paper, she started with the first page and read it front to back. Even the ads. You never knew what you might find for sale. There was a letter to the editor that caught her eye because Harold Peabody had written a disclaimer above it, indicating that he didn't usually print a letter without a signed name, but he was making an exception. She had to read the letter twice, but she could see why Harold had published it. It gave her the shivers. She wondered if her dad had seen it yet.

It had to be about the Schuler murders. The date was

right. They never did know the truth about what happened. Sometimes her mom would talk about the incident, saying that she missed her sister Bertha every day of her life. "She was a good wife and a good mother and a good sister and she could bake a peach pie like you wouldn't believe." High praise from her mother.

One time, after her mother had died, and Arlene and her father had gone out to look at the old homestead, Arlene brought up the murders with her father. He wouldn't talk about what had happened. All he'd say was that it was a sad story that didn't bear repeating.

Her parents had inherited the Schuler farm. Otto Schuler had had no family in the area. All his relatives were still in Germany and couldn't be found. Her dad farmed the land, but he didn't want to rent out the house. He did little to keep it in repair, but he kept a roof on it. Her dad claimed no one would want to live in it after what had occurred there. Finally, he rented it to the Danielses not long ago.

When Arlene was little, she would sneak over and climb into the house through a broken window. The house was kinda spooky. There had been brown stains on the kitchen floor that she imagined came from the blood of the murdered children—her five cousins. She would have had a different life had they lived. She would have been part of a big family. As it was she was raised all by herself.

Hearing a noise, she lifted her head to see her father's truck come barreling down the road, raising a cloud of dust behind it. He pulled into the driveway and drove right up to where she was sitting.

"All through working for the day?" he asked her.

"Just taking a break. You want a cup of coffee?"

"Naw, just thought I'd check and see if I was welcome for supper."

"You know you always are, Dad. Come by around six." She shook the paper at him. "You see the *Durand Daily* yet?"

"No, I don't bother with that paper. Nothing in it I want to know about."

"There's a letter that I think might be referring to the Schuler murders."

He stared at her.

"Says that they want to find out the truth about what happened."

He shook his head. "They're dead and gone. What good's the truth now? It's too late."

Opening the door to the basement, he smelled the scent of darkness. He found it a comfort, allowing him to feel safe and away from the world. He stepped down the first step and closed the door behind him. This was another of his holy places—the basement. His wife never went down into it, hating the cold and damp. They kept the freezer out in the garage and she stored all her canned goods in the pantry, so she had no reason to go down there.

It wasn't even a full basement. The old farmhouse had been built in pieces, and the basement was only under half the house. It was built of old limestone and seeped water most of the summer, but he liked it down there. His father had built a workshop in the room right under the stairs and now it was his. He still kept all his father's tools in their proper places. A diagram drawn in pencil on the wood backboard made it easy, outlining each tool hanging on its nail.

Above the tools hung his mother's graduation picture. In it she wasn't smiling; she was watching. He knew she finally understood what he was doing. Even she had to admit the time had come.

Upstairs, his wife was stretched out on the couch, watching one of her soap operas. He couldn't tell one from the other, even though she would talk about them as if the people lived just down the road and he saw them at church every Sunday. They filled her life and he was glad of it. She needed something.

He had a lemon, a jug of water, and a little vial. He had brought down a good cutting knife from the kitchen. Slicing the lemon into quarters, he had decided, would be the way to go, as a quarter was the best size for squeezing the fruit. Plus, four was a good solid number. He had always liked it. It might be his favorite number. Like an animal that moved on four legs, it seemed alive and solid.

He cut and squeezed until he had gotten all the juice he could out of the lemon. Not as much juice as he had hoped, but it would do. He added a cup of water, then dumped the contents of the vial into the jug. After screwing the top on tight, he shook the jar and the dark granules dissolved. Then he poured as much of the liquid as he could fit into a silver flask, the old drinking flask of his father's.

The next step would be taken tonight. Even though he would be the one to carry it out, he could not control what would happen. Four times seven was twenty-eight. It was always twenty-eight. You counted the numbers, you followed the steps.

The letter had been in the paper today. Now everyone would know what this was about; everyone would be thinking about it. The collective energy of the county would be on the old Schuler murders. This next step would start the talking. Everyone would be talking about it, and the truth, like the juice from the pulp of a fruit, would squeeze out.

It could be held inside its skin no longer.

The truth could save them all. If it would come in time.

The last step. He took out his special box, the one he had made when his mother died, and he opened the lid. A pile of delicate bones like links on an ivory chain were arranged inside. Gently he lifted out the smallest bone—Arlette's, probably—and put it next to the jar. He was ready.

CHAPTER 9

Originally, Claire had asked Rich to come over and spend the day. She had promised to make everything for their holiday feast—a real American celebration: grilled chicken, potato salad, and rhubarb pie. She had asked Rich to pick up a six-pack of beer and just bring himself.

It was his idea of the perfect Fourth of July—complete with fireworks at the end. He had great hopes for this day and set the engagement ring out on his chest of drawers so he wouldn't forget it.

But this morning, when the phone rang before nine, Rich had a bad feeling. Sure enough, when he picked up the phone, it was Claire.

She started right in. "Plans have changed. I have to go in to work. I'm taking Meg with me. I won't stay long, but let's keep it simple. How does wieners and potato chips sound?"

"Fine."

"Sorry, I know you were looking forward to my potato salad."

"Don't worry about it."

"Did you see the letter in the Durand paper?"

"Yeah. Kinda cryptic."

"I think this guy is nuts. I just hope we catch him soon."

"Do you think he's going to do something today?"

Claire didn't say anything for a few seconds. "I hope not."

Because her hope sounded rather fragile, he decided not to push the subject. "What time do you want me to come over?"

Claire paused, then asked, "Can I call you?"

He hated the idea of waiting the whole day for her to call. "Give me a guesstimate."

"No later than seven."

There went their day together. He had finished his chores first thing in the morning, assuming he would meet her around noon. "Fine."

"I'm sorry."

He was peeved, but he didn't feel like discussing it with her. "Don't worry about it."

"I'm worrying."

"You've got enough on your mind."

"What do you know about the Schuler murders?"

"I was only a toddler."

"I know. I want a full report tonight. Love you. 'Bye."

He liked how easily and casually she had said she loved him. As if it were that much a part of her life. That felt good. So she had to work. Big deal. Maybe he would wander down to the beach. He hadn't spent any time looking for arrowheads in quite a while.

But before he did anything, he would call his mother. She expected him to at least check in on holidays.

"Happy Fourth of July. Beatrice Haggard here."

"Hi, Mom."

"Oh, Rich, I've been waiting to hear from you. What did she say?"

"Who?"

"Claire. Did she say yes?"

Shoot, he had forgotten to call his mother and tell her what had delayed the proposing. Since he had gotten the

ring from her, he should have known she would be waiting on tenterhooks, as she might say. "Oh, I haven't
asked yet."

"Why ever not?"

He didn't need his mom to get all nosy on him.
"Hasn't come up."

"Rich, what's going on?"

"Nothing. It's no big deal. It will happen and you will
be among the first to know. Claire's been busy with
work. I wanted to pop the question at the right moment."

"Of course, that's important."

"I'll let you know." He decided it was time to change
the subject. "Hey, Mom, what do you remember about
when that farm family—the Schulers—were all murdered? You were living down here at that time, weren't
you?"

"Yes, I was, and it was just awful. Why do you want
to know?"

"Well, it's a long story, but it's come up in Claire's
work, and she was asking me about it."

"Well, that was right after I married your father. I had
just moved out to Fort St. Antoine to live on the farm.
And I was scared to begin with, having been a city girl
and all. Everything scared me—the animals, the thunderstorms, the trains at night—you name it. I was so
young." His mother's voice faded off.

"Then this horrible massacre happened and I was petrified. They never found out who did it. Can you imagine? All I could think of at night was that he might take
it into his head to come and kill us all at the Haggard
farm. Wasn't so very far away from where the Schulers
lived. Everyone was scared."

"Were there any rumors about who did it?"

"Well, the Schulers weren't very well liked. Otto

Schuler was a recent immigrant from Germany, and anti-German sentiments were still running high after the war. His English was very bad and he wasn't a very good farmer. Most everyone liked Bertha, but Otto was too proud to ask for help. I think they were deep in debt. Close to losing their farm. Then all the kids. Although everyone had a lot of children in those years. As far as who did it, I never heard of particular accusations. Although I'm not sure I would have. I was still pretty new to the community."

"Well, if you think of anything else, let me know."

"Well, if you propose tonight, you let me know." With that, she hung up.

Ray Sorenson woke up with a boner. He ached with desire but he was alone in his twin-sized bed and he could hear his mother down in the kitchen, putting the pots and pans away loud enough to wake him up. He didn't think he should do anything about it.

First he looked at his watch, which he always wore except when he took a shower. Ten o'clock—not so late. Then he lifted up the sheets, stared at his "soldier," as Tiffany liked to call it, and apologized to it for having to ignore its demands.

He shouldn't have thought of Tiffany. He ached all the more. She was one hot girl, or *woman*, as she wanted to be called. He had heard of guys who had to beg their girlfriends to even touch their privates. Tiffany was different. She had shown him what it was all about, giving him a blow job in the custodian's closet when they stayed after school one day. When she had decided it was time to go all the way, she had brought the condoms. Plural, because she said he was such a stud.

She had moved here from Chicago and explained that the kids were all doing it there. She wouldn't tell him how many guys she had been with before him. "What do you care?" she would say. "I'm with you now."

Sometimes he actually felt a little used. She said she thought he would be good in bed because he had such nice, strong hands. Tiffany made no bones about the fact that she was leaving Pepin County—and wouldn't be looking back—as soon as she graduated. "I don't belong here," she would tell him. "I'm not sure which coast I'm going to go to."

The first time she said that he hadn't realized she had been talking about New York or Los Angeles. He thought she meant she wanted to live by the ocean. He had learned to not talk too much around her. She liked him quiet and ready. He never knew when she might want his services.

His mother's voice reached him. "Ray?"

He sat up in bed, knowing he'd better answer her or she'd come up and barge into his room. That thought caused his soldier to go "at ease." He hollered back, "What do you want, Mom?"

"Do you want to get up?"

What a question. "No."

She was quiet. Then she said, "I'll make you some breakfast."

He knew that she was lonesome. He was the last kid at home, and his dad was gone a lot, working at the co-op. She loved to cook and look after everyone and now they were all gone. Except him.

He crawled out of bed, opened his bedroom door, and yelled down to her, "I'm coming."

"Do you want pancakes or French toast?"

"Either."

She was quiet again. That wasn't the right answer. She really *did* want to know what he wanted.

"Pancakes sound good."

He threw on an old Farm Feed T-shirt, a band that he had seen in Milwaukee, and pulled on the jeans he had worn last night. After stopping in the bathroom to pee and rinse his mouth out, he went downstairs, taking the steps two at a time.

"Raymond," his mother admonished him, but with no sternness in her voice.

He poured himself a cup of coffee and sat at the counter, where she had already set out a plate for him.

"What time did you come in last night? I didn't hear you."

"Not that late."

"I was up till twelve."

"Maybe about one."

She raised her eyebrows.

"Mom, it's a holiday. I'm going to be a senior. We were just goofing around."

"Were you with that Tiffany?"

"No." He didn't have to lie about that. She had gone up to Chicago with her folks for the holiday. That was why he had been in such a needy condition this morning. Missing her.

Her mother poured the pancake batter into pools on the cast-iron pan and while it was forming bubbles she showed him the paper. "I don't know if you've heard us talk about the Schuler murders, but there's a letter in the paper that troubles me. I've been trying to get hold of your father. It might have to do with the pesticides that got stolen, too."

"Huh?" he said.

"The Schuler murders—so horrible. Whole family killed. I was only a little girl, but I can still remember my mom crying and holding me. All those children. Just awful."

He stared at the pancakes. They were almost ready. She followed his eyes and flipped them over. Perfect.

"But you probably don't know a thing about it."

Actually he did—thanks to Chuck Folger, the agronomist at work. The murders were like an obsession with the guy. Folger had a whole scrapbook about it in a drawer in his office: newspaper clippings, photographs, even a plat map showing where the farm was. Sometimes, when it was slow in the store, Ray would go visit with him and he would talk about the murders.

His mother carefully stacked up the three pancakes and plopped them on his plate. "How many can you eat?" she asked.

"About twelve."

His mother turned and poured out three more pancakes, then looked off in the distance. "The oldest boy was ten," his mother said.

Ray looked at his mother as if she had lost her mind. What was she talking about? What boy?

"Denny Schuler. He was just ahead of me in school. He got teased because he was German. I sure thought he was cute. I couldn't believe that he had died. Mom wouldn't let me go to the funeral."

"So you had a crush on him?"

His mother laughed. "Nothing that serious. I just thought he was cute."

Ray wondered if he would still be here in the kitchen, eating pancakes, if that kid had lived. Maybe his mother would have married Denny instead of his father and he would never have been born. Odd to think those murders so long ago might have changed the course of his life. He poured syrup all over his pancakes. Flooded them.

"Ray!" His mother slapped his hand with the spatula and surprised them both.

As Ray dug into his pancakes, he thought that maybe he should mention Chuck Folger's obsession to his father. Maybe not. Probably didn't mean a thing.

At first glance, it was an innocent enough photograph, an old black-and-white eight-and-a-half-by-eleven, showing a table set for dinner, seven plates spaced around the table with silverware and napkins, but it broke Claire's heart.

She had pulled it out from the Schuler file and then couldn't stop staring at it. A large platter with a big slab of meat was set down at one end, a bowl of potatoes in the middle of the table, and at the other end of the table was a cake with one single candle stuck in the dark frosting. One white candle.

Claire closed her eyes for a moment. She wondered if they would ever know what had happened to that family. How was the murder linked with the pesticide incidents? Claire had come into work late that morning to check on the pesticides robbery. As an investigator, she had to put in more time when the cases called for it. Not a bad trade-off for a steadier lifestyle.

Claire didn't think the sheriff was taking the whole matter seriously enough. He was hoping these recent incidents were merely pranks. She hoped so, too, but doubted it.

No new news. Nothing from Eau Claire about the forensic work that was being done on the bones. All she had heard was that, after a preliminary glance, the pathologist had said, "Human bones. Fingers."

After looking through the Schuler file, she realized this was the link that might connect the pesticide attacks with the murders in 1952. It was not common knowledge because the sheriff's department had kept it under wraps, but each member of the murdered family had

had a finger cut off. The fingers had never been found. She wasn't sure that Sheriff Talbert knew about the missing fingers. He hadn't lived in the county at the time of the murders.

It drove her crazy that the forensic work was taking so long. She needed to talk to the sheriff about the possibility of digging up the Schulers' bodies—if, in fact, this latest crime was related to those murders. They could get a DNA match on the bones. It would be a positive link between the two cases, and it might give them the lead they needed to solve the theft of the pesticides.

Claire decided to call the sheriff at home. She would keep her voice down so that Meg wouldn't hear the conversation. Mrs. Talbert answered and said it would take her a minute or two to fetch her husband.

She glanced over at Meg, who was sitting in a chair at another deputy's desk, reading a book. One of the Harry Potters. The ultimate child fantasy. Your cruel parents are not your real parents. What child doesn't dream of that? And you are the only one who has the power to save the world. When kids fantasize, they do it big.

When Meg had first started reading the series, she had complained because the main character was a boy, but she was halfway through the third book and seemed totally lost in it, oblivious to the world around her.

When Sheriff Talbert came on the line, Claire told him what she had discovered. He didn't say anything for a moment. "Wish it wasn't a holiday."

She decided she'd better push him on this. "Can you call the forensic lab and ask for a rush?"

"I think I'd better."

"I'm taking the file home with me. I'd like to meet with you in the morning and go over anything else I discover."

"Yeah, I think I need to study up on this one too. Good work, Claire."

After she hung up, she looked back at the old photograph and felt tears well up in her eyes.

What broke her heart wasn't at first obvious; it only showed slightly under the lip of the table: a small hand stretched out on the floor, tiny fingers curling up as if reaching. The baby had fallen under the table. Just one short year in the world. And one of the fingers was missing.

CHAPTER 10

He could not hide in this place, he thought as he walked down the gentle incline to the park by the river. Everyone knew him. That didn't matter, he told himself. They didn't really see him. People nodded and helloed him on either side, but no one stopped to talk. No one would ever think of him. They never did. He could come and go and no one would ever notice. That was the kind of man he was: insignificant.

He liked being insignificant. It was another way of being safe. He had studied being safe all his life.

Darkness would come soon. It would fall over the land, a sort of blanket of unseeing. Then he would really be invisible. That was how he had been saved. He walked slowly down toward the lake.

His wife had not come with him to the park. She did not like crowds, she did not like noise, and she hated fireworks. That was fine with him. He had not encouraged her. Always a homebody, she let him wander around at will. She asked very little of him, but liked him to be home for supper. Her perception of him was that he was a busy man, going about his business. That suited her fine. She liked to be a housewife—cooking and cleaning—and she watched her soap operas for company.

He had the flask with him, tucked into his bib overalls. He patted it from time to time, just to make sure it was there. As he continued his walk down to the park, he said howdy to many people: friends and neighbors, folks he had known all his life. He meant them no harm. When the truth came out and washed all the sins away, he hoped they would understand that he had to do this. He had a job to do, which meant he had to be watchful. There would be an opportunity and he would take it.

As he got down close to the lake, he could see the crowds of people setting up chairs on the beach. The smell of the lake came to him, not unpleasant—sweat and seaweed. He swatted his arm as a mosquito found him. He had said hello to twenty people. He liked numbers that were divisible by ten. It was a good sign.

The fireworks would go off straight across the lake from Lake City and everyone in Fort St. Antoine would have front-row seats. Families laid out blankets; kids ran to the edge of the water, lit off firecrackers, and threw them up in the air. Small bursts of noise, screams of delight and terror rose from the crowd.

He had always figured that fireworks were just another way for the country to get its people ready for war. If the boys came to have pleasant associations with loud bangs, then maybe when they marched off to war, it wouldn't frighten them so much. Another lie the country perpetrated on its people.

He knew how evil war was. It had destroyed his father. He had never been able to stand any loud noises and so had imbibed far too much to calm his nerves the rest of his life. His mother had always been shushing him, telling him to be still, whispering to him, "Do not startle your father or we both will pay." He had learned to move quietly.

The sun was close to setting. Another fifteen minutes and it would fall into the lake at the northwestern tip.

Just on the other side of the summer solstice, the length
of daylight shortened by about three minutes a day. This
time of the year the sun set way to the north. Seagulls
soared over the lake, white dashes in the darkening sky.

He walked to the water's edge and stared down at
the shoreline. Zebra mussels encrusted rocks and shells,
black snarls of crustaceans. They were taking over, slowly
clogging up the waterways, destroying the clam beds
that had once thrived in the river. They were a small evil
that was impossible to fight. He patted the vial in his
pocket. You needed to fight the ones you could.

Then he turned back and started to walk toward the
concession stands. He counted his steps. They mattered.
It all mattered. How you did everything. The smallest
change or deviation could change the course of everything. He knew. He had seen it happen. Look at the
Schuler murders. He had to get the truth to come out
so everyone would know what had happened that day
when the sun set a few minutes sooner than it would
this day.

Harold strolled up from where his wife, Agnes, was sitting on the beach in one of the folding chairs they had
brought with them. Agnes didn't want to walk around.
She said the sand got in her shoes. She'd stay put. The
people would come to her. He needed to get up and
move through the crowd and see who was there. It was
part of his job and it was all of his life.

The letter in the paper had not stirred up as much talk
as he thought it might. Possibly because it was the
Fourth of July, everyone was too focused on family and
eating to give a prank letter in the paper much thought.
Harold had thought of little else.

Even last night in bed, he had wrestled with it. He
hoped it meant little or nothing, but he had a very bad

feeling, and as old as he was, having seen as much as he'd seen, when he had a bad feeling he paid attention. Just as bones might ache from cold, his psyche seemed to ache from evil. He smelled it. He sensed it.

Once or twice he had thought of calling Deputy Watkins to discuss possible scenarios, but he kept deciding to wait, to give his mind time to sort through all he knew of the case history.

The night was a perfect July evening—enough humidity in the air so that smells floated easily on the water molecules—and what he smelled made him hungry. A cheese-curd stand was set up near the middle of the park, but much as he might lust after a greasy bag of that delicacy—plasticky leftovers from some cheese-making process, dipped in batter and fried in a tub full of grease until the cheese turned molten—he knew that he and his wife would suffer all night long if they ate a bag: he with indigestion and she with his thrashing.

But just beyond was a lemonade stand. Agnes liked lemonade. He was feeling slightly parched. It sounded like a good idea. He made his way and stood in line.

As he waited, he noticed Andy Lowman walking his way, carrying a large plastic cup full of lemonade. He hadn't seen Andy in a few years. Since Andy's mother died and his father was down in Tucson, Harold had no reason to get together with the younger Lowmans.

In years gone by, Earl Lowman and Harold had been friends. Not close friends, but they had both started at their jobs around the same time—Earl as a deputy sheriff and Harold as a cub reporter on the Durand paper. They would often have coffee together at the drugstore in town, Harold picking Earl's brain for the latest crime, Earl using Harold as a sounding board for what was going on in town.

Earl was a decent fellow. Andy had been a good son

until right before his mother died. Then the two of them had gotten into it and, as far as Harold knew, hadn't talked since. Such a shame. To have children and not have a relationship with them . . .

Harold had wondered about their quarrel; he had speculated about the reasons why they might have argued; and what he had come up with was that they had argued about Florence, Earl's wife, Andy's mother. She had been very sick near the end, dying of cancer, and there had arisen the issue of whether to tube-feed her to keep her alive. They had chosen not to do this.

Earl had told Harold about their decision over coffee. "Flo had just about stopped talking to us. It happened fast. One day she could hold a normal conversation and the next she could hardly say a word. Well, you know Florence. If she can't talk, what good was life?" He rubbed at his eyes.

Harold had thought it a good decision—Florence had had a good life. Why make her suffer at the end of it? But he feared that Earl had not wanted to tube-feed and Andy had disagreed with him. As husband, Earl would have had the final say. So sad to see a death split people up rather than bring them together as it should. As far as he knew the two had not talked since. But he would ask.

"Andy, how're the crops looking?"

"Hey, Harold. You're looking mighty spruced up."

Harold was wearing a light linen shirt his wife had bought him. It was perfect for this hot weather, but not many men in Pepin County wore linen shirts. He had undone the button at the neck and rolled up the sleeves, but it still looked rather dressy. "The wife," he said. "She keeps me in clothes."

Harold was surprised how Andy had aged. Now in his forties, Andy had lost his hair and weathered significantly from the constant sun that he got farming. He was wearing an old football jersey with the arms cut short and a pair of jeans. "The corn looks good. The soybeans are doing fine. Think it's going to be a good year, except it's going to be a good year for everyone, so nothing'll fetch much."

Harold decided to not beat around the bush with Andy. "How's your father doing? I haven't heard from him in a while."

Andy turned and looked toward the lake as if he were hoping there might be fireworks starting and he wouldn't have to answer the question. When he turned back to Harold, he said, "Dad's fine, I guess. He called today and talked to Marie."

"Still in Tucson?"

"I guess."

"You still aren't talking to him?"

Andy shrugged. "Not so's you'd notice."

"I should send him the paper. I think he'd be interested in that letter I printed today. Had to do with the Schuler murders. Did you see it?"

"Yes, Marie pointed it out to me. In fact, I was thinking I'd talk to you about that. About what actually happened. Dad would never say much about it, but I think he knew more than he'd let on." Andy took a swallow of his lemonade.

"Well, he was the first one on the scene," Harold started to say, when he was stopped by an odd look on Andy's face.

First, Andy looked like he had bitten into a lemon, which made sense, since he was drinking lemonade. Then he looked like he had had a lemon forced down his throat. Then he looked like the lemon was choking him. Andy's arms went up to his neck and he tried to speak, but no sound came out except a gasp for air. Harold stepped forward as Andy fell into his arms.

As they walked down to the park, Rich was reminded of this same walk only a few days ago and how that had ended—Claire running off to work. He hoped that the only excitement tonight would be the fireworks.

Meg tugged at his arm. "Can I have a piggyback ride?"

Claire, who had seemed a bit snappish all evening, said, "Leave Rich alone, Meg. You're too big. You can walk."

He thought of stepping in and contradicting Claire, but quickly reconsidered. Let her calm down, he told himself. In the meantime he simply tugged on Meg's arm, and when she looked up at him, he gave her a wink. They had started this communication between the two of them; it meant: *Wait a while; she'll get better. Then we'll get what we want.* Meg burst out into a big smile and started to skip next to him.

"I love fireworks," she announced to the night air.

"Noise and fire—what's not to like," Claire said, but with a tug of a smile.

"But Mom, they're beautiful. Sparkles and flashes of color and pictures sometimes even."

"Yes, I know, honey. They are beautiful."

Rich chimed in. "Almost as good as northern lights."

"Oh, Rich, it's been a long time since I've seen them," Claire said. "Probably ten years or so. I was driving to Fargo, on a case. I was alone in the car, heading north. It was late at night."

"How old was I, Mom?"

"You were a baby."

"Where was I?"

"You stayed home with Daddy." Claire rubbed the top of Meg's head and then continued, "I noticed something off to my right, which was north, and when I took my eyes off the road and looked into the sky, I almost drove off the road."

Meg giggled. "Mom."

"Meg, you have to see them. We should go up north this summer, Rich. Up to the Boundary Waters. Stretch out on our backs on a dock by a lake and stare up into the heavens. I've seen them where they look like white water swirling down a drain in the middle of the black sky. But that night, driving to Fargo, they were like green curtains undulating."

Meg repeated the word. "Undulating, undulating." Each time she spoke it, she did a small belly dance to illustrate what the word meant. Rich was choking back laughter. What a kid she was.

They came to the park and saw the throngs of people lined up by the lake. Rich had a sleeping bag tucked under his arm for them to sit on. Meg was dancing and jumping at the end of his other arm. Claire cupped the back of his neck with her hand and said, "I'll try to get into the spirit of things. It looks like a party down here."

Meg wanted to run off and play on the swings, so they let her go, telling her to find them at the beach in a few minutes. Rich slung his now free arm over Claire's shoulders.

"I take work with me too much," she confessed.

"That's a good thing about you. You make our county a safer place to live."

"You sound like an ad," she said, but she was laughing.

"Let's go get a good spot to watch from," he suggested.

"Oh, Rich, I ate too many potato chips. I need a glass of something."

"Beer?"

"No alcohol. I might need to do a little more work tonight."

"They've got some kind of food stand. We'll swing by and get you something on our way to the beach."

They walked slowly, exchanging greetings with their neighbors and watching the night settle over the bay. Rich stood in line with Claire to get the drink and when she got to the front, she ordered lemonade.

As they turned to head toward the beach, Rich saw Harold Peabody over Claire's shoulder.

Who was that with Harold? he wondered. When the man turned and faced Rich, he could make out that it was Andy Lowman. He wondered what those two could be talking about. They didn't have much in common. Suddenly Andy clutched his throat.

Rich stopped walking and gave his full attention to what was going on with Andy.

Claire lifted the glass of lemonade toward Rich and said, "Do you want a drink?"

Rich shook his head, not saying anything. He was watching the glass of lemonade Andy had in his hand as it went flying. Then Andy collapsed.

"I'm so thirsty," Claire said as she lifted the drink to her mouth.

Rich's hand rose up and just as the plastic cup touched her lips, he knocked it away, lemonade spraying them both.

CHAPTER 11

———+

Claire felt herself splitting into pieces as she tried to determine what to do. She had to help the man who had fallen. She had to stop what was happening. She had to find out who had done it. It was too much. Her greatest fear was that whoever had stolen the pesticides was at work again.

The first thing was to ask for help. Rich had told her that he thought it was the lemonade that had made the man sick.

"Rich, you gotta stop them from selling any more of that lemonade. Go up and talk to the owner. Don't let anyone drink it."

As Rich ran to the stand to shut it down, Claire turned to help Harold Peabody, who was about to collapse under the big man's weight. They held him together and then gently lowered him to the ground.

"Who is he?" Claire asked.

"Andy Lowman," Harold said as they settled him on the dirt. He was trying to hold Andy steady, as the afflicted man held his stomach, twisting and moaning in pain.

"What happened?" Claire asked Harold as she pulled out her cell phone. Harold shrugged. She knelt by Andy and, as she punched in the numbers of the station, she tried to reassure him. "Andy, you're going to be all right. We're right here. I'm calling for help right now."

Harold leaned him forward and encouraged him to hang in there, but Andy was fading. His face was pallid and he seemed to be having trouble breathing.

Claire needed to get help for him immediately. Her call was picked up by Judy. Thank God, she was one cool cucumber.

"I think we've got a poisoning in Fort St. Antoine. The park. At the fireworks. Send the ambulance and tell them we may have a case of Parazone or Caridon poisoning. Tell them to refer to my memo. And make sure they do it."

"Got it," Judy said back to her.

When Claire clicked off the cell phone and turned her attention back to Andy, she remembered what Bridget had told her about what the pesticide could do. As she knelt by the man, she started to check him over. He was sweating and salivating profusely, gagging reflexes shaking his whole body. All these responses were what she would expect to see in someone who had ingested one of the pesticides. Andy barely seemed conscious, and she shook him gently. His eyelids lifted slightly.

"Let's try to keep him awake and keep him partially sitting up so he doesn't choke," she said to Harold.

At her words, a spasm of nausea hit the man. He leaned forward and vomited on the grass.

A woman came running up and tried to fling herself at him, but Claire moved to block her. "I'm his wife," she told Claire. Then the small, dark-haired woman turned to her husband. "Andy, what's the matter with you?" she screamed as she reached out a hand to touch him.

"God, help me," Andy managed to get out, and then he passed out, sprawling limp on the ground.

Andy's wife tried to pull him into her arms and Claire

had to be a little rough with her to let him go. "Ma'am, you need to let me take care of him." The woman looked at her with horror in her eyes as Claire pushed her away. "I'm sorry. I need to help him."

Harold Peabody put an arm on the woman and pulled her back, saying, "Marie, let the deputy do her job."

Claire knelt down by the big man and started to arrange him in the recovery position. He was already prone, so she turned his head to the side, making sure he was breathing; then she put an arm up on that side to give him some support and pulled up the leg on that side too. She had learned in her latest Red Cross class that this was the safest position for victims who were unconscious but breathing—as long as they hadn't been seriously injured.

Rich came to get her. "Another person, a little girl, is throwing up."

Claire turned to him, horrified.

He guessed her thoughts. "Meg is fine. She's still at the swings."

"Watch her," Claire begged him, then turned back to Harold and Andy's wife. "Can you take care of him? I need to check on someone else. Watch him. Make sure he's breathing. Try to keep him from vomiting until we know what it is. The ambulance should be here in moments."

Claire went to minister to the girl, an eight-year-old blonde named Shawna whose mother told Claire that she had taken only a sip of the lemonade. The young girl was lying with her head in her mother's lap.

"Shawna," Claire said, bending over the child. "What happened when you drank the lemonade?"

"It made my throat feel dusty." The young girl clawed at her tongue, trying to get the drink out of her mouth. "It tasted like grass."

Claire worried that such a small child would suffer much worse effects. But she was relieved that Shawna seemed more alert than Andy.

By the time the ambulance arrived, four people were sick with whatever had been in the lemonade. The emergency technicians took over and examined the casualties before loading Andy into the first ambulance.

Claire stepped back from them all for a moment and looked around for her daughter. She saw that Rich was standing at the swings, pushing Meg into the sky. She wanted them to go home and lock the door. She wanted her daughter out of here, away from this danger.

She took a deep breath and headed toward the lemonade stand to find out what had happened there. As she approached it, a large bang went off and she jumped. Then glowing lights filled the sky. The fireworks blazed from the far shore of the lake, seemingly arising from another, more peaceful country—a country where it was still a holiday.

When the man came charging up, yelling at them to stop selling the lemonade, Dot decided to shut down completely. It could kill her business if someone got sick from something she served. She was racking her brain, trying to imagine anything she'd done wrong, but she knew she had meticulously followed the state's thorough guidelines. She hoped that it wasn't botulism or E. coli.

She thought of taking a sip of the lemonade herself to test it, but then she saw a man stretched out on the grass, throwing up. She didn't need that.

Remembering something, she checked the lid on the big silver cylinder that contained the latest batch of lemonade. She had seen something there when she had moved the new lemonade dispenser into the trailer to start selling it, but had been too busy to stop and see what it was. Sales had been brisk. It was a nice hot evening and everyone had eaten too much and needed something to drink to wash it all down.

She had been hoping to make enough money from this event to make the last payment on her trailer. When Guy had left her last year, telling her he couldn't sleep with a woman (actually he had said *cow*) when she weighed more than he did, he had left her with all their bills to pay. Since he had left, she had tried to lose weight, hoping he might show up again, but the harder she tried, the more weight she gained. It didn't help to be working with food.

Just as she had remembered, there was a small white plastic joint under the handle on the lid. She didn't touch the lid or the cylinder. She had watched enough TV to know that you don't touch anything. But she bent her head down and stared at the little plastic piece.

Maybe it wasn't plastic. It was off-white and looked like a small tube or joint or something. She looked closer.

It was a bone. A small bone like from the leg of a bird or a frog. A delicate ivory bone.

She felt the urge to pick it up and feel it, but she resisted.

It might mean nothing. It might have been dropped from the tree that was above the cart in the park. Those cottonwoods were notoriously messy. Maybe a bird cleaning out a nest. The remains of a fledgling that didn't make it.

When the woman deputy came running up to ask them about the lemonade, she asked who was the owner of the stand. Dot looked her over. Pretty woman, nice dark hair, great teeth. Probably smart, too, weighing well within the normal range. Dot hated her on principle.

Dot stepped forward. "I am."

"Did you make the lemonade?"

"Yes, I made it last night."

"Could it be contaminated in any way? Did you leave it sitting out overnight?"

"I didn't. And I don't think lemonade contaminates. I follow the rules that the state told me to follow. I do everything just the way it should be done. You can ask anyone. I've been doing this all summer and never had a problem."

"Where did you keep the lemonade right before you were serving it?"

"Out behind the trailer." Dot pointed to the refrigerated area that attached to the back of her trailer.

"You don't keep it in the trailer?"

"There's not enough room."

"So anyone could have had access to it?"

Dot realized what the woman was saying. "I guess."

"Shit," the woman said.

Dot was surprised to hear a deputy sheriff swear, especially this pretty woman. Dot decided that she should tell her what she found. "I don't know if this means anything, but I found something on the lid of this particular canister."

"What?" The deputy lifted her head.

"A small bone."

Stewy had been pretending to watch TV with his eyes closed. It was too early to go to bed, only nine o'clock, still light outside. But probably he was tired because he had gotten up early to mow the lawn. Really, he should blame it on the three beers with dinner. He didn't drink much anymore. Just couldn't keep functioning when he did. A couple of beers made him fall asleep. Sad state of affairs.

But a sharp, insistent ring kept nudging him awake.

As he opened his eyes and saw someone shoot someone on TV, he realized that he was hearing his cell phone. Where was the blasted thing? What could be so important on this summer night that work would call?

Then he remembered the pesticides, the letter. He bolted up in his chair and the thing folded up on him, the footrest sliding under him and the back pushing him down. Couldn't move fast in that chair. It could kill you. He managed to extricate himself from it and he looked down at a pile of newspapers and realized the phone was in there someplace. Scrambling through them, he could still hear the ringing.

Hold on; I'm coming, he thought.

As he stirred around in the newspapers, the phone popped out of the comics section. He grabbed it and pushed the right button the first time around. He hated having a cell phone, but the sheriff insisted.

"Hello," he said.

"Stewy, it's Claire. We've got several poisonings down in the park at Fort St. Antoine."

"Bad food?"

"I'm not sure. I think there's a chance it might be the pesticide guy using some of the stolen goods."

He hated to ask the next question. "Any fatalities?"

"Negative. Not so far. But the ambulance from Maiden Rock just took two people out of here, and the ambulance from Pepin is loading up. Five people in all were affected. A little girl is one of them."

"What happened?"

"I think something was put into a vat of lemonade that was being served from a refreshment stand here."

"Why do you think that?"

"All the victims had just consumed the lemonade."

She paused. He didn't like the way this incident sounded. Then she added what turned out to be the clincher for him. "A small bone was found on the lem-onade container."

Stewy caught himself on the verge of swearing. The words came out too easily. Now that he had grandchildren, he was trying to curb that impulse.

"Have you called Sheriff Talbert?" Stewy asked.

"No. Could you do that? I need to organize people here. We've got a couple of patrol cars."

"I'll call the sheriff and the lab."

"Thanks."

"Claire, what've we got going on here?"

"Possibly some kind of vendetta."

Stewy heard her hang up. He had to call Dan Talbert. But he needed to breathe for a second. He would drive down to the park as soon as he got off the phone with the sheriff. He'd brush his teeth and gargle with Listerine so the evidence of his beer would be washed away. But first he turned to the dictionary that perched on top of the bookshelf in the living room. It was always left opened to the last word he looked up.

He looked up *vendetta*. The first definition read, "a feud in which the relatives of a murdered or wronged person seek vengeance on the wrongdoer or members of his family." The Schuler family were the murdered people.

Stewy called the sheriff, trying to sound alert. "You know what a vendetta is?" he asked.

"Yes," Talbert answered. "Why?"

Stewy pressed on. "And do you know if there's anyone left in the county who is related to the Schuler family?"

"Stewy, where you going with this? Why?"

Then Stewy told him why.

CHAPTER 12

Earl was hammering the last nail into a stool he was fixing for Stella, his next-door neighbor, when he thought he heard something. It took him a few moments to figure out that the phone was ringing. He dropped the hammer. A call this late scared him to his bones.

When he picked up the phone and heard Marie's voice, his hand flew up to his heart. In Tucson it was eleven at night, so he knew it was one A.M. in Wisconsin. He knew the only reason she would contact him at this hour would be about something bad.

"Why are you calling me?" he asked, his voice shaking.

"Earl, I'm at the hospital."

"What happened?" he yelled. "Tell me."

"They think Andy was poisoned. Maybe pesticides."

"What did he do? Was he mishandling them? What was he doing using pesticides this time of year?"

Marie raised her voice, saying firmly, "Earl, calm down and listen to me. It wasn't like that. Someone put it in some lemonade he drank."

He didn't comprehend what she was saying, but that wasn't important right now. "Is he going to be all right?"

Her voice deepened. "The doctors aren't sure. They're using charcoal to get it out of his system. One doctor talked to me a few minutes ago. He said that they should know in a few more hours if he's going to make it." Suddenly her voice broke and she wailed, "Earl, I can't lose him. I won't be able to stand it."

He wasn't going to argue with her. She was one strong woman, but no one could stand to lose a loved one. He still missed his wife every day.

"Marie," he said soothingly, "start at the beginning."

So she explained that she and Andy had gone to see the fireworks and that Andy had bought some lemonade. "They think there was something in it."

Then she explained what the sheriff had told her, that a crazy person had stolen some pesticides and was going around the county using them for destructive purposes.

"Seems to be tied in with the Schuler murders," she said in conclusion. "That's what they think."

The irony. It didn't matter how far away he went, that damn murder case was going to haunt him all his life.

"Was anyone else hurt?" he thought to ask.

"Yes, four other victims. One of them was a little girl. But she's all right. She spit it right out. The mother doesn't think she swallowed much. They sent her home an hour ago. The other three are in worse shape, but all of them seem to be recovering. They figure Andy drank half his glass in one gulp. Man, I've always told him he has a big mouth." She started laughing and then she was crying again.

Earl knew what he was going to do. He wasn't going to tell Marie, because he didn't want her to dissuade him. "He's a strong man, Marie. He's not going to let this stop him. You can count on him to come back to you."

Marie had gone silent on the other end of the line. She sniffed and blew her nose. "Thank you for saying that, Earl. I needed to hear it. You're right. If anyone can make it through this, he can."

"Are you going to stay there all night?"

"Where else could I be? I can't leave him. What if he wakes up? I need to be with him."

"Of course. Listen, give me the number there and let me call you in the morning. It can be on my nickel."

Marie did as he asked.

"Thank you for calling me, Marie. It means a lot." His voice was trembling and he needed to get off the phone. He needed to move.

"You're welcome."

They both hung up. Earl sat for a moment, fighting back the urge to kick or punch the wall, knowing it would do no good. He would just end up with a broken hand or a bruised leg—might even put a dent in the wall.

He walked over to his coffeemaker. The timer was set for six in the morning. He turned off the timer and turned on the machine. It made a small gurgling that he found reassuring. He would need to tank himself up on caffeine if he wanted to get to Wichita by tomorrow night. Then it would be another day's drive to get to Pepin County.

If he could stand to fly, he would do it, but he hadn't been able to get on a plane since he was twenty—when the first and only plane he had ever boarded had felt like it was going to fall out of the sky.

He hoped he would still have a son to talk to when he got to the hospital in Wisconsin.

The frogs in the slough alongside the lake were so loud that they sounded like they were screaming themselves hoarse. Claire was sure that their calls were something about love, but she didn't want to think about their yearning.

Sitting by herself at a picnic table in the park, she watched the last patrol car pull out onto Highway 35. Claire knew she should stand up and go home and try to sleep for a few hours, but she wanted to sit for a moment. She needed this time of stillness to gather herself together. Over the last few hours, she felt she had flown into fragments.

A small prayer had pulsed through her as she worked with everyone on this crime scene: *Please let no one die.* A few minutes ago she had called the hospital to learn that they had released the little girl; that news had lifted her spirits. However, Andy Lowman's condition had been given as critical. The nurse told her that the other three were stable.

The lemonade stand, with police tape wrapped around it, had been shunted off to the side of the road that led down to the lake. The lab hadn't wanted the stand to be moved, even though they took half of the poor woman's equipment with them.

The ambulances had left first. The interviews had gone on until after midnight. The sheriff had gotten right in with the rest of them, asking questions, writing down names. They had needed all the hands they could get.

Out of the full sheriff's department of twenty deputies, ten had been in the park, transcribing the testimony of eyewitnesses. At first questioning, no one had seen anything suspicious.

There must have been over two hundred people in the park when the poisonings occurred. How many of them were men? How many of them had a farming background? They could start narrowing all this down in the morning.

However, she couldn't be sure that the pesticide had been put in the lemonade while it was in the park. It could have happened at the woman's workplace. More to check on.

Claire desperately hoped this incident didn't escalate into a murder investigation. When she had seen the five victims off into ambulances, four of them had looked pretty good. But not Andy Lowman. Apparently he was the one to worry about.

This whole scene reminded her too much of the street dance she and Rich had gone to last summer—a festive gathering of people that was blown apart by violence when a man had been stabbed to death. This wasn't supposed to happen out in the country.

She slumped over the picnic table. It was after two o'clock. She had to go home. She hoped Rich was sleeping. She didn't want to rehash everything with him. Not that he wasn't a good sounding board—he was. But she was weary from thinking about what might happen next.

However, before she went home, she was going to make one more phone call. She took out her cell phone and dialed a number she knew by heart.

A sleepy man answered. The tone of his voice reminded her of the man she had loved for most of her adult life. Steven's dad sounded so much like her late husband that she couldn't say anything. He said hello again.

"Sorry, Thomas. It's Claire."

"Claire, what's the matter?" His voice rose at the question.

"Not anything to do with us. Meg and I are fine. But we're having some problems down here, and I know you and Beth said you'd like to have Meg for a week or so this summer."

"Yes," he said, and waited.

"Could you come and get her bright and early tomorrow morning?"

"Of course. Is nine okay?"

She hated to do this to him, but she knew she would need to get to work before then. "How about eight?"

"Eight will be fine. We'll see you then. Go to sleep, Claire." He hung up.

He was a good man. Asked no questions. Did what he could. His son had been like him. Talking to Thomas made her miss Steven more than usual.

Rich hated this. He knew he would always hate Claire's work demands: the waiting, the worrying, the putting the kid to bed alone, the attempt to sleep, the attempt not to sleep. It stank.

Here it was nearly three o'clock in the morning, the fifth of July, and Claire still wasn't home. He was sitting on the edge of her bed, in her house, holding his head in his hands and feeling mad.

What would she have done if he hadn't been there to take care of Meg? He knew he didn't dare ask because she would only get mad and tell him she could manage without him. One of the things he liked most about Claire was how independent she was. It also drove him crazy.

He wondered if she could manage without him. He wondered if she had any suspicion that she couldn't.

But he couldn't do anything about that. Claire had to resolve those things herself. What he needed to work on was his own attitude. If he were going to marry this deputy sheriff, then he needed to learn how to be a supportive, understanding, calm partner—not always typical male characteristics, and certainly ones he needed to improve on.

He had been angry when he climbed the stairs to go to bed. He had left all the dirty dishes piled next to the sink. Washing dishes was good for the soul, his grandmother used to tell him.

Rich stood up from the bed and pulled on his jeans and a T-shirt. He felt a bulge in his pocket, and when he patted it, he remembered he had slipped the box with the ring in there just in case. With Claire deep into a new case, he wasn't sure when he'd ever have the chance to propose. What did all this say about their relationship?

He walked down the stairs quietly, so as not to wake Meg, and started running hot water into the sink.

And that was how Claire found him—elbow-deep in warm, soapy water, digging the last few utensils out of the bottom of the sink.

She walked in, gently closing the door behind her. She leaned against the door, then saw him. "Oh, you're up."

"Couldn't sleep. I tried. Thought of going down to the park, but knew that wasn't a good idea."

"Oh, Rich, you wouldn't have wanted to be there." She walked into the kitchen and stared at all the dishes stacked in the drainer. "Thanks for cleaning up."

"What happened?"

Claire looked exhausted. When she got tired, her hair seemed to get messier, out of control. Wisps of black hair had come loose from her ponytail and floated around her face. She had a smear of dirt on her cheek that looked like a blurred beauty mark. Her eyes were red-rimmed.

She shrugged her shoulders. "I don't really know. We talked to everybody. Nobody saw anything that we know of yet. Maybe when we go over all the notes tomorrow, something will jump out at us."

Rich knew that Claire had thought she would have the next day off and had no day care set up for her daughter. "You want me to watch Meg for you tomorrow? I've got some errands, but she can come along with me."

"No, that won't be necessary. She's going to stay with her grandparents. It's all set up."

This was the first he had heard about Meg's going

away so soon. When had Claire arranged that? "Oh, that works out well." He hated the edge he heard in his voice.

"Well, I know you've got your work to do and I just didn't want to have to worry about her."

"I don't mind watching her."

"I ask enough of you already, Rich. I need to save you for special times."

"Special times—what a load of crap! What does that mean? You don't have to save me for nothing."

"I don't?" Claire looked up at him with trepidation. "What does that mean?"

He decided to be very clear. He pulled out the box with the ring and handed it to her. "I want you to marry me."

"Oh!" Claire held the box out in front of her as if it might explode.

Rich knew he was deep into it now and there was no way to go but straight ahead. He plunged forward.

"I want to be next to you when these things happen. I want to have a reason to get so worried about you. I want to know that if anything happens to you, I'll be the first person to be notified. I'm in love with you and I want to make a life with you. Will you marry me?"

Claire opened the box and saw the ring. Then she sat down in a chair at the kitchen table and burst into tears.

July 7, 1952

Louise Schuler was sitting on the floor in her bedroom, showing Elisabeth how to put clothes on a paper doll. Louise didn't really like to play with them much anymore—she was almost too old for that—but she loved to cut them out.

She heard a loud bang downstairs in the kitchen and then Arlette cried for a moment and then another bang and the baby stopped. Louise stood up. It must mean something, that noise. It nearly sounded like a gun. She hoped it meant it was time for dinner. Usually her mom hollered out the front door to tell them to come in and eat. Maybe she was trying something new. Or maybe her dad had dropped something.

She hoped he hadn't dropped the birthday cake. Mom had let her help frost it and she had dipped her finger in the frosting when her mom wasn't looking. It was so delicious her mouth watered just thinking about it.

Louise stood up and told Elisabeth to put her paper dolls away. It was time to go eat.

"I didn't hear Mom."

"*Mach schnell*," Louise said, imitating her mother. She didn't know many words in German, but her mother said those words all the time. It meant, *Make it snappy; be quick about it.*

Elisabeth couldn't do anything fast. She carefully put

her paper dolls back in their folder and put all their clothes away. Louise decided to practice her pirouettes in the middle of the floor. She was wearing only her stockings, so she could turn better. She wanted to take ballet lessons but her mother said they didn't have enough money.

She heard some steps coming down the hall and stopped turning around, but her head was still dizzy from all the spinning and she couldn't walk straight. A third loud bang happened, only this time right outside the door. Elisabeth fell down on the bed.

Louise stood very still, her arms stretched out for balance. The fourth time the gun went off she didn't hear it.

CHAPTER 13

Meg sat out on the front steps in the shade of the crab-apple tree. Another hot day. Too hot to even think about being productive. All she felt like doing was going down to the beach. But it didn't look like the day was shaping up that way.

She wanted to have her life be the way it was supposed to be: her mom with the day off, Rich and her mom smiling and happy, her visit to her grandparents' not for a few weeks yet. Instead her mom had woken her up early this morning and helped her pack a suitcase. Now she was sitting on the front steps, waiting for her grandparents to pick her up.

It wasn't that she didn't like her grandparents. They were great, even if they tried too hard. She always felt like they were trying to make up for their son, her father, being dead. They always gave her toys and took her to movies. They did some kind of major activity every day—went to the science museum, took a bike ride—but sometimes she found it exhausting.

It was hard to adjust when things changed so rapidly. She needed to get her mind ready.

She wasn't bored with summer yet. If it were the end of summer, she would be ready to go and stay with them, but she still could think of so many things to do. She wanted to stay home. But looking at her mom's face, she knew a tantrum would do little good. Claire was bustling about at top speed, making sure Meg hadn't forgotten to take anything. Rich was nursing a cup of coffee and pretending to read the paper. But it was yesterday's paper and he wasn't turning the pages.

Meg decided to go along with the plans. She had a feeling her mom and Rich needed to have it out, and it might be easier for them to do that if she wasn't there. She wanted to have Rich as the permanent guy-dad in life, but she wasn't the one who had to marry him and pledge for better or for worse. She could only give her mom so much advice on these matters and then she was on her own.

Meg walked into the house and let the screen door slam behind her. A small protest. "Mom, how long am I staying for?"

Her mom stopped what she was doing, turned her head, and then said, "What?"

Meg knew the *What?* wasn't a real one. It was a stalling *What?* She sat down on a porch chair and just looked at her mom, waiting for her to provide a real answer.

"How about a week?" Her mother looked over at her with her face slightly crinkled.

"That's a little long."

"Maybe it will be shorter."

"You just want me out of here, don't you?"

Her mom wiped her hands on her pants and walked over and sat down next to Meg. "In a way. I'm not going to lie to you. You know this job of mine is demanding sometimes." She flicked back a strand of Meg's hair. "We've talked about this. I need to focus on this case. People got hurt last night."

"Poisoned?"

"It appears so."

"Did anyone die?" Meg had to ask the question she had been framing since she woke up.

"No, just got very sick."

"God, Mom, you almost drank that stuff."

Her mother's head jerked up. "Meg, don't say that word."

Meg clamped her hand over her mouth. How had that word come out? She had only said *God* a couple of times in her life, and then it had been around friends. But she knew she should never have even tried out the swear words. Once your mouth got used to saying them, you never knew when they might pop out. Words had a life of their own.

"I just don't want you to worry," her mother said.

"That's stupid to tell me not to worry. It makes me know there's something to worry about."

"I'm sorry."

"Oh, Mom. It's okay. Will you promise to call every day?"

"Yes, I will."

"Will you promise to let me come home as soon as I can?"

"Yes, the very moment."

Meg felt her mother's arms fold over her the way the wings of a mother bird covered her young. But she didn't sink into the embrace and close her eyes and cuddle. She kept watching—because there was something out there that was trying to get them all.

Five people were poisoned in the Fort St. Antoine park as people gathered to watch the Fourth of July fireworks. It appears that the lemonade sold at one of the concessions had been spiked with a toxic product, possibly a pesticide. The sheriff's office believes there might be a connection to the pesticides that were stolen on July first.

"How's it coming?" Sarah popped her head in his office door. They were on a tight deadline. Usually they didn't have breaking news that needed to go above the fold on the front page. It meant a major reordering of all the other articles.

"I'll have it done," Harold promised.

With that, Sarah returned to the outer office.

Harold paused in his typing. Maybe he should have let Sarah write the lead article. He could work on layout and she could interview him as a material witness. Harold still remembered the weight of Andy Lowman as he fell into his arms. It was urgent that this piece get finalized in the next hour, but Harold felt his mind wander into the past to another Fourth of July celebration.

Sitting at his desk with a pile of old papers in front of him, Harold remembered the first time he had seen Bertha Schuler. She had been Bertha Ostreich then. Eighteen years old and brimming with life. Blond hair down to her waist, green-blue eyes that called to any man, a full figure, and strong arms. She was a farm girl. Even though she was born in Wisconsin, she had a bit of a German accent left over from her parents.

He had seen her at a dance. He had been only fifteen, but he thought of asking her to dance. He mentioned it to one of his friends, Danny Swenson, who had laughed at him and slapped him on the shoulders, saying, "Don't dance with her. Don't you know she's a kraut?"

Harold had thought to tell his friend that he, too, had German blood in him, but decided not to bother. He didn't really know how to dance well enough to have the courage to ask her. Watching her spin around the

floor in the arms of one older man and then another had
been good enough for him.

Two men had vied for her attention: Carl Wahlund
and Otto Schuler. Wahlund had gone off to the service a
few months later, and Bertha had married Otto Schuler
that same year. Harold had finally danced with her for a
short moment at her wedding.

Years went by. He had hardly thought of her again
until the murders.

He had gone off to Madison to the university and had
met his lovely Agnes there. He had brought her back
home and started working at the paper.

Two years later, the Schuler family had been murdered
and he had written about it in the *Durand Daily*. He
picked up an old issue, dated July 8, 1952.

The headline read: FARM FAMILY MASSACRED, NO SUS-
PECT

Last night the Otto Schuler family, five children and
their two parents, were found shot to death on their
farm outside of Fort St. Antoine. A young deputy
sheriff discovered the bodies at about seven P.M. when
he returned a saw he had borrowed. No one was at
the scene when he arrived. The house had not been
ransacked and the table was still set for dinner. It is assumed the killings took place in the late afternoon.

Sheriff Runsfeld said he had never seen anything
like it. "It's been five years since Leroy Kent was shot
to death in a bar in Durand. That was the last murder
we had in Pepin County. Now we have seven deaths
on our hands."

Harold stopped reading and took off his glasses.
Made him tired to read about it. At the time he had been
excited to the marrow of his bones. Driving out to the

crime scene, he couldn't wait to get there. The sheriff's men had blocked everyone from going into the house, but he had seen the feet of the oldest son sticking out from under a blanket in the barn.

At the time he had thought this story would be his ticket out of rural Wisconsin. His writing was being picked up by newspapers all over the country. There was something about a farm killing, the isolation of it, the supposed idyllic nature of farm living, that got urban readers going.

When it had changed, when the story had hit him full in the chest, was when he had gone to the funeral. The size of the coffin for Arlette, the littlest girl, the baby of her family, had thrown him. Too small. No one should die that young.

Then all the coffins lined up. A whole family wiped out. What they might have done in the world gone. Agnes had not been able to stop crying through the whole service. They had gone home and gone to bed and he had held her gently all the night long. In the morning she told him that she was glad they couldn't have children.

"I couldn't bear it if anything happened to them," she said. "We're fine the way we are."

And they *had* been fine. Surprisingly, they never left Durand. A couple of offers had come in, but Harold hadn't accepted them for varying reasons. They had settled back into their lives. The Schuler family had stayed dead, and no one else had been murdered for years.

After Harold bought the paper, he gave up on his idea of ever leaving the area. He gave up on some of his lofty ideas about what a real newspaper should do for a community. He had come to see, unlike his college professors who had never written for a small-town newspaper, what his community actually wanted from the paper: a chance to have their names on the front page for baking the best oatmeal cookies at the state fair, the honor-roll list from the high school every quarter, the weddings, the funerals, the births, the swap meets. A minor skirmish at the school board meeting was enough excitement for them.

When he bought the paper, Harold was in his late forties and he understood his readers better. He cared about them more. It seemed to him they wanted life to go on in a calm and gentle way—for it to appear under-standable and controllable. When you were trying to grow soybeans for a living, you didn't necessarily want the paper to challenge your way of life.

And now he was faced with the second big story of his life and he was seriously thinking of handing it over to Sarah Briding. Maybe it would be her way out of town and he would see her byline in the *New York Times* in years to come. Everyone deserved a chance.

"Sarah, could you come in here please?"

The girl—woman, he supposed he should call her—appeared in his doorway. She reminded him a little of Bertha all those many years ago. Hair was a little darker blond, but she was equally full of life. It was all ahead of her.

"Yes, Harold." After her first month of working at the paper, he had been able to persuade her to call him by his first name, but it still rolled uneasily off her tongue. "What can I do for you?"

"The park poisonings, the Schuler murders . . ." He pointed at a nearby chair, then paused. Where to start? "Come in here and let me tell you everything I know."

"Human for sure?" Claire asked, holding the phone wedged between her shoulder and her ear so she could take notes.

"Quite sure." Sarah Morgan, the forensic anthropologist, cleared her throat, then added, "Although the small bones could be from a bear."

"Really?"

"Well, I don't think so, but bear bones are the ones that most closely resemble human and they resemble them especially when they're young. And most of these bones are from younger humans."

"How many people?"

"Hard to tell exactly. From their varying sizes, I'd say there's a good chance that the bones are from four to six different people. One's pretty small. Baby-sized."

"Well, there was a baby involved. Can you tell what bones in the body they are?" Claire had told her nothing about the Schuler murders. She wanted to see if she would match it or not.

Sarah said, "All the bones are phalanges or digits."

"Translate, please."

"Fingers. Probably baby fingers."

"That's what I wanted to hear. Can you tell me the sexes?"

"No, nor can I tell you anything about their ethnicity."

"One last queston. Can you tell how long they've been dead—so to speak?"

"I can tell you they weren't dismembered yesterday or even three months ago. But they could be a year old or they could be fifteen hundred years old. Until they get old enough to do carbon dating, I can't tell you much more."

"But they could be fifty years old?"

"Yes."

Claire told Sarah she would be sending her another bone. Sarah said she'd fax her the full report when she had finished with the tool-mark analysis.

"What's this about?"

"A family was murdered here about fifty years ago."

"With a baby?"

"Yes, it was her first birthday."

Two hours later, the sheriff called a meeting with everyone to go over all that was known about the poisonings. He reported that four of the poison victims had left the hospital. Andy Lowman was still in critical condition. He sent off a crew of deputies to go back to the park and scour it for anything they might have missed last night. He told Claire he wanted her to be on hand to take the forensic reports as they came in and to coordinate all activities from the office. Among all the deputies there was a sense of urgency and a more pronounced sense of not knowing how to protect themselves or the community from what was happening.

"We have to understand what has led to this," Claire stated.

The sheriff nodded. "I want you to work on that."

Since the meeting, Claire had been at her desk, poring over the Schuler case. She read every report, looked at the file inside and out, stared at the photographs. Seven people killed. Five in the house and two outside.

When she lifted up her head to clear it, she thought about Rich. He had asked her to marry him, as she thought he might. But she hadn't said anything definite, just put him off. They had agreed to talk again in several days. She had awakened in the night and felt his body sprawled against hers. She would lose him if she couldn't commit to him. He wouldn't stick around for long. Why did she have to be so unsure? It should be easy to link up with this gentle man.

"I've called in reinforcements," the sheriff told Claire, standing over her desk like a totem pole.

Claire stood up, not liking the way he was towering over her. "I'm all for that."

Sheriff Talbert shook his shaggy head. "I have a bad feeling about this. Have had all along."

"We all do. We need help. I think this guy might do worse to the county before he's done." Claire pointed out to the sheriff, "The Schulers were murdered on July the seventh."

"I realize that."

"We need to talk about what this guy might be able to do with the pesticides he has left. When will they be here and who's coming?"

"They said they'd try to get here by late afternoon. Two guys from the Department of Criminal Investigation. Can you line up the rest of the folks that should be included in this discussion?"

Claire nodded. "I'd like Sorenson to come from the cooperative. Maybe Harold Peabody. He seems to be quite in touch with this case. He knows everything there is to know about the county."

"Who do you want from the department?"

"Everyone we can spare."

The sheriff nodded and turned to walk away.

Claire said after him, "I've been looking at the Schuler murder case. I think our answers might be there."

He turned back and asked, "What are the questions?"

"Who killed the Schulers?"

"We have only this note in the paper that tells us it's connected with the Schulers," the sheriff pointed out.

"We have the bones. And the most likely person to have the bones is the man who killed them. He might be at it again, except it looks like he might want us to catch him this time."

CHAPTER 14

A plat map of the county covered Claire's desk. The date was 1950, two years before the Schuler murders occurred. The drawings were in black and white with dotted lines for the roads, doubled lines for the sections, and single lines for the property divisions. The names of the owners of each property were written in a clear, slanting print. Names like *the Vogl brothers, John Green et al.,* and *Paul & Martha Moody* explained relationships.

Claire let her eye follow the road up the bluff from Fort St. Antoine. Turning a page, she continued her descent and curved around the road as it meandered between streams and farmland.

There it was—the Schuler place. An L-shaped, sixty-acre piece of property right next to the Carl Wahlund farm. That name sounded familiar to her. She'd have to see if he was still alive.

"What you poring over there, Claire?" Scott Lund, another deputy, leaned over the desk next to her and stared down at the map.

"Do you know this area, Scott?"

"Sure."

"Is Carl Wahlund still alive?"

"Alive and kicking. Last I heard he was still farming." Scott reached down and traced the edge of the Wahlund property and then followed it around to encompass what had been the Schuler property. "He's farming all that piece of land."

"He now owns the Schuler property? How'd that happen?"

"Well, he inherited it. He married Bertha Schuler's sister. When the whole family was killed, they were the closest of kin. I guess you could say that his wife inherited it. She died about ten years ago. Nice woman. But Carl ruled the roost."

"But I thought that was the Daniels farm?"

"Naw, they just rent from Carl. I think they rent the farmhouse and about five acres right around the homestead. He farms the rest of it."

"Who's back here?" Claire pointed to the farm behind the Schulers'.

"That's the Lindstrom place. Theo Lindstrom is dead now. So's his wife. But their son, Paul, is working the farm. He's a nice, quiet guy. Married. You see him around once in a while."

"How old is he?"

Scott thought for a moment. "Jeez, I'd guess about fifteen, twenty years older than me. Don't really know."

"So in his late fifties, which would have made him pretty young when this all happened. But he's probably worth talking to."

Scott stared at the map and then pointed his finger at a swampy area marked by slash lines on the property to the west of the Schulers'. "You ever been up here?"

"I don't think so. What is it?"

"It's that trout farm. You can go up there and fish. They'll fillet your fish and send you home with them ready to fry up. I took my nephew up there once. He thought it was great."

"I bet Meg would like it," Claire said, and felt her

heart lurch slightly at the thought of her absent daughter. How she missed her when she was gone, like an amputated limb that continued to tingle.

"Let me know if I can be of more assistance," Scott said before he walked away.

Claire continued to study the map. *This is where it all happened,* she thought. *This piece of land at the top of the bluff.* It was pretty up there. She had always admired it when she had gone up to get eggs from the Danielses. She'd have to ask them if she could come up and walk around, get more of a feel for the place.

She wondered what it was like for them to be living in a farmhouse where such vicious murders had taken place. She'd have to ask Celia Daniels if she had ever heard any gossip on what had really happened that day. One of the old-timers might have let something slip when they came over to buy eggs. It was worth a shot.

Just as she was about to close the map, she noticed a marking at the top of the Schuler land, right next to the Lindstroms'. A circle with a line bisecting it. What did that mean? She turned to the legend and read aloud, " 'Well or cistern or spring.' " This country was dotted with springs that dug coulees out of the sides of the bluffs on their way down to the lake. Water was plentiful.

Arlene wiped at the kitchen counters and wondered what she should make for lunch. It was still the big meal of the day for her men. She could count on her dad coming to eat today. She had seen him out in the field, baling the hay he had cut a couple of days ago. It was a good day for haying—hot and dry. If the weather went right, he'd get another harvest out of the fields. It could be a good year.

He had been out there bright and early, considering

that she had seen his pickup truck drive past their house at eleven o'clock last night. How unlike her father. He usually tried to watch the news if he managed to stay up that late, then went right to bed. Maybe he had gone to see the fireworks.

She didn't think her husband would be back in time for lunch. He had told her he was off to Eau Claire to get a piece of something to fix the mower. She hadn't really listened. She'd put something aside for him to eat when he got in.

Arlene went to the fridge and took out a pound of hamburger. She could always do something with hamburger. Once in a while Dad liked meatballs. That was one dish her mother had made that was German—meatballs in a sour-cream gravy. She checked and she had a little sour cream left in the container, enough to stir in and make it work. Seemed kind of hot to make the dish, but Dad always wanted something that would stick to his ribs.

One day, a few weeks back, she had tried to make him a salad. She had seen Martha Stewart prepare it on her television show and it had looked so good. Arlene couldn't pronounce the name of it. Salad Neeswaws— something like that. Potatoes and green beans and tomatoes. She had all that coming out of the garden, so she thought she'd try it.

Her father had looked at it and said, "Nice salad, but where's the dinner?"

She wouldn't fix it again.

Funny how she had gotten stuck with her father. When she was a kid, Arlene had sworn she'd leave Pepin County and never come back. Then, in tenth grade, she had started going with Larry. They had married right out of high school.

Larry didn't want to leave the area. There was no get-

ting around that. He wanted to live on the family farm
and work for the railroad. So they moved down the
road from her parents and then her mother died.

She missed that woman like a comforter on a cold
night. She actually didn't think her father was going to
last without her. What was odd was that they never had
seemed to get along that well while her mother was still
alive. She did everything he told her to do. But there
didn't seem to be much love.

Arlene had heard through the grapevine that her father had been in love with her mother's sister. She had
never asked him about the gossip. It was so long ago, it
didn't seem to matter anymore.

Arlene felt like she was getting to the age where she
had started to redefine love. Lust had gotten her and
Larry in trouble. She had been sure she was going to get
pregnant before they got married. But love was gentler
than lust. It lasted longer. It didn't tend to hurt as much.
It was about living together and doing the chores and
fighting a little and mending a lot.

From the bread drawer she took out a box of Ritz
crackers, left them in the inner wrapper, and smashed
them with her rolling pin. When they were all crumbs,
she opened up the wrapper and poured them in a bowl
with the hamburger. Then she chopped up a little raw
onion, dumped in some Worcestershire sauce, and stirred
in an egg. She never had to measure anything. She had
done it too many times. Plus, a recipe like this wasn't
exact. It was about what you had in the cupboards.

With a big spoon, she scooped up a handful of the
meat mixture and rolled out the meatballs.

She lifted out the big cast-iron frying pan and got it
heating up. She cooked the meatballs slowly; they held
together better if you did them that way.

Precisely at noon, her father showed up.

"Hey," he shouted in at her from the back door.

"Hi, Dad."

"Smells good."

He washed up and came and sat at the table. She poured him a glass of water, which he drank down, and then she poured him a glass of milk. He drank milk with every meal.

"Where's Larry?"

"Had to get a thingamajig in Eau Claire."

"I don't know if they have them there."

A bark of a laugh came out of Arlene. Her father had made a joke. He must be in a good mood.

"Where were you last night?" she asked as she set his plate down in front of him.

He spilled his milk. "Why?"

How like him to answer a question with a question. Nothing was easy. "I just wondered. Saw you coming home."

"What're you, spying on me?" He started stirring his food. He always did that, and it bugged Arlene. Why couldn't he simply lift the food off his plate with his fork and eat it? Why did he have to move it all around?

"Dad, I was washing the dishes and looking out the window. Don't think that counts as spying."

"Went for a drive." He stabbed his fork into a meatball and ate it. He nodded his approval.

"Nice night for that." She would leave it at that. No need to stir him up. She wished she had never asked.

Claire parked in the Danielses' driveway and sat in the squad car, staring out at the buildings. She had studied photographs of the crime scene so carefully that she knew where all the bodies had been found on this farm. Most of them in the farmhouse, but the father and old-est son had been outside. The son's body had been found right in among the cows, beside buckets of milk sitting out, gathering flies.

The trees around the homestead had grown up since 1952. The thicket of arbor vitae that Bertha had planted around the side of the house was as tall as the roofline, forming a courtyard. The maple, only as high as the clothesline in the photos, now towered over the house, creating a canopy of green leaves for the kids to play under.

Chickens were scratching away at the ground. One was sleeping in the hollow of the maple tree. She wondered what the Danielses had decided to do about them. According to Rich, they didn't feel they could use them anymore as egg layers.

Why had she come up here? It didn't make a lot of sense. There would be nothing here, after fifty years, that would help her understand what had happened. But she felt clear that she needed to look around.

As she opened the car door, the smallest Daniels came running out. What was her name—Julie, Jilly?

"Hi," the girl said, stopping a few feet away and standing so her belly stuck out under her sunflower T-shirt.

"Hi, yourself. Your mom home?"

"Sure, she is." The little girl waved her arms up and down. "I know you."

"You do?"

"Yeah, you're Meg's mommy."

"I am."

The girl tilted her head and squinted at Claire. "So why are you dressed up like a policeman?"

"This is my job."

"Oh. That's a funny job."

"Not always."

Claire heard the screen door slam behind her and

turned to see Celia Daniels jogging down the path, worry tightening her face. "Is anything wrong? Why are you here?"

"Hi, Celia. Nothing that you need to worry about, but we did have another poisoning last night."

Celia stopped a few feet in front of her and folded her arms in front of her waist. A tall, thin woman, she had muscles that showed through her shirt that were from working, not working out. "Where? Who?"

"Down in the park at the fireworks. Five people went to the hospital, but all but one are doing fine."

"Who isn't doing fine?"

"Andy Lowman."

Celia shook her head. "I don't know him."

"He's from around here. His father was a deputy."

"Was it pesticides again?"

"We're pretty sure."

"What can I do?"

"Well, the reason I came out—" Claire stopped to collect her thoughts. "I'm not sure if you've heard, but it seems that this wave of activity is tied in with the Schuler murders."

Celia gave a slight nod of her head, then said, "Jilly, I want you to go find Thomas and help him with whatever he's doing."

"Mom, I want to be with you."

"Jilly!" At the sound of her mother's voice, Jilly scampered off.

"Come on in the house." As they walked down the gravel path, Celia told Claire, "I haven't really told the children much about what happened here. Actually I don't know much myself. When we rented the place from Carl Wahlund, he told us about the murders, but he didn't go into great detail. I got the impression it was a painful subject for him. He knew we'd find out and he didn't want us to feel like we had been duped. The house was in real bad shape when we moved in. No one had lived in it for over forty years. Carl had kept a roof on it and that saved the structure."

The kitchen was lovely. Sunshine came through white dotted-swiss curtains over the sink. A row of white ceramic pots lined the windowsill. The sink was full of white and red radishes, the chore Celia had been in the midst of when Claire arrived.

Claire looked around the room, which seemed sunnier than she remembered it from the photographs. "You've made this such a nice place to live. Hard to believe what happened here. Why would someone have killed the whole family?"

Celia answered, "Love or money."

This answer surprised Claire, and she gave Celia an odd look.

"I read mysteries. That's what it always is in the end—love or money."

"Maybe in books, but in real life the reasons are usually more basic—stupidity, anger, or craziness."

"I suppose."

"Why did you rent this house?"

"It's not that easy to get a farm around here, and we figured this way we'd get a foot in the door." Celia looked around. "We'd love to buy this place. But I don't know if Carl will sell it. We've brought it up a couple of times, and we can't get him to say anything definitive. I suppose it's hard to sell because it was in the family."

"Well, not really his family. His wife's family."

"That's right." Celia pointed her to a stool. "Can I get you something to drink?"

"Just water would be fine. What I'd like to do, if you don't mind, is look around the house."

Celia filled a large glass with water from the tap and

handed it to Claire. "Sure. It's a mess, though. This is our busy time of year and we don't do much to keep the house straightened."

"Don't worry about that."

"Do you want to do it on your own?"

"If you don't mind."

"That'd be fine. I've got more to do than I can manage. Just wander around. If you need anything else, let me know."

Claire stepped out of the kitchen and looked back in at it. Whoever had done the killings must have started outside. First the boy, then his father. Then the killer must have come in through the kitchen door and shot Bertha Schuler as she was putting food on the table. Then the baby had been shot.

The rest of the kids would have been upstairs, hearing the noise of the gunshots. It broke her heart to think of them. What a horrible time it must have been. What had they tried to do? Three were shot in their rooms— one of them had even tried to crawl under a bed to get away.

She walked up the stairs, hearing the sound her shoes made on the treads—impossible to sneak up on anyone. She turned down the hallway and looked in one room. This was where the two girls had been found. One by the door, the other over by the window.

Claire squatted down and looked at the wood floor. Right by the door frame there was a small mark on the floor, a marring of the wood surface.

She stood up and walked into the other room. The bed had been up against the wall. A large braided rug covered the floor. She rolled it back and knelt down, stared at the floor. She found the same mark again. A sawing mark, where a knife had chewed into the floor.

Maybe this was why she had come here—to examine

the crime scene. Maybe it didn't matter that the crime had happened fifty years ago. Like a bloodhound getting a faint scent from the old clothes of the hunted, she needed to sniff around and get a feel as to what had happened on that summer day.

Claire rubbed at the mark, feeling it with her fingertips. She was afraid she knew what had caused the old grooves.

The fingers had been cut off as they lay dead in their warm blood. The terrible marks were still on the wood floors.

CHAPTER 15

The new issue of the *Durand Daily* was so in demand that people weren't waiting for the paper to be delivered at home; they were coming into the front office to buy a copy. The story of the poisonings in the park took up most of the front page. Sarah had done an excellent job on the piece. The headline read: PARK POISONINGS POSSIBLY STOLEN PESTICIDES.

Harold had given her the opening of the story, but she had written the rest of it on her own. He especially liked the way she had quoted him. She was going to be a fine journalist. He hoped she would stay with him long enough so he would get a chance to teach her the tricks of the trade.

Harold was standing at the counter talking to Mrs. Plummer when Deputy Watkins came in and asked for a paper.

"On the house," he said, handing it to her. "Although you certainly know the breaking news story."

She tossed her quarter in the jar. "Best money I've ever spent." She stood there, reading the paper, until Mrs. Plummer left. Then she looked up. "I'd like to talk to you. Do you have time now?"

"Yes, of course. Come into my office. There's not much privacy here." He walked her through the outer office and then shut the door behind her as she followed him into his space.

As soon as she sat down in the chair, she burst out with, "I keep thinking about the fingers."

As usual she impressed him, leaping right to the heart of the matter. Harold could see she wanted to solve this one. She knew the poisonings were just an outcropping of the terrain she must travel to solve the real mystery—what had happened to the Schuler family. "Yes, the fingers. They are puzzling."

"Why would the killer do that—chop off all their fingers—what purpose did that serve?"

"I think, my dear deputy, that if you knew the answer to that question, you would know it all."

"You were at the scene, weren't you?"

"Yes, I was there. But the sheriff's men kept us out of the house."

"So you were at the murder site early on?"

"Nothing had been disturbed. Lowman had called the sheriff, and I heard about the call minutes later."

"Who told you?"

"I had my connections."

"Tell me about it, what the scene was like."

He tipped his head back and stared at the ceiling. The old wet spot in the corner still hadn't been painted over even though the leak had been fixed. It always looked like a spotted cow to him. He enjoyed looking at this flying cow. He had driven by cows on his way out to the farm. In fact there had been cows in the farmyard. They had gotten loose from their stanchions and wandered out.

He brought his head back down and started his account. "There were cows out in the yard milling about. They had gotten loose from the barn. It was frantic. Too many people were there. The sun was setting and a pale ghostly light settled over the farm. I remember everyone whispering like they didn't want to wake the dead."

Claire had her notebook in her hand, but she wasn't taking notes. She was listening, just as he wanted her to do. Listen, take it in, be there for a few moments. That was the way to figure it all out.

"They wouldn't let us in the house. I sneaked around and got a look in the barn, but didn't see much, the boy's shoes sticking out from under a blanket. I walked around to the front trying to see if I could talk to the sheriff, but as you can imagine he was very busy."

"Yes, I'm sure."

"Earl Lowman was still there. He was the one who found the bodies."

"Yes, I know."

"He wasn't needed. They told him to go home, but he couldn't seem to leave. He was in deep shock. I could hardly believe he was still on his feet. I don't think he had ever seen anything like it before. None of us had. All the bodies. The blood. The children."

"Did you talk to him?"

"I did talk to him. For comfort more than trying to get more news for my story. He was the one who told me about the fingers, but I didn't put it in the *Daily*. The sheriff called later and asked me not to. It would be the way that they knew who had really done it. You know how they keep an important fact out of the news so they can sift the truth from the talkers who yearn for some weird kind of fame? Turning themselves in for something they hadn't done."

"So Lowman told you?"

"Yes, he said they all had one of their little fingers missing. He was acting very odd. Walking around in front of the house, kicking the ground, like he was looking for something."

"Did you ask him what he was doing?"

"I did, and he said he was looking for the fingers."

"What?"

"Yes, he said he didn't know where they could have gone to. He was talking crazy. I think it really spooked him. I told him it was time for him to go home. I got him to go with me. I got him in the car and drove him home. When we arrived at his house, I went in with him and asked his wife to get out some booze; as I recall she brought out some bourbon. I poured him a large shot and one for myself and we drank them together. I poured him another and watched him drink it. I told him to go to bed and try to sleep. I drove back to the *Daily* and wrote the first story about the Schuler murders."

"I think I need to talk to Earl Lowman. I didn't find his name in the phone book. Do you know where he is?"

"Last I heard he was in Tucson, Arizona. I don't know more than that. You'd have to talk to his family."

Claire stood up to leave, but she didn't turn around. She stared into the air as if she were reading something. "Remember the first time we talked and you analyzed the kind of man who wrote that threatening note?"

"Yes, of course."

"Can you do it for this—can you tell me why someone would cut off the victims' fingers?"

Harold didn't even have to think about it. He had always understood that. "For souvenirs. To remember them by. Nothing in the house was disturbed. Nothing was taken. This family was murdered by someone who felt strongly about them, and whoever it was wanted to keep something to memorialize what he had done."

Marie Lowman was standing in the hallway across from her husband's hospital room when Claire found her.

Leaning against the wall with her hands covering her mouth, she was trying not to cry.

Claire recognized Marie from the night before but was sure the woman didn't know who she was. For one thing, she hadn't been in uniform. In those moments, that was all people saw—a woman in a deputy sheriff's uniform. A cop. Marie was still wearing the clothes she had been wearing at the fireworks. Claire could tell because there was a dark smear of dirt from last night.

"Marie, I'm Claire Watkins." Claire stood fairly close to her. She had found that people who were traumatized could focus on you more easily if you were closer.

"Do I know you?" Marie asked, her hands coming off her mouth, but hovering near her face.

"I was there last night. I helped get your husband into the ambulance. How is he?"

"They don't know—" Marie said, then stopped.

"They don't know what?" Claire bumped her.

"They don't know if he's going to come out of this. You hear about people in a coma. I mean, you read about it, you watch those trashy news shows, but you really don't know until you're standing there in the room with him and he doesn't know you're there."

"I'm sorry. We're trying to find out who is responsible."

"I know I should care. I know I should be angry and all that, but all I can think about is Andy. Is he ever going to be in this world again? Am I going to have my husband back?"

Claire flashed back to her own husband lying at the edge of her lawn after he had been run down by a truck. She remembered those same feelings, praying with her whole body that he would be all right while she ran as fast as she could outside, to be with him if he was still there to be with. He hadn't been. When she knelt down next to him, he was gone. She could see that his body was only a shell of skin and muscle, that the essence of him had left and gone elsewhere. She had no belief structure strong enough to let her think that she would ever see him again.

Claire couldn't help herself. She reached out and took hold of Marie Lowman's hands. They seemed like frantic birds to her. She stroked them. "I hope he's going to be all right. I'm sure he wants to come back to you."

"My Andy's strong. You don't know how strong he can be. If anybody can pull out of this, Andy can."

"Good."

Marie looked at Claire suddenly as if she had finally seen her. Then she looked down at her hands and slowly pulled them away. "Why are you here?"

"Do you want to go sit down?"

Marie turned around in the hallway. "It's so hard to be away from him. I try to go and get something to eat, but I keep thinking he'll wake up and I won't be there and no one will notice."

Claire waited. She understood how hard it was to pull away even for a moment. "We could go and talk in Andy's room, if that would make you feel more comfortable."

"No, I need to do this. I need to leave him for a while. He will come back."

Claire followed her down the hall to a waiting room, a small room with no windows, but what looked like a Mary Cassatt picture of a woman holding a child. There was one other woman in the room and she was reading a thick book. They sat on the opposite side of the room from her.

"Do you want some coffee?" Marie asked Claire.

"Yes, I could use a cup."

"It's not very good, but it's awfully nice of them to provide it for us."

Claire thought of the price this woman's insurance was paying for every moment of her husband's stay in the hospital, but decided not to mention it. "Black is fine," Claire told her as Marie lifted up a Styrofoam cup and held it out to her.

"Thanks." The coffee looked like beef bouillon in strength and tasted like stewed leaves. "Marie, I'd like to talk to Earl Lowman, Andy's father. Do you know how I can get in touch with him?"

"Earl? Why do you want to talk to Earl?"

Claire didn't think this was the time to go into the whole long story. "About something that happened a long time ago."

"I talked to him this morning. I can give you his number in Tucson. He's usually there." Marie dug around in her purse and found a napkin on which a number was scribbled. "I called him last night from the hospital to let him know about Andy. He and Andy haven't gotten along so well the last few years, but I knew he would want to know. He's taking it real hard."

Claire copied the number down.

Marie looked puzzled. "Something that happened a while ago? What does that have to do with Andy?"

"Did Earl ever talk about the Schuler murders with you and Andy?"

"Not often. It was a touchy subject for him. He and Andy didn't agree about something that had to do with the murders. I never knew what it was. It all happened when Florence was dying—Andy's mom. They were both so mad about her dying and they took it out on each other. Sad when that happens."

*   *   *

As Ray Sorenson was walking out to pick up a bag of feed, he ran into Chuck Folger, the agronomist, whose office was close by. It looked to him like Mr. Folger had been waiting for him, or waiting for someone to come along. Or maybe he was just leaning against the wall of the long building, working on his tan. It could use some work—the man looked like a ghoul.

"You got a second, Ray?"

"Sure, Mr. Folger." Some of his buddies who worked at the co-op thought Mr. Folger was a pervert, but Ray could never be bothered to be rude to the guy. Folger had helped him out a time or two, even if he was kind of weird.

"Come on into my office."

It wasn't too busy in the store, so Ray didn't figure he'd be missed for a few minutes. He followed Mr. Folger down the long hallway that ran along the front of the building, small offices off of it until they got to the end and the hallway ran right into Mr. Folger's office. It was as neat as a pin. That was an expression of his mother's and he had never understood it. Ray had wondered once or twice if the man was a queer. It would explain some things about him. However, Mr. Folger was married.

A bookcase full of reference books about all the various products they sold to the farmers covered the back wall. Mr. Folger had been at his job so long that he remembered when they could use the really bad pesticides, like DDT and Alar.

"You want something to drink, Ray?"

Mr. Folger had his own refrigator tucked under a shelf in his office. Ray always figured it gave the guy a sense of safety knowing his food didn't mingle with everyone else's. Maybe it was just about control. Having a cold drink when you wanted one. A cold drink sounded good to him. "You got any Mountain Dew?"

"No, but I have Diet Coke."

"Whatever."

Folger handed him the can of Coke. "You hear the latest news on the stolen pesticides?"

"You mean the poisonings in the park? Hey, I thought I saw you down there at the fireworks?"

"Yeah, I was there. So were half the people in the county. What have they told your father?"

Ray thought back to what his father had said this morning at breakfast. "Not much. I think he's going in later on today to talk to them. He did say something about it being connected to that letter in the paper and those murders you talk about."

"Yes, that's what I thought. That's what I'd like to know more about. Can you let me know what they tell your father?"

Ray stood up and said, "Why are you so interested? I don't usually tell other people about my dad's business."

"I could tell your dad some pretty interesting things about you and that slutty girlfriend of yours."

Ray sat back down.

Folger continued. "I worked late one night. She showed up and I saw her go into the back storage area with you. I thought I'd check on the two of you, just to make sure everything was all right."

Ray remembered that night. Why did he let her persuade him to do that? He had not wanted to do anything with her at work, but it was like all she had to do was touch him and he was on high alert. She thought it was fun. She liked the danger. What would she think if she knew they had been watched? Knowing her, she'd probably like that too. He wasn't sure he would even tell her.

"I might mention to your father that you let your friend come into a secured area. And I do mean *come*."

There was no subtleness about this guy. The leer on Folger's face made Ray reexamine his thoughts about him being gay. "It won't happen again. Please don't tell my dad."

"No, I'm afraid that won't be good enough, Ray. I think that I am going to need to get some information from you or I will be forced to talk to your father about your animal behavior. There are some things I want to know."

"Like what?"

"How do they think this ties into the Schulers? Who do they suspect? I want to hear about it tonight, tomorrow morning at the latest."

"Why are you so interested?" Ray let his full can of pop drop into Folger's pristine wastebasket and watched dark liquid spray the insides of it. His little moment of resistance to this man's nastiness.

"I've thought about what happened out on that farm a long time. I think it's all going to come out pretty soon and I want to be one of the first ones to know about it."

CHAPTER 16

When he saw the big headline about the poisonings emblazoned across the front of the *Durand Daily*, he was surprised that he wasn't feeling more excited about how well his plans were working out. He sure had everyone's attention. And so far no one had died. He guessed that was good. People who died never came back. He had tried once to bring them back and it hadn't worked at all.

But as he sat there reading over the article, he felt hollow. It was a familiar sensation. He had had it since he was small. He felt as if he didn't have a heart, as if his body were made of plastic and that he was a fake, a robot, but no one knew it. In this familiar story, the fact that he was a robot had been kept a secret even from him, but he had his deep suspicions.

Sometimes he wanted to cut himself to see if he bled, to see if he would cry, if he would feel the real pain, the deep pain that meant he was connected to the rest of the human race.

His wife was busy cooking his lunch. She would eat her cottage cheese and tomato slices, claiming she was on a diet. A thin woman, she didn't really like to eat much. She didn't like anything to do with her body very much. But she took good care of him and left him alone.

He had work to do today. He had scouted the area

and figured he could go over to the pond right before sunset. The last of the pesticides were all ready to go in the back of his truck.

After this event, he had only the grand finale to do. All the other poisonings would dim in comparison.

His wife set down a plate of fried eggs. He liked two eggs and two pieces of bacon and a piece of toast cut in two equal pieces. He liked it laid out so there was a symmetry to the plate. Two was a very safe number. It was about pairing up, which he had done with his wife, which all the animals had done to go into Noah's ark. There was a balance to it that felt like the right way to be in the world. Being with his wife didn't make him stick out so much. He appeared more normal.

His wife had learned how he liked things at the very beginning of their marriage, and she easily went along with his requests. She had always felt bad that they could have no kids and so she worked harder at being a good wife to him.

"Isn't that terrible about those poisonings? Aren't you glad we didn't go down to the fireworks? You must have known something was up. Maybe you're psychic," she said, and gave a little laugh.

"Too old for fireworks."

"Oh, I wouldn't say that. Sometimes I think you appreciate things like that more as you get older."

He cut his eggs in quarters and humphed at her. She took it for an answer and filled his cup and her cup with more coffee. Without demanding anything more of him, she went back to her book.

They ate in silence. She was reading one of her romance novels while he browsed through the paper. She was a good wife. She lived in her own world, too. It was safer for her to read about romances than to have had to live through one. He understood. They were meant for each other. He would miss her if she had to die in the end.

When Claire walked up Carl Wahlund's sidewalk and found him sitting on the front steps of his porch, he looked like the archetypal picture of the old farmer: white band of skin circling the top of his forehead from where his hat sat on it all day long, face lined like a dark, furrowed field, and the finishing touch was the blade of grass sticking out of his mouth.

Claire introduced herself and asked how the grass tasted.

"It's good this time of year," he said, removing it from his mouth to talk. "Timothy grass. Nice and sweet. Perfect time to harvest it. It's been a good growing summer. Turned hot just when we needed it."

"Plenty hot," she agreed.

"You look a little warm in that uniform. Come up here on the porch out of the sun and sit."

She was surprised by his solicitude. She walked up on the porch and sat in an old yellow wicker chair. When she sat down in it, it sank a little more and then sprang back. The movement of the chair surprised her and she let out a little yelp.

Wahlund chuckled. "That's called a Rockerfeller. Darn comfortable chair. Got them when I was first married."

"I came to talk to you about the Schuler murders," she said abruptly.

He nodded. "Wondered if someone might not show up, asking some questions."

"What do you remember of what happened?"

"Well, it was a hot day like today. My wife had just had our daughter. I remember that. She and her sister were real close. We would have gone over for Arlette's birthday if my wife had felt up to it. Maybe then they wouldn't have been killed."

"It's hard to say."

"Yes, it is."

"When did you hear about the murders?"

"Pretty quick. I think it was the sheriff who called us. I went over there before it was dark. I wouldn't let the wife come. It would have been too hard on her. He wanted me to identify the bodies, but everyone knew who they were. I looked at Otto. But I didn't want to look at the kids or Bertha." He stared out at the field alongside the house. Claire noticed that his eyes were blue, reflecting light like a pond in dark earth. "I didn't want to see her dead. She had been so alive. When she was in her teens, men just wanted to eat her up. She was a peach of a woman."

"I know no one was ever charged with the murders, but did you have any ideas about who did it?"

"Sure, I did. I made no bones about it at the time. I told anyone who cared to listen. But the sheriff couldn't get the evidence against him."

"Who did you think was responsible?"

"Theo Lindstrom."

Claire remembered that name, but wasn't sure where she had heard it. "Who was he?"

"A neighbor of Bertha and Otto's."

Then Claire remembered. In her mind she saw the plat map and saw Lindstrom's name on the plot of land to the north of the Schulers'.

"Why did you think he had done it?"

"You gotta remember when this all happened. It was only a few years after the war was over. Theo Lindstrom had been through some very tough battles. He had been one of the few survivors in his platoon. He hated the Germans. That might have been what it was all about. It didn't take much to set him off. But I think he and Otto were also arguing over the border of their property. Also, some weird things had been happening at the Schulers'. He had found some dead cattle out in his field."

"Did the sheriff look into it?"

"Yes, but supposedly Theo Lindstrom was gone the day the Schulers were killed."

"Where?"

"He was in Milwaukee. Buying some piece of machinery. He had an airtight alibi. Or so the sheriff told me. I still didn't buy it."

"Why not?"

"Milwaukee's not that far away. Four hours if you know what you're doing."

"Is Lindstrom still alive?"

"No, he died about twenty years ago. Never a happy man. The war really took it out of him. I always felt sorry for his wife and kid."

"Are either of them alive?"

"His wife died a few years after he did, but Paul is still living on the farm. He's an odd one. I think his dad scared the crap out of him when he was a kid and he never could do much with himself after that."

"Well, maybe I'll talk to him about his father."

"You know who else you should talk to? An old army buddy of Theo's. They went into the service together and came out together. Tight as clams. Chuck Folger. You know him?"

"Yes, I think I've had the pleasure."

Wahlund scratched the front of his head. "If it was a pleasure, it must not have been Chuck."

Rich sat at the bar of the Harbor View Café and watched the sailboats on Lake Pepin. They weren't much to watch. Late afternoon the wind had dropped off and they bobbed on the silky surface of the lake, becalmed.

That was how he felt waiting for Claire. He had been ready to move forward, ready to begin a new phase of his life with the woman he loved, and she had taken the wind from beneath his sails—as the old saw went. He was adrift.

But he was trying to snap out of it. He decided they needed to do something fun, so he had loaded the canoe in the back of his pickup and he hoped to persuade Claire to go out on the river with him tonight. Maybe she'd want to try to make love in the bottom of a canoe. He had brought large lifesaving cushions for padding.

One of the bartenders of the Harbor View placed a bottle of Leiney's in front of him without asking. Rich nodded his thanks. The bartender asked, "You waiting for the lovely deputy?"

"I am."

"She working on that poisoning that happened last night?"

"Of course."

"Must be hard for her to even take time to have dinner."

Rich felt his shoulders rise in anger, but calmed himself. "Yup, but she has to eat like the rest of us."

Claire walked in and said hi to some friends near the door and then made her way back to him. She was in her uniform, but had the top buttons on her shirt undone and her hair down. He saw people watching her as she walked back to where he was sitting. She leaned in and gave him a quick kiss.

"Can we just stay at the bar? I don't have much time. I've got to go back to work in an hour or so."

This was a test for him, he decided. "Sure. I like eating at the bar. Sorry you have to go back to work." He hoped it was safe to say he was sorry.

She smiled at him. "I'm sorry too. The guys from DCI were supposed to show up late afternoon, but they called a couple hours ago and now they're not going to be here until around eight. We're meeting with everyone and I need to be there."

"Sure. Let's order. Do you want a drink?"

"Not a good idea. I need to keep my wits about me with these fellows coming in."

"The competition?"

"I hope not. I'm sure they'll be a big help. But they're going to assume we don't know what we're doing and they're going to want to take over. They don't know I've worked much bigger cases than this."

"You'll just have to tell them."

"No. I'll have to nudge the sheriff to tell them. I can't be seen bragging about my career. Not proper."

"Police etiquette."

"Exactly."

They ordered—Claire just wanted soup and salad, but Rich went for the salmon. He had worked hard and was hungry for a real meal.

As soon as the waitress left, he turned to Claire and asked, "How's this latest case going?"

"You know, for once I'd rather not talk about it. My head is bursting and I'd like to just have a pleasant meal with you. I'll probably call you at one tonight and want to talk, but right now I need food." She pulled her hair back from her face and stretched her neck.

He reached up and rubbed her neck. She pushed into his hand and he could feel how tight she was. "Listen, my timing wasn't good last night."

She pulled away from him and took his hand in hers, squeezing it. "Rich, your timing was fine. I forget that you don't really understand the nature of my job. You know, Steve and I were together so long and we got married before I was even on the force. My police work was part of the fabric of our marriage. It was a given. Sure, he didn't like it sometimes when it interfered with plans we had, but hey, I didn't like it either."

She paused and then looked around the room as if she were trying to sort out where she was. "It's much easier down here in Pepin County. My life is much more predictable than it was in Minneapolis. But these incidents—the stolen pesticides, the poisonings—this is bad. This is as bad as it gets. This guy is holding the whole county hostage, and we've got to find him quick."

She paused and so he quickly said, "I agree with that. I wouldn't stand in your way."

"No, I know, but I need to focus all my wits and desires in order to figure this out. I need to stop this man. And I can't think about anything else. I probably shouldn't even be here having dinner with you, but a girl's got to eat."

"Why don't we just table it?"

"Really?" She sounded so hopeful.

"Yeah, pretend it didn't happen until you have your mind and your desires back, especially your desires."

A blond waitress placed the salads that came with their meals in front of each of them. They thanked her.

Claire laughed. "This looks great. I'm hungry."

"That's a good sign. My mom told me to mention a guy named Carl Wahlund to you. She said she remembered people suspecting him of coveting his neighbor's possessions."

"I'm on it."

CHAPTER 17

Even driving slightly over the speed limit, Claire was ten minutes late getting back to the sheriff's department. When she walked into the meeting room, she was glad to see only familiar faces look up at her. The DCI agents hadn't arrived yet.

The sheriff was writing on the white board at the front of the room. He loved using the board and he was good at it. He could have been an elementary school teacher. He had *Schuler Murders* written at the top of the board and underlined, then halfway down the board: *July 1st: Pesticides Stolen*. He was writing something else below that.

"Anything new?" she asked.

"Relatively quiet here today," the sheriff answered.

They were all on tenterhooks, waiting to see if the pesticide man would decide to destroy anything else today. She wasn't sure if she should feel relieved that so far he hadn't. It could be happening as they were meeting.

Claire sat down next to Harold Peabody and whispered, "I talked to Carl Wahlund."

"What did he have to say for himself?"

"He told me about Theo Lindstrom."

Harold pursed his lips. "One thing you should know. Those two never got along. Since they were kids."

"Who? Lindstrom and Schuler?"

"No, Lindstrom and Wahlund."

"Why didn't they get along?"

"Who knows how far back it goes? Those two were at each other all the time growing up. But it got worse as they got older. When the war broke out, Wahlund didn't join up right at first. He stayed home and farmed. Lindstrom called him a coward on more than one occasion."

"So you think he might have been trying to pin the murder on Lindstrom to get back at him?"

Harold thought for a moment. "I wouldn't put it past Wahlund, although why he'd bother now with Lindstrom long dead I'd be hard put to say. There probably was some truth to whatever he told you."

As always Claire was astonished by how the lives of the people in Pepin County swirled around each other. Most of the people who lived in the county had lived there all their lives. They had been kids together, grown up together, fought for and against each other, loved each other. There was no easy way to read what went on between any two of them. Their history was so deep, it was hard to plumb.

Two men came to the door. It was obvious they were the agents sent from Madison. For one thing, Claire didn't know them. For another, they wore suits, not uniforms. And finally, the taller of the two had darker skin than even Carl Wahlund's, and it wasn't from sitting out for a thousand hours under the sun.

They came in and Sheriff Talbert introduced them to everyone. "Agent Sean Tyrone and Agent Phil Singer." Phil Singer was short, with frizzy blond hair and a wide face that made him look surprised. Sean Tyrone was at least six feet tall but quite slim, with a dark chocolate complexion and a pair of Malcolm X glasses. Claire wondered which one of them was the leader and which the follower.

Singer spoke up and said, "Sorry we're late. Traffic was bad on Ninety. We're mainly here tonight to hear where you're at with this case. I will serve as the liaison to the forensic labs at DCI. Tyrone will work with your investigator coordinating the investigaton. But we're here to help you out. Just let us know what you need."

Sheriff Talbert filled them in on what had been happening in Pepin County since the first of July. He did it by talking and writing on the white board as he went. The two men listened and wrote and asked questions.

Talbert asked Scott Lund and Billy Peterson to summarize their interviews with the people who were at the park last night.

Scott stood up and began his report. "Nothing seems out of the ordinary. The couple of people who weren't from the area turned out to be relatives of people we know. From what we could gather today and from the interviews last night, it appears that whoever did this was from around here. There were no strangers unaccounted for." He resumed his seat.

The sheriff turned the meeting over to Claire, explaining, "I've done the overview, but Claire Watkins is in on all the particulars. She's been out in the field all day long and I haven't even had a chance to touch base with her. What have you learned?"

"Well, this isn't all just from today," Claire said as she rose to her feet, "but what I'd like to add to what Sheriff Talbert has laid out here is that we're dealing with two separate crimes. The first happened nearly fifty years ago. Many of the people who have information about it are dead or gone. But I think in order to hope to catch whoever is doing the most recent series of crimes, we'll have to understand what happened to the Schulers. If not solve the murders, at least understand how they impacted this community. However, there is a very good chance that our pesticide guy is also the Schuler killer."

Tyrone raised his head and Claire nodded at him. "Why not just focus on what's at hand and try to catch the perp like you would anyone who steals something?"

"Because I don't think we have the time. I'm afraid that this guy is counting down to the seventh of this month, which is the fiftieth anniversary of the Schuler murders. I don't think the forensic evidence is going to come back fast enough or that there will be anything significant if it does. He was careful. If he is the killer, he's been planning this for a long, long time.

"Let me tell you what I know about the bones. Sheriff Talbert mentioned the bones that have been found at the scene of every crime. Although we do not yet have the forensic support to prove it, they are most probably the smallest digits from each member of the Schuler family. Therefore, whoever is doing this ended up with the bones. This probably means that he is the murderer. Although the note that he sent to the newspaper makes it sound as if he is *not* the murderer, since he is demanding that the truth come out and would probably not need to make this demand if he knew who had killed them."

Claire walked up to the white board, where she wrote three names. As she began to speak, she pointed to the first one. "There are three men who have been mentioned as possible suspects in the Schuler murders. The first is Carl Wahlund. He was in love with Bertha Schuler before she married Otto Schuler. He, in turn, married her sister, which meant that when the whole Schuler family died, he, or rather his wife, inherited their farm. Which gives him two reasons to kill them all—revenge and greed. Both valid reasons. Carl Wahlund is still alive."

Claire pointed at the next name on her list. "Then

there is Theo Lindstrom, their next-door neighbor who was in a land dispute with Otto Schuler. More important, Theo never liked Schuler. Theo had fought during the war in Germany and came back with a huge grudge against all Germans. He has been described as never having gotten over the war. However, Theo Lindstrom died twenty years ago, so we will learn no more from him."

Then she pointed at the last name. "Finally, there's Earl Lowman. This man is still alive. He was the first person on the scene at the Schuler murders. He was a deputy sheriff for this county, but was very new to his job at the time. I don't see him as quite as strong a contender for being the murderer. Still, one always has to look at the first person on the scene as a suspect."

Singer lifted his pencil, eraser tip pointing at the board. "How did he happen to go there? Had he been called there? Was he there as a deputy?"

"No, he was a neighbor and had borrowed a tool from the Schulers. He had stopped by to return it when he discovered the bodies. He's still alive—living down in Tucson. I've been trying to reach him today, but so far no luck." She paused in reflection. "I suppose there is a chance he's here in Pepin County."

Claire sat down on the edge of the table and looked at everyone. "The problem is, these three men were certainly scrutinized at the time, and I don't think we know anything that the sheriff's men didn't know then."

The light was fading gently on the horizon. At this time of year, the sun was almost setting in the north. He didn't think anyone could see him from the house, but he didn't want to take any chances. Until it got dark, he would sit in the tall grass at the edge of the field and bide his time.

He liked hiding at the edge of the field. It reminded him of when he was a kid and had hidden from his father.

He had learned early on that when his father was in one of his moods, it was best to give him a wide berth. Wherever he was, when he heard a certain mean tone of voice coming from his father, he disappeared. He hid behind the woodpile, he hid in the laundry hamper, he hid behind the furnace. He had hidey-holes scattered all over the farm. After a few hours it would be safe to come out. His mother would have made dinner; his father would calm down again.

It had served him well, this ability to disappear.

He had spelled it out in his latest letter. He wanted the sheriff's deputies to know that he would never forget that they had not done their job. But he felt it wasn't enough. It had to do with the numbers. Seven people had died, but it had never seemed right to him. Eight was a better number—it was even, and he had always equated evenness with good. An odd number was a hungry number, waiting for one more.

He kept track of everyone who died. He had since he was young. Every year he wrote down the total of the people who had died in the county. Last year, twenty-eight people had died. It was a high year, but nowadays more people lived in the county. You had to keep that in mind.

One summer he tried to count the stars. No one had told him you couldn't do it. He worked on it for nights, mapping out the sky, working on a section at a time, but the sky moved. He never told anyone what he was doing. Finally, after a couple of months, he gave up.

The next year, in high school, he learned that it was impossible. The teacher told them about the layers of stars on stars, the possibility of the universe being shaped like a saddle, the concept of infinity, and he had felt like he was looking down a well that had no bottom.

The light had leaked from the sky. It was time for him to make his delivery. He stood up in the field and walked down to the house. The new people who had the house had worked hard on it. He hoped it would be their house someday. They deserved it. The house was not bad. It was just what happened in it.

He had brought the bones back to where they had been severed from their bodies.

As he walked up to the house, he saw a little girl sitting on the front steps with a kitty in her arms. The kitty was sprawled against her and she was waving its tail back and forth under her nose. They both seemed quite happy.

"Hi," she said. "I'm Jilly."

She didn't seem afraid of him. He was surprised she wasn't in bed yet. Her light brown hair hung to her shoulders in a cloud of soft curls. How easy it would be to take her by the hand and walk away with her. But that wasn't in his plans. He would let her be. She could be his messenger.

He handed her the tin.

"For me?" She smiled at him. "Can I open it?"

"Sure," he said.

He watched as she attempted to pry open the tin. It was pretty stuck together, but she seemed determined. He was sure she would get it open. At least it would keep her busy for a while. Before anyone else came out and found him standing there, he slipped away into the starlit night.

Sitting on the front steps of her house, Claire could feel a light breeze picking up. It felt like good sleeping weather. She was exhausted. She had to get up early to beat the boys from Madison into work. She felt that old competitive edge creeping into her life. The one she really needed to beat was the man behind all this.

When the phone rang, she wished she didn't have to answer it. She had talked to Meg a few minutes earlier and there was no one else she wanted to talk to. It was probably work.

Claire answered, "Watkins."

"He was here," a woman's voice shouted at her over the phone.

"Who is this?" Claire asked, not recognizing the voice, not knowing what the woman was talking about.

"You need to come up here. This is Celia Daniels. He was here, I don't know how long ago. He handed—in person—handed Jilly a tin full of bones. I found her outside playing with them."

Claire turned and hit the door with her hand. "Who was it? Did she recognize him?"

"All Jilly can tell me was that it was a man and he was wearing a hat. She's so little. I'm trying not to scare her."

"Have you called the sheriff?"

"No, I called you first."

"I'll be right there. Is your husband home?"

"Yes, he was already sleeping. I just woke him up."

"Lock the doors. Stay put until we arrive. Don't try to find him. He might still be there and he might be dangerous."

After calling the sheriff and asking him to meet her at the Danielses', Claire decided not to waste the time putting her uniform on. She knew it was against the regulations, but time was of the essence. She grabbed her keys, slung her gun and holster over her shoulder, jumped into her car, and sped up the hill. She made it to the Danielses' in nine minutes.

When she got out of the car, she stood quietly for a

moment or two. She listened. He could still be close by. He could be watching to see what would happen. She had her hand on her gun.

An owl hooted from the edge of the field. She could make out a bat or two flying in the light on the barn, feeding on the insects that circled there.

Celia Daniels stuck her head out the door. "Thanks for coming so fast."

"You're welcome." Claire walked toward her. "Jilly still up?"

"Yes, but she's getting ready for bed."

Claire wanted to talk to Jilly before the little girl went to sleep and forgot everything she might have noticed about the man. Celia presented her to Claire. The little girl's face was scrubbed to a soft pink and she was wearing dinosaur pajamas.

"Nice pajamas," Claire said.

"My best pajamas," Jilly told her.

"She'll hardly wear anything else," Celia said, patting her daughter on the head.

Claire sat down on the floor so she was the same height as the little girl. "Jilly, I'd like to ask you some questions about the man who was here."

"Mom already did."

"I know. But could you answer a few more for me?"

"Sure." She rubbed her nose.

"Did you know this man?"

Jilly scrunched up her face. "Not really."

"Have you ever seen him before?" Claire dared hope she might get something.

"I don't think so."

"Was he as big as your daddy?" Claire glanced over to where Jeff Daniels was standing. He looked to be about six feet tall and probably carried about one hundred and ninety pounds.

"No."

"Was he old or young?"

"Pretty old."

"Older than your daddy?"

"I think so."

"He was wearing a hat?"

Jilly nodded.

"What kind of hat?"

"Like Thomas wears."

Claire looked at Celia. "A baseball cap," she said.

"Was he fat or skinny?"

Jilly turned her hands out. "Not fat, not skinny."

"In between?"

"Yup."

"What color of hair?"

"Don't remember."

"Could you see his eyes?"

"They were black."

"Did he wear glasses?"

"Huh-uh." Jilly shook her head.

She answered no to Claire's questions about a beard and a mustache.

"Anything else you can remember?"

"He seemed nice."

Celia wrapped her arms around her daughter. "I think it's time she went to bed."

Claire nodded and wished she could go with Jilly. Bed was where she wanted to be right now, but as she stood up she saw a squad car pull in behind her car. She had a long night ahead of her.

CHAPTER 18

The light was on at the Sands Hotel just outside of Wichita, Kansas. The sign overhead advertised rooms at thirty-nine dollars a night. When Earl Lowman tried to stand up from his car seat to check into the motel, he thought his legs were going to go out from under him. He was bone-tired, had to pee so bad he could taste it, eyes were dry in the sockets, and he was hungry to the pit of his stomach. He should have stopped four hours ago, but now he could make it to Wisconsin in a day's time.

Things like that were important to him. He figured out how long it would take him to get someplace and then he wanted to get there on time. As if time were a special commodity. As if being on time was the same as being holy. If it were, he'd be a saint.

He held on to the car and steadied himself. It was a typical Kansas summer night, hot and muggy, weather only mosquitoes liked. Enough water in the air to lay a slick on your body.

It had been a sweltering day like this when he had gone over to the Schulers'.

All the long day driving he had been remembering what had happened that day, nearly fifty years ago. If he could have that moment back and live it over again, he would do it differently. He had been so young.

He pushed himself out of the car and headed toward the motel registration. Walking up to the desk, he saw a dark-haired young woman bent over something behind the desk. When he got closer, he saw that she had a baby with her. It was sleeping in a carrier and it looked pretty close to a year old. Same age as the youngest Schuler had been.

"Evening," Earl said.

"Can I help you?" The woman snapped to attention, swinging back her long black hair and looking at him with dark brown eyes like a doe. She looked exotic in Wichita. Probably from India. He had heard that Indians had bought up all the small motels in middle America. Fine by him as long as they ran them clean. He hated a dirty room.

"Do you have a room?"

"Sure."

"Do you give a discount for seniors?"

"Absolutely." She gave him the once-over. "Would you qualify?"

"Don't get smart on me." He laughed. Here he was in the middle of Kansas on an adventure and a young woman was teasing him. Things could be worse. Then he remembered where Andy was and remembered why he was traveling and realized they *were* worse.

He gave her his credit card. After sliding it through a machine, she handed it back to him and gave him a map, drawing a big circle around his room. His room was on the far side of the motel.

He parked right in front of it and took out his bag and walked in. Nothing fancy, but it was clean. The king-sized bed looked great to him. He sat down on the edge of it and called the hospital. The number that Marie had given him rang and rang.

Finally he hung up and decided to call Andy's house.

Maybe Marie would be home from the hospital and she might have some good news.

Their boy, Ted, answered.

"This is your grandfather," Earl explained.

"Who?"

"Your dad's dad."

"Oh, yeah."

"I haven't seen you since you were two."

"I'm twelve now."

"That sounds about right. How's he doing, your dad?"

"Not great. He's in the hospital."

Not very forthcoming, this kid. "I know. Is your mother home?"

"No, she's still down there. She called and said to go to bed. I think she's sleeping there tonight."

"Has he come out of the coma yet?"

"Nope."

"I'm sorry."

The boy didn't say anything. Earl wondered if he was crying. He didn't know what to do about that, so he kept talking. "Listen, I want you to let your mom know that I'm on my way there. To Wisconsin. I should get in sometime tomorrow night."

"Are you coming here?"

"I'll probably go right to the hospital. Can you tell her that?"

"You're Dad's dad and you're coming to Wisconsin?"

"That's right."

"I'll tell her."

"Thanks, I'll see you."

"I'll see you, Grandpa."

Grandpa—that did him in. Earl sat on the edge of the bed and hung on to the bedspread. He hoped he would get there in time.

*   *   *

The phone rang and he jerked up and answered it. *"Durand Daily."*

"Harold, do you know what time it is?"

He propped himself up and tried to focus on his wristwatch. "Agnes, it appears to be nearly eleven o'clock."

"Wouldn't you say that's time to come home?"

"I was on my way when I stopped to look up one more article. I must have dozed off." Harold looked at the bottle of brandy that was sitting next to a glass by his hand. Maybe once a month, he'd have a snort or two. Tonight had felt like one of those nights.

"Are you sober enough to drive?"

"I will be by the time I lock up."

"Come right home."

"Yes, dear." After she hung up, he stood up and wandered around the empty office. He was getting too old to be running a newspaper. Maybe he'd go right from running a full-time business to addleheaded in a nursing home. If he didn't get home soon, Agnes would divorce him and he would be forced to go to the nursing home.

Nothing had happened today. He had heard no reports of anything amiss. Maybe this whole thing would blow over. The Schulers could go back to being dead and buried. Poor family! What had they done to deserve any of their misfortune? *But then, what have any of us done,* he thought.

He checked the back door. It was locked. He couldn't always count on Sarah to remember to lock up. She was a bit flighty.

He gathered up his lunch box and his briefcase. Silly of him to be dragging a briefcase back and forth, but it had been with him more years than Agnes and had held up nearly as well as she. It was part of him. He put his calendar in there and a copy of today's paper. Agnes, poor woman, was always a day behind on the news.

He turned off the lights in the back office and walked out to the front.

He almost missed it.

He walked out the door and then turned back to make sure it was locked. That was when he saw it, the letter, lying on the floor in the office. He must have walked right over it. Another letter.

Quickly he unlocked the door and picked it up. He set his briefcase down on the counter and put the letter down next to it. Deputy Watkins had left him some plastic gloves. He found them under the counter and put them on. Holding it carefully, he cut through the top of the letter. The same handwriting. A longer note, it read:

The day is almost here. The day of reckoning. When the truth will come out or the people will pay for it with their lives. Just as the lives of the Schuler family have been poisoned, so will the water be poisoned. Let the truth be known or the innocent will pay.
I mean it.
Wrath of God

Harold read it through a couple times and thought of the water that ran through their lives. Poisoning the water would be horrible. It could ruin everything in the county. How did this guy think that he could get at the water supply in an area where most people had their own wells? The water-holding tank in town? He needed to call the sheriff and let him know about the letter.

They didn't find anything. Claire hadn't thought they would. There were trails going from the fields off into the woods, but they were deer trails. All someone had to do to camouflage their steps would be to follow those paths.

At midnight the sheriff called the search off. He said he would send some more officers over tomorrow to look more carefully in daylight. Scott Lund volunteered to stay the night at the Danielses' in case the man showed up again.

Claire drove down the hill to Fort St. Antoine a little more slowly.

When she got in the door, she decided to make one more call. One more try to reach Earl Lowman. It was only a little after ten down in Tucson; maybe he'd come home from wherever he'd been all day long. The phone rang five times and she knew what would happen next.

The answering machine picked up. Earl Lowman's gravelly voice said slowly, "Don't seem to be here at the moment. I'd like to know you called. Please leave me your name and number. I'll get back to you as soon as I can."

Claire wondered if it would be soon enough. "Mr. Lowman, this is Claire Watkins again. I very much need to talk to you. It's an emergency. Please call me no matter when you get this message." She left her home number and the number at the sheriff's office, adding, "You might still remember this number. I don't think it's changed since you left. Thanks."

That was all she could do. She hung up.

She wished Rich were waiting for her upstairs, but she couldn't even think of calling him. Their dinner hadn't gone too well. She needed to think about what she had to tell him, but she couldn't do it now. Hard to have a life when you were trying to work a crime of this breadth.

She just hated feeling so jangled. She knew she'd have trouble getting to sleep. She thought of having a nice big glass of wine, but in the long run it wouldn't help that much either.

Instead she went down to the basement and folded a

load of wash and brought it upstairs to her room and Meg's room. She set the piles of clothes on Meg's bed. Meg liked to put her clothes away herself. She had a special system. She had tried to explain it to her mother once, but Claire was glad to let her take care of her own things. Meg was growing up.

Claire sat on the edge of her daughter's bed and thought about what had happened with Jilly. The pesticide guy could have done something awful. He could have taken the little girl, but he hadn't. If Jilly hadn't been sitting outside, Claire was guessing that he might have just left the tobacco tin with its bones on the Danielses' doorstep, where they might not have discovered it until morning. Still a creepy thing to do, but not so threatening. What did he want, and what was he willing to do to get it?

July 7, 1952

Schubert sneaked out to the hallway to see what was going on, but there was no one there. Loud shots had exploded in his sisters' room. Firecrackers? Balloons? That was what they had sounded like.

He could hear someone doing something in there, but he couldn't hear his sisters talking or laughing anymore. They had been playing together and talking. He had been waiting to hear his mother call them for dinner. The cake was what he was really waiting for. Arlette's birthday cake.

His birthday had been in April. He had turned six. There had been balloons and they made a loud noise when they popped. But maybe the loud bangs had been something else. If it had been balloons, his sisters would be laughing, and he couldn't hear them doing anything at all. It made him feel nervous. He didn't want to go any closer, because he felt so nervous.

If only he knew what had made that noise.

He didn't know who was in their room. Maybe it was Denny, playing a joke. Where was his father? Where was his mother? Why didn't they want to know what was happening? Why didn't they come?

His mother didn't call and there had been two bangs and he felt like he was going to wet his pants. He went back and stood in the middle of his room, trying to think what he should do.

Schubert felt like he was playing a game they played at school called Statues, where someone would twirl you around and then let you go and you had to stay perfectly still, like a statue.

Maybe if he stayed perfectly still, nothing would happen to him. Maybe whoever was in the next room, moving things around and making odd noises, would go away and they could have dinner and eat the cake.

Schubert was afraid that he would never get to eat the cake. He heard footsteps leaving his sisters' room and coming down the hallway toward his room.

Dropping to the floor, he lifted up the blanket edge and tried to crawl under the bed. He had to get away and hide. He should have done it before. But there were too many toys stuffed under his bed. He couldn't get under it far enough. He heard the footsteps stop close to him.

"Dad, please, Dad," Schubert yelled into the darkness under the bed.

He heard a loud blast and his leg burst into flames and then he didn't know anything more.

After the second shot, the boy was pulled out from under the bed and his hand placed down on the floor. It didn't take much effort to cut off a finger with a hatchet. Just the way he'd take the head off a chicken.

The man stood and knew he was nearly done. He walked out of the room.

The room was quiet. The boy lay stretched out on the floor, a bloody pool around his hand.

Then the clothes in the closet moved.

CHAPTER 19

When Mrs. Lindstrom answered the door, Claire felt as if she were looking at a woman from the fifties. Mrs. Lindstrom's hair was up in curlers and she was wearing a snap-down-the-front housedress. Claire couldn't remember the last time she had seen a woman wearing curlers, but at least she wasn't out in public. Mrs. Lindstrom was thin and pale, hunched over as if she were cold in the midsummer heat. Her hair was a light brown without much gray in it, but she looked close to sixty years old.

"I wasn't expecting anyone," Mrs. Lindstrom said, her slight hand flying up and patting at her curlers.

"Sorry, I called and talked to your husband. Didn't he tell you I was coming?"

"Paul isn't much of a talker. I think he's out in the barn. Let me call him in." Instead of walking out the door and heading toward the barn, Mrs. Lindstrom went back into the house. Claire stood on the steps, as she hadn't been invited in, and watched the woman push a button on an intercom in the kitchen.

"Paul," Mrs. Lindstrom yelled, not counting on the intercom to carry her voice adequately. "Paul, there's a woman in a police uniform here to see you."

Claire had nearly brought Tyrone with her to interview Paul Lindstrom. She wondered how Mrs. Lindstrom would have described him—a black man in a business suit? That was what happened when you were in the minority—you were seen only for your difference.

"I think he's coming." Mrs. Lindstrom came back to the screen door and pushed it open. "Please come in. He won't be a minute."

Claire walked into the kitchen and sat down at the kitchen table. It was definitely from the fifties—metal legs with a yellow Formica top. Very cheery. The kitchen was painted yellow, and a red rooster ceramic plaque crowed on the wall above the stove. Everything was clean, but a little worn-looking.

"Can I help you with anything?" Mrs. Lindstrom asked.

"I need to talk to your husband about the Schuler murders."

Mrs. Lindstrom looked blank, then said, "I haven't heard about anyone being murdered. When did this happen?"

"About fifty years ago."

"Oh, are you still trying to solve it?"

"More like again. Have you heard about the pesticides that were stolen from the co-op?"

"No."

Paul Lindstrom walked in the door. "My wife isn't from around here. She doesn't follow the local news much."

Mrs. Lindstrom stood by the sink, hovering with a dish towel in her hands. Lindstrom sat down and turned to his wife and said quietly, "Why don't you go read one of your books, honey. I've got to talk to this deputy woman and none of it has anything to do with you."

Claire noted that he didn't say it meanly. He was just clearly telling Mrs. Lindstrom what to do. His wife seemed relieved and scurried out of the room.

Lindstrom settled into the chair across from Claire. Like his wife, he was on the thin side. He had clear dark eyes, high cheekbones, and an aristocratic nose. If he had been an animal, he might have been a mink—dark, handsome, and a little furtive. Farm work had made him wiry.

She pulled out a notebook. "Do you know about the stolen pesticides? The poisonings in the park?"

"Yes, the fellas down at the Kum and Go are talking about it. Gives them something to chew on while they drink too much coffee." He stated it as fact.

"Well, we feel that these incidents are tied into the Schuler murders. I wanted to ask you about your father."

Lindstrom jerked as if she had given him a slight shock. "My father? Whatever for? He's been dead awhile."

"I've heard that he didn't care much for the Schulers."

Lindstrom snorted. "What's that got to do with anything? They weren't anyone's favorite people after the war. You know, the father had just come over from Germany before the war broke out. He could hardly speak English."

"Did your father argue with the Schulers?"

Lindstrom looked at his hands, then rubbed them and kept rubbing them together like he was cold, but it was eighty degrees out. " 'Argue' might be a little strong. It was no secret that Dad didn't like them. Dad didn't like any Germans. Didn't like Catholics, for that matter, and the Schulers were both."

"Was there some kind of land dispute?"

"Oh, I sorta remember that. Dad claimed that Mr. Schuler's fence was infringing on his property. They threatened to get a surveyor, but then when the family was killed, I don't think he did anything about it."

"How old were you?"

"Well, I'm fifty-seven now. You can do the math."

"Do you remember the murders?"

"Of course. My mother was petrified. She was a fearful woman anyway. I thought she'd never let me go anyplace on my own again. She became so protective of me. Dad didn't say much. I think he might have felt uncomfortable about the bad feelings between him and Otto Schuler."

"I heard your father was away from home when the murders took place."

"Yeah, that's the truth. He left that morning for Milwaukee and didn't get back till the next day. I expect the sheriff checked his alibi out carefully at the time. Like I said, Dad made no secret of his feelings about the Schulers."

"When did you find out that the family had been murdered?"

Lindstrom tipped back in his chair and let his eyes half close while he was thinking. "Hard to think back that far. All I can remember is some neighbor—maybe Folger, Chuck Folger—coming over to tell my dad. I'm not even sure if it was that night or the next morning."

Claire wasn't sure what to ask him next. It was so long ago, and he had been just a little boy. What right did she have to suggest at this late date that his father might be a murderer? On no evidence to speak of. Then she remembered the ages of the Schuler children at the time they were killed. Paul Lindstrom would have been close in age to the two boys.

"Did you ever play with any of the Schulers?"

He picked at the steel edge of the table, then said quietly, "At school. Schubert and I played a bit. But my dad wouldn't let me play with them when I was home. My mother and I couldn't have anything to do with them."

Claire closed her notebooks, disappointed in what she had learned. But you just had to keep asking the questions. She sat still and willed herself to devise one more. "Who did your dad think had killed them? Did he ever say anything?"

"I can't remember him trying to place the blame on anyone." Lindstrom paused a moment to clear his throat. Then he continued, "The only thing I remember him saying was something about the deputy sheriff who found them. How he could remember Earl Lowman stealing a car and nearly wrecking it, and wasn't it something that he had ended up on the right side of the law after all."

Harold felt oddly elated sitting at his desk. Sometimes that happened to him after he had had a little too much to drink the night before. He had realized early on that he had the potential for being a drunk, so he had put all sorts of limits on his alcohol intake. And he had married a wife who didn't imbibe at all. But from time to time he tied one on, and occasionally that experience left him slightly euphoric. It gave him a little remove from the world and made him feel he was above it all and could see what was going on around him more clearly.

Sarah walked into his office, holding the copy of the threatening letter that had come in last night from the pesticide guy. "How do you want to handle this? What would you like me to do?"

"I think this time we should run something about the letter," Harold said.

She looked down at the letter. "This is getting pretty weird. All this biblical language, and then he ends with 'I mean it.' This guy's nuts."

"Probably. But that might be to his advantage. He believes that what he's doing is righteous. It gives him a kind of biblical power and authority. What have we got on the front page right now?"

She looked at her notes. "The results of the county

fair baking contest, the crop report, and the two-car accident on Deer Island last night."

"What happened? They can't have been going very fast. The island's not long enough to pick up any speed."

"An older woman stopped for a rabbit that was crossing the road and one of her neighbors rear-ended her."

"Oh, I like that. Any pictures?" he asked hopefully. "Of the rabbit?"

Sarah giggled.

"Keep that story below the fold, but bump the fair story onto the next page. Above the fold I want a picture of the letter, a quote from the sheriff, info on the two guys that DCI has sent out, and a short piece on the Schuler murders."

He patted an old stack of papers that was sitting on his desk. "Here's most of the pieces we ran on the Schuler murders, written by yours truly. Read them all through and you'll know most of what was known at the time—or at least everything this reporter knew. Then write up a summary of the events, leading into what is presently happening."

She stood up and picked up the papers. "I'll try."

"Bother me whenever you need to, but I'm going to let you run with this. Get those other two pieces written up."

"Already done." Sarah looked at the top paper and asked, "Who do you think was responsible for what happened to the Schulers? I've read a little about it. Did you ever come up with a theory?"

Harold steepled his fingers and touched them to his lips. An affectation, he knew, but it gave him time to think. "Not really. There was something about the whole disaster that seemed off to me. I mean, I guess that goes without saying. You have a whole family shot to death on their isolated farm and something obviously went wrong. But I never felt like we knew what really went on. That there was something everyone was missing. See what you think when you read everything."

Sarah was a good kid. If she ever tried to buy the paper from him, he would dissuade her. No one should stay in one place so long that the mysteries of your youth come back to haunt you.

When Claire walked in, Judy told her that most of the deputies were still over at the Daniels farm, but that Sheriff Talbert and Stewy were back in the conference room with those two DCI guys.

Judy rolled her eyes, but Claire could tell she liked all the excitement. "They've still got their suits on today. And they've been tromping around in the fields. They've gotta be hot as the dickens in them." Judy shook her head and pointed toward the conference room. "I just delivered lunch."

When Claire walked into the room, Stewy held up a bag for her. She had been starving when she left the Lindstroms', but had decided she needed to get back to the office to check in before eating. She thought she had had a piece of toast for breakfast, but couldn't quite remember. Tyrone was talking about the new letter the paper had received.

"What strikes me about this letter is that it's handwritten. That element tells us something very important about this man," Tyrone was saying.

Not wanting to interrupt him midthought, Claire leaned against the wall by the door.

Singer saw her and nodded. Tyrone was in full sermon and didn't notice her. The sheriff and chief deputy were listening, but looking into their lunch bags at the same time. Not much threw them off their feed.

Tyrone leaned over the table. "This guy wants us to

catch him. Or maybe to put it more implicitly, he doesn't care if we catch him, he doesn't care if we find out who he is. One thing that's in his favor, and he knows it, is time. He's running the schedule and we're just trying to catch up. Even though we have his handwriting, we have no way to trace it back to him, no database that we can plug it into. He might well realize that, but more probably he just doesn't care."

There was silence; then Claire spoke up. "It might also tell us that he doesn't own a computer or for that matter a typewriter. This is a farming community. I'd guess that only about fifteen percent of the county is plugged into the Internet; maybe another twenty percent have computers. In fact, it's hard to get service down here."

Everyone turned around to look at her as she walked up to the table and slid in next to Tyrone. "What I noticed was that he didn't just handwrite it; he used a pencil. My guess is he's a farmer. They always have pencils on hand to mark things, to jot things down. They work better in dust and grease than an ink pen."

Tyrone looked at Claire with some interest. With a nod in his direction, she added, "But I think you're right that he doesn't care if we find out who he is. Also obviously by the way he sauntered up to the Danielses' house last night and dropped off the rest of the bones. He's a man on a mission and he wants it done and figures it will be done before we can stop him. He's wrong about that."

Singer spoke up. "What I don't understand is that if he really wants this information, the truth about these old murders, then why does he put such a tight time limit on it?"

Claire had given the deadline issue quite a bit of consideration over the last several days. "I think this date is very important to him. He probably has watched it roll around for many years. This year he wants everyone to remember what happened on the seventh of July. He's never forgotten."

Stewy slapped his sandwich down on the table. "I think it's because he's nuts. He just wants to raise hell. And he's doing it. People in this community are scared. I'm getting calls from all sorts of people demanding that we catch this guy and make the county safe again. When this next letter is published today, I expect all-out panic to erupt. We've got to do something. But first let's eat." Swanson dug into his bag and everyone else followed suit.

Claire opened the bag lunch that was waiting for her. Tuna-salad sandwich. Not her favorite. She wrinkled her nose.

Tyrone noticed and looked over at her food and said, "I'll trade you a half a turkey sandwich for part of that tuna."

"That's awfully kind of you." She handed him half of her sandwich. "I guess my mom made me too many tuna-fish sandwiches for school lunches when I was growing up."

"My mother specialized in olive loaf." He smiled at her and she envied his straight, white teeth. Teeth always looked better next to dark skin. His skin, seen close, was the color of the dark soil in her garden. Good growing soil.

He said, "I heard you used to work for the Minneapolis police department."

"Seems like a long time ago, but yes, I was an officer there."

"That's a big agency. Nearly the size of Madison. I've done some work with them. Quite a change to come here."

She had expected a note of condescension in his voice, but was surprised to find a bit of envy. "Yes. I've enjoyed having more of a life."

"I hear you. I like working for the DCI, but I enjoy the traveling less and less. My idea of fun is not sleeping in the Durand Hotel without air-conditioning. Like I had to do last night."

"I'm sorry. What happened?"

"My air-conditioning unit didn't work. I ended up bunking in with Phil. We get along, but too much to-getherness is not good. Neither of us was too happy about the sleeping arrangement. But it gave me some time to go over the file on the Schuler murders. Man, that's some grisly reading."

"You find anything up at the Danielses'?"

Her question caught him in midbite. He carefully took his time finishing chewing and then patted his mouth with his napkin before answering. He looked at her and then said, "No. But what occurred to me was that there is a good chance this man walked over there. I mean, he might have had a truck tucked into the weeds on a side road. But maybe he's a neighbor, just waiting for an opportunity to teach everybody a lesson."

CHAPTER 20

Bridget stretched out on the lounge chair on the screened-in porch. Even though it was going into the eighties today, there was a slight breeze from the east and it was cool. She patted her belly. She had almost lost all the weight she had gained with the baby. She had ridden Joker this morning before her husband went to work. Rachel had just gone down for a nap and would probably sleep for a couple of hours. Bridget thought of all the things she should do while she had the chance.

First she wanted to call her sister. Bridget hadn't heard from her since Claire had called asking about the pesticides.

The fact that she hadn't heard from Claire in three days made her nervous. They usually talked every day or two. She picked up the cordless phone and punched in her sister's work number.

"Watkins here." Her sister's voice was crisp and so sharp that Bridget wondered how many cups of coffee she had had so far this morning.

"This is your darling sister. I haven't heard from you in a few days. What's going on over there? I read about the poisonings."

"Sorry, I've been busy. I should have called you. The man who stole the pesticides is wreaking havoc."

"Mom used to use that phrase—*wreaking havoc*—but as I recall it was about the way your room looked."

"Thanks for that reminder."

"So are you working nonstop?"

"Yes."

"What about Meg? Do you want her to come and stay with me for a few days?" Bridget didn't know how Claire managed on her own, trying to raise a daughter with the hours her work required.

"Thanks, but she's taken care of. She went to stay at Steven's parents. They're happy to have her. She's having a good time. They dote on her."

"I bet. How are you and Rich doing?"

Claire didn't say anything for a moment; then her voice sounded lower. "What, do you have extrasensory perception or something? Why do you ask?"

Something was going on. Bridget had felt that those two were ready to take another step forward. They had moved up to spending nearly every other day together. She wouldn't be surprised to hear they were going to move in together. "I don't know. Just wondering how he handles it when you get so busy."

"Not great." Claire took a deep breath and then confessed, "Bridge, he asked me to marry him."

"Oh, a wedding. I love it." When Claire had married Steven, they had done the justice-of-the-peace route. Bridget had been so disappointed. This time she would insist on more and offer her help. Maybe a simple church wedding, early fall, great flowers, and a buffet dinner. They could do it at her house in Wabasha. It would be perfect. Too bad Rachel wasn't old enough to be a flower girl.

"Slow down, Bridget. I haven't said yes yet."

"And why not?" Bridget thought Rich was perfect for her sister. A little on the quiet side, but he had a real solid sense of humor that would get them through the tough times. And he loved Meg.

"I'm not sure I want to get married again."

Don't argue with her, Bridget coached herself. *Whenever you argue with Claire she gets stubborn.* "I can understand that. Losing a husband the way you did might make a woman jumpy."

"Maybe that's it."

"How do you feel about Rich?"

"I think he's great. He's one of the kindest men I've ever met. So considerate. Solid."

"Boring?" Bridget asked, wondering what could be wrong. It might be the sex. Claire had her needs.

"No, I wouldn't say that. But certainly traditional. I think that's one of the reasons he has such a hard time when I'm not available to him, when I have to work such long hours. He has this image of the good woman by his side. Not necessarily doing everything for him, but available."

"The man can go out into the world and the little wife is supposed to be home with dinner ready whenever he arrives, but it can't be the other way around."

"In all fairness to Rich, I think he wouldn't mind having dinner ready. It isn't that he wants me to take care of him. I actually think he'd rather take care of me. But he wants me to be there. His idea of a relationship doesn't allow for much room to move. He's surprisingly needy."

"So what did you tell him?"

"I told him I needed time to think."

"How much time?"

"Well, I wasn't specific."

Bridget knew she had pushed as far as Claire was comfortable. They needed to have a longer talk. Maybe it was time for Rachel and her to go visit Auntie Claire. "Take your time. This is a big decision."

"Bridget, I gotta go. I can't think about anything else but this pesticide guy. It might be over tomorrow; it might be starting tomorrow. It depends on if I can figure out what is going on. It's hard to think about love when people are in danger."

Ray Sorenson walked into the sheriff's department and asked to see Claire Watkins. "Do you want to go back? Her desk is right in the main room," the woman receptionist told him.

"I'd like to see her out here, if that's okay," he said. He didn't want to talk about Folger with a whole room listening. "Could you go get her?"

It took a minute, but then Claire appeared. She had her hair pulled back from her face and the top button on her uniform undone. She looked tired and preoccupied, but when she saw Ray she smiled. It made him feel worse.

"Ray," she said. "What can I do for you?"

"Can we go outside?"

"Sure, that sounds good." She followed him outside. She looked around like she hadn't seen the day yet. "I can use a break."

"My pickup's over there. In the shade. I left the windows open, so it shouldn't be too hot. We could sit in there."

"Fine."

When they got to his Ford Ranger pickup truck, Ray walked around and opened the passenger-side door for her. She thanked him and climbed in. He circled the truck, jumped in his side, and pushed back the seat. He didn't know where to start. She was looking at him, waiting.

"This is hard," he said.

She didn't say anything. He took a deep breath, then started. "I'm kinda being blackmailed."

"Really?" she said, and waited.

"You remember about Tiffany," he said, making it half a question.

She nodded.

"Well, once she came to see me at the co-op."

This time she asked, "At the co-op?"

"Things got out of hand."

She waited.

"It was Tiffany's idea."

"What did you do?"

"We kinda did it in the storage area."

"Oh." The deputy turned and looked out the windshield.

He thought maybe it would have gone easier if they were driving. They could have driven down to the river or anyplace. If they were moving, they would have something else to look at while he told his story. "Someone saw us."

"Who?" she asked.

"Mr. Folger."

"The agronomist."

"Yeah."

"He's blackmailing you?"

"I guess."

"What does he want?"

"He said that if I told him about what's going on in this investigation about the stolen pesticides and everything—anything that I could get out of my dad he wants to know—that he wouldn't tell my father about what I did with Tiffany."

As he spoke, Ray couldn't help remembering what he and Tiffany had done. She had wanted to do it like the animals, she said. Being in with the feed and all, she wanted him to take her like a horse, from behind. She had dropped her jeans and offered her white buttocks to him. He had been unable to resist. He hated to be thinking about it with this woman deputy in the car with him. He felt like she, in her quiet way, would be able to read his thoughts.

Claire sat for a moment, then asked, "Why is he so interested in all of this?"

"He's got an obsession with the Schulers."

Claire turned and looked at him. "Really? How do you know that?"

"It's gone on forever with him. He's shown me the newspaper clippings. He has a whole file on the murders. I think it was the most important thing that happened in his life."

"That's interesting."

"What am I going to do?"

"I think you've already done it. You've come and talked to me, reported Folger. What he's doing is against the law. I'll take it from here."

"Are you going to let my dad know?"

"No, but I think you should. You don't need to lay it all out for him. But I think you should let him know that you did something inappropriate with Tiffany at work and that you're really sorry. Assure him it won't happen again. That way if Folger does tell him, it won't be as big a shock. But I think I'll take care of Folger for you. I don't think he'll be divulging anything to anybody."

"Tell my dad?" It was the last thing in the world Ray wanted to do. The thought of having his dad know anything about Tiffany made him want to gag. Maybe it would have been better to let Folger tell him. Then he wouldn't need to see his father's face when he heard the news of his son's bad behavior.

"Give him a heads-up. Don't go into gory detail. He was young once, too. He might even understand."

"Oh, God."

Claire touched him on the shoulder and made him look at her. "You need to pull in the reins on this young woman you're seeing."

Wearing plastic gloves, Claire lined up and counted the ivory-colored objects. Eight. Then she counted them again. Still only eight. The number didn't seem right to her. There were seven people killed at the Schulers'—two adults and five children. Seven baby fingers cut off. There were three bones in each finger. That should make twenty-one bones. They had found seven bones when the pesticides were stolen, one by the dead flowers, one by the chickens, and one with the lemonade. That made ten bones they had found. That left eleven, but all she had was eight.

There was one whole finger still missing.

"You need to get those ready to send off to the crime lab," Tyrone told her when he walked into the back room.

"I know. I want to take some pictures of them. Some close-ups. They are like pieces of a puzzle. I think one of the fingers is missing."

"What do you mean?"

Claire explained to him what she had realized. "I'd like to figure out whose finger is missing."

"How can you do that?"

"By trying to match up the bones we have found and see what size they are. We might be able to figure out whose finger isn't there." She pointed out two very small bones. "These are obviously the baby's. However, even if we puzzle this out, it might not tell us much. Maybe some of the bones were lost. Maybe the pesticide guy still has some. But it's worth a try."

"Do you have pictures of the other bones?"

"Yes, but they're not exactly to size. It might be hard to match them up."

"What about the pipe tobacco can?"

"That's ready to go." She lifted up a Polaroid. "I have a picture of that. I talked to an antique dealer in town, and she said this particular tin was being made in the late forties, early fifties. Fairly common, she said. Worth about ten bucks now. I wonder if it would be worthwhile to ask around and see if anyone remembers who used this particular brand. It was so long ago, it's hard to say what someone might remember. I might call Harold Peabody at the paper. He seems to have a mind like a steel trap."

"The sheriff just stationed someone at the water tower to watch it until we catch this guy. He said he was going to poison the water, and that might well be where he would plan on doing it."

"Good thought."

CHAPTER 21

———|———

Earl Lowman had forgotten the lush green beauty of the Iowa farmland in midsummer. He had pulled over at a rest stop to relieve himself and stretch his legs. The fields around him were in full growth and the grass leaned in the wind like the plush nap of green velvet. Tucson was brittle and dry this time of year, and he avoided going outside in the middle of the day.

The sun was still quite high, but it was getting toward the end of the afternoon. He had been driving for ten hours already. He had gotten up at five and left by six. He had another six hours to go before he drove into Wisconsin.

He didn't know how he was going to do it. His head felt like it was full of water and if he leaned to one side it all sloshed over, pulling him that way. Sleep was what he needed. Just a short nap. An hour or so and he would still get into Durand before midnight.

When he had talked to Marie this morning before he left, she had said that Andy was holding his own, but hadn't come around yet. He was stirring, she said, and all the nurses had been encouraged, saying it was a good sign. Earl was worried that his son would not wake from this coma, but he worried more that Andy would come around and not be able to function in the world.

How hard it would be to see his healthy, strong son turned into an invalid.

Marie had also said something about a deputy coming around, wanting to talk to him about the Schuler murders. Would he never be rid of that family? Would he sleep with their bones the rest of his life?

Earl lumbered back to his car. He pushed the driver's seat away from the steering wheel and tipped it as far back as it would go. To catch the breeze and let it blow through the car, he opened all the windows. He was facing north, so he would be sitting in shadow.

When he closed his eyes, he saw the Schuler farm as it had been the night he went to return the saw he had borrowed. He had called when he got to the house, trying to raise someone, but no one answered. It struck him as very odd, seeing as the front door was wide open and it was dinnertime. He stuck his head inside the kitchen door, and that was when he had seen Bertha. She was lying on the floor. He couldn't figure out why she would be doing that. The oddest thing he had seen. He took one more step and he understood. She had a bloodred corsage on her housedress. A pool of blood circled her hand. The baby was partly under the table. He hadn't even looked at her.

He had to force himself to walk through the kitchen to pick up the phone that was attached to the wall. His hands were shaking so hard he could hardly even dial, but he called the sheriff.

"They're murdered out at the Schuler farm," he had said. "I'm afraid they might all be murdered. Please send help."

Then he had gone to sit on the steps. He knew he should walk through the house and see if anyone was still alive, but he didn't think he could even force himself back into the same room with Bertha.

As he sat there, trying to get up his courage and find the rest of the family, someone had come out of the house to talk to him. He had never told anyone about that person being there alive. He had decided not to, and he had lived with that decision. It might be time to tell what had really happened that long-ago summer night.

He would do anything to bring Andy back. Whoever was threatening the county with the pesticides wanted the truth; he could give it to them. The more he thought about it, he might do it no matter what.

He clung to the steering wheel with his hands and slept. In his dreams, he was heading north, trying to find his way home.

Claire decided she had someone else she had to talk to—Charles W. Folger, born seventy-one years ago. Claire remembered him telling her he was that old, bragging about it. Claire decided to look through the databases to see if she could pull up anything on Charles Folger, but she found nothing. He might be a weirdo, but he was a quiet, prudent weirdo. Possibly until now.

Thinking back to her first interview with Folger, she remembered how antagonistic he was. Maybe he just didn't like women law-enforcement officers, but maybe he didn't like women. Maybe he didn't like authority figures. She wanted someone else there to watch how this man handled himself. Because she was going to push him hard to find out what he knew.

This might be the break they'd been waiting for.

Tyrone was on the phone in the conference room. He and Singer had set up in there. He thanked someone, then hung up. Looking up at her, he asked, "What can I do for you?"

"You want to take a run with me?" she asked him.

"Sure. Where we going?"

"Check on an agronomist."

She pointed out a patrol car to him and he climbed into the passenger seat. After they drove out of town, he wrinkled his nose. "Something smells around here."

"Good fertilizer," she told him as she waved her hand.

"So that's what's been coming off the fields as we drive through this county." He laughed.

They drove a while in silence, and then she asked him where he was from. "Chicago. The Big Chi town."

"How do you like Madison?"

"I dig it. For a smallish city, there's a lot going on. The university saves it from just being another dairy town."

"Do you miss Chicago?" she asked.

"Do you miss Minneapolis?" he returned.

"Yes," she said. "But not as much as I would have when I was younger."

"How old are you?"

She looked at him, surprised at his question, not sure what to do with it. "Are you serious?"

"Want me to guess?" he said.

"Absolutely not. That might ruin any chances we might have of getting along. I'm slightly past forty."

"My, my, but you're holding your own against time."

"And what about you?"

"Thirty-five and climbing." Tyrone looked out the window and said, "This is beautiful country. I didn't realize Wisconsin could be so hilly."

"Yes, this bluff country is gorgeous."

Again, they drove a ways in silence. He shifted in his seat and asked her, "How do you get treated as the only woman in the sheriff's office?"

"How do you get treated as an African American at DCI?"

"Touché," he said.

"To answer your question—mainly fine. I think the

younger guys—Billy, Scott—are easier with me. The older deputies don't like it that I've jumped over them as the investigator for the office. They might grumble, but they do it softly, not so's I can hear."

"Yeah, I've had one or two problems, but I actually think some of the guys think it's cool to work with a black guy. I'm more apt to run into problems out in the field."

"How've you been doing in Pepin County so far?"

He gave it a thought, then turned and smiled at her. "Fine."

Dinner had been good fresh green beans from the garden, homemade bread, and meat loaf. With just the two of them, they finished only half the meat loaf. That would be good, since his wife might not be up to cooking for a while. He knew what he had to do tonight. He wouldn't wait too long to get it done, but he felt like sitting another moment or two and allowing his meal to digest.

"That was a good dinner," he told her.

She looked over at him, surprised. He didn't often praise her cooking.

"We should be getting some of the new corn any day now," he said just to say something.

"That'll be nice." She started to clear the table.

There had never been enough fingers. There should have been seven and there had been only six. The sheriff's office would know that by now. He had decided he needed to give them one more. The numbers had to be right. Maybe that was what had been wrong all along. Maybe that was why the truth had never come out. The numbers hadn't added up. The more he had thought about it last night, the more clearly he saw what he had to do.

"You want some dessert?" she asked.

"What've we got?"

"I could offer you a bowl of ice cream or some peanut butter cookies."

"How about both?" he asked.

"My, but you've worked up an appetite today. What about your cholesterol?" she reminded him.

"I'm not sure I want to live that long anyway. Especially not without ice cream and cookies."

She gave a nervous little laugh. An odd sound in the house. This house had never heard much laughter. She pulled the ice cream out of the fridge, ran the scoop under the hot water, and dug out three nice round scoops for him. Then she put two cookies next to the ice cream in a bowl and handed it to him. She gave herself one scoop and stood up at the counter, eating it.

"Come and sit down," he told her.

"Naw," she said. "If I sit down it's just that much harder to get up again. I want to get this kitchen clean before I go in and watch my show."

She liked to watch the quiz shows on TV. Normally he would go out into the barn and putter around, but tonight he had different plans.

She grabbed his bowl away from him as soon as he was finished and put it in the soapy water in the sink.

He stood up and walked to the window. Clouding up a bit. Tomorrow was the big day. It would have been fifty years ago the Schulers were killed. His wife didn't know a thing about it. He had never talked to her about it. He had never talked to anyone except his mother. He wondered what his wife would say if she knew what he had been doing. Soon she might get an inkling of what he was made of.

"There's something I'd like to show you in the basement," he told her.

Turning from the sink, she gave him an odd look. "In the basement?"

"Wipe your hands and come on down."

"Can't you bring it up?" she asked. "My show's almost on."

Firmly he took her arm. She resisted for a moment, then gave in as she always did. He walked her over to the basement door and opened it.

She looked wild-eyed at him. She hated the basement. As he started her down the stairs, he said soothingly, "I'll help you down. Don't worry. What I want to do won't take a minute."

CHAPTER 22

Claire knew that Charles Folger lived up the bluff from her, but she hadn't realized he lived so close. She figured, as the crow flew, his house was probably only two miles away, but as the road wound, it was more like six miles. As they rounded a bend a few miles down the bluff from Folger's house, they caught sight of a view of the lake.

"What's that body of water?" Tyrone asked.

"Lake Pepin," Claire said, surprised he didn't know. "That's right, you came from the east and you haven't had a chance to see the lake yet. The lake is really the Mississippi River, but since it runs so wide and deep they call it a lake for this twenty-three-mile stretch."

"This is a first. I don't think I've ever seen the Mississippi before."

"Since it meanders between St. Paul and Minneapolis, I've spent my life crossing it. My dad made us spell it out every time we went over it and, of course, as a kid saying the ending, I-P-P-I, seemed pretty risqué."

As the road took another turn, they lost the lake. Claire came to Folger's driveway and drove to the end of the lane. Two cars were parked in front of an open garage. Claire remembered hearing that Folger was married. She wondered what his wife must be like to be able to put up with him.

When Claire got out of the patrol car and looked over

at the house, she saw that Folger was sitting on his front porch, watching them. He didn't stand up, he didn't give a howdy wave; he just watched.

Tyrone came around the car and they walked up to the porch together. "Mr. Folger, may we have a word with you?" Claire asked.

The older man glared, but motioned to two hard-backed wooden chairs sitting next to his on the porch. When she had seen him at work, he had worn a button-down shirt and dress pants. He had rolled up the sleeves of his shirt and had put on tennis shoes, but otherwise was dressed the same.

Claire took the chair closest to him and moved it around so she was half facing him. She introduced Tyrone. He swung his chair around so they formed a half circle. Very cozy.

Folger squirmed as they moved in on him. He looked like he was about to bolt from his chair. "What's this about?"

"I had a visitor today," Claire started. "Ray Sorenson. He told me about a recent conversation he had with you."

Folger stood up with a jolt and his chair tipped over backward. "I don't need to say a thing."

"No, of course you don't. But then we might need to take you back to town for questioning."

"I was just trying to warn the boy about his immoral behavior. I would think he would be grateful that I came to him and not to his father."

"A warning is one thing, Mr. Folger, but the threat of blackmail is another." Claire pointed at his chair. "Why don't you sit back down?"

Folger perched on the edge of his chair as if he were ready for instant flight. "Ray must have misunderstood."

"I don't know. He seems like a pretty smart kid to me.

He seemed very clear about what had happened between you two. He was even considering talking it over
with his father."

"He wouldn't dare."

"I think he would." Claire paused, then went on. "But
that isn't really what we've come to talk to you about.
Ray also mentioned that you're quite interested in the
Schuler murders. That you have files on what happened.
We were thinking you might be able to help us out."

"It's nothing. I have a few newspaper clippings. I'm
sure most of the older people in this community have the
same."

"Why this interest?" It was the first question Tyrone
had asked. Claire felt it was well timed.

Folger tucked his chin into his chest and stared at the
porch floor. "You wouldn't understand."

"Try us," Tyrone urged.

"What do you know about what it's like to live in a
small community?"

"I'm learning," Claire said.

"Those people were our neighbors. They went to
church with us; they sent their kids to school. As far as I
know nobody had a big beef against them. And then,
boom!—like that they were killed. And nobody saw anything; nobody knew anything. They never found out
who did it. We were none of us safe after that. We all
followed what had happened. People talked of nothing
else."

"So you kept track of it all."

"Yeah, to try to understand. I always felt like if we
would just know what had happened we'd be a little
safer. You could guard against it happening again.
But the not knowing was horrible. It ate us up. It
changed us."

Tyrone leaned in a little closer to Folger. "It sounds awful."

However, Tyrone's sympathy had the reverse effect on Folger. He reared back. "There's no law against keeping a scrapbook."

"No," Tyrone said. "Could we see it?"

"Stay here. I'll go get it from the house." Folger walked into the house and was gone about five minutes.

Claire gave Tyrone a what-do-you-think look and he shrugged. When Folger returned, he had a big scrapbook with a picture of a doe and a fawn on the cover. The pages and the clippings inside were golden brown with age.

"Would you mind if I looked this over?" she asked him. "It might help with the case." She wanted to see what he had gathered. On first glance it didn't look like he had anything she hadn't already gotten from Harold Peabody.

"I guess, but I want it back. I do bring it out from time to time and I did show it to Ray Sorenson. He seemed interested. Not many of the young kids are. I've always wanted to know the truth of what happened." Folger looked at both of them. "And now it looks like I'm not alone."

"I'm desperately hungry," Tyrone announced when they climbed back in the car. He felt like he hadn't had a good meal since he left Madison. He lusted after a juicy falafel sandwich from the Middle East Café or enchiladas with plenty of salsa, but doubted anything like that was available. There might not be any spicy food available in all of Pepin County.

"I think I can take care of that. If you're not particular. We're pretty close to the Fort."

The Fort, he thought; he wasn't even going to ask. "How about a beer?"

"This little joint I'm thinking of specializes in beer," she paused, then added, "and hamburgers."

Tyrone paged through Charles Folger's scrapbook as Claire drove down from the bluff and into Fort St. Antoine. Nothing struck him as out of the ordinary. Even though the press clippings usually had the date on them, someone had written the date and the paper's name below. Thorough, anal, but not that unusual. Then he found some loose photographs stuck into the back of the book.

"You see anything in there?" she asked.

"All the usual clippings, but he's got a couple of photographs from the scene of the crime. I wonder how he got those?"

"Everyone knows everyone. It probably wasn't too hard for him to find out who photographed the crime scene. I'm assuming they are the same photos that we have in our files?"

"They look like it." He set the scrapbook down. "I'll leave this with you. You can check it over tonight and bring it in tomorrow."

After driving down through dense woodlands and dropping out of the farmland that crowned the top of the bluff, they drove into a small town that was right on the lake. Claire took a sharp turn up a hill and pointed out a white clapboard house. "That's where I live," she said.

It looked like a small run-down farmhouse. He wasn't good at commenting on housing stock. "So you have a lake view?"

"I only glimpse the lake through the trees in the summer, but in the winter I see it much better." She smiled over at him. "Do you want to drive down to the lake?"

"Hungry," he said. "Barely able to talk."

She laughed. "I hope you're not a vegetarian."

"Nope. I eat meat with the best of them."

When they walked into the bar, Tyrone felt the cool air wave across his body. His hand instinctively reached up and undid his top button. The smell of the place was fried food, yeasty drinks, and loud laughter. Two men were playing pool in the center of the room. Two women were sitting at the bar holding beers by the necks.

"Hey, Claire" came from the window into the kitchen behind the counter.

"Hey, Clarence," Claire shouted back.

Claire grabbed two menus from the holder by the cash register and pointed him toward a table. "By the window suit you?"

"Great."

When they sat down, she explained, "The soup is made homemade every day. And it's good. Everything else is frozen and fried. Burgers are not bad. The soup is written up on the board. Looks like bean with bacon. Leinenkugel is on tap."

"You're making this easy."

When the waitress came, Claire ordered a grilled cheese sandwich, a cup of soup, and a beer. Tyrone went for the Lakeside Burger, which featured mayonnaise, a side of fries, and a beer. But when Claire's cup of soup came immediately, he decided he had to have that, too.

The waitress came back with another cup of soup and set down their frosty beer mugs. Claire lifted hers and he clacked his against it. "What're we celebrating?"

"The end of the day." She pointed at the sun setting over the lake.

He felt it necessary to point out what came afterward. "But the beginning of the night."

"What did you think about Folger?" Claire asked him while she crumbled some crackers in her soup.

"Are you going to eat all your crackers?" he asked.

"Didn't you eat anything today?"

"No midafternoon snack and it's almost nine o'clock."

"How do you stay so slim?"

"By not eating. I just think about it a lot."

"What about Folger?" Claire came back to her question.

"Guy gave me the willies, but seemed nonlethal."

"Yeah, that's how he struck me this time around. When I saw him the first time at his office he was much more belligerent."

"The scrapbook still might tell us something. It's worth looking at carefully. I guess it wouldn't be uncommon for someone from around here to be fascinated by the murders, but that is also behavior we see in killers. Tracking their crime in the paper. Their fifteen minutes."

"You going back to the office after this?"

"Yeah, the sheriff wanted me to be there ten to two. Do cell phones work here? I wonder if the pesticide guy has struck again."

"Not well, because of the bluffs. Let me use the phone at the bar to check in." She picked up both of their empty soup bowls. "Ex-waitress," she explained.

He watched her walk up to the counter and lean over to grab the phone from behind the cash register. Claire wasn't his type but she was sure fun to ogle. Good hair, great lips, nice ass. Not so skinny as many white women tried to be. She looked like she'd be a handful in bed. Five years ago he probably would have tried to find out, but five years ago he hadn't met Sandy yet. She was good enough to be faithful for.

Claire came back to the table shaking her head. "Nothing's going on. No calls have come in."

"Maybe he's taking a day off."

The food arrived. The fries looked like a pile of straw, but were nice and crispy. The hamburger wasn't bad. Tyrone was facing the door and looked up from his food as a man walked in. He stood in the doorway and looked over at Tyrone with an odd, determined look. Tyrone was accustomed to the look. It happened from time to time when someone walked into a place where they didn't customarily see a black man and there he'd be. He usually ignored it. Did no good to even think about it. But he was surprised when the man pushed open the door and went back out. He hadn't looked so redneck to Tyrone that he wouldn't even have a drink in a place serving a black. Tyrone lifted his beer mug again.

Claire knocked hers against it. "What're we celebrating now?"

"Satisfaction," he said.

Rich didn't know what to do with himself. He felt like an idiot. Why had he backed out the door? Why hadn't he walked in and gone over to the table and kissed the woman he loved? Instead he had acted like he had done something wrong, or found her in a compromising position.

He walked down toward the lake and thought of going back to the Fort, but his stomach turned.

Rich felt like something broke in him. Seeing her with another man. Even though he was sure the guy was official—some deputy or sheriff or agent or cop. That was her world; that was her life. She was the only woman in an arena of men. She could handle it. Why couldn't he?

He wasn't sure he could share Claire the way he would have to if he wanted to be part of her life. It would always be like this. One case or another would take her away from him. She would go out for drinks with the guys after work and he would not be included.

Why, if it was so important to him to have a wife who stayed close to him, had he fallen in love with a deputy sheriff?

The lake stretched out greasy and hot under the setting sun. When he turned back to go to the bar, he saw their patrol car pull away.

He missed her.

CHAPTER 23

Debby didn't usually work the late shift. It had been one of the requests she had made when she took the job, that she not have to work at night. Everything was screwed up these days. She had started to hate to come to work since her flowers were dead. Everyone was working longer hours. All because of that guy who had stolen the pesticides and something that had happened fifty years ago. She didn't get it.

Debby had agreed to fill in at the front—she was tired of answering the phones. She had only another couple hours left and she could go home. It was nearly ten o'clock and she thought of her husband, her new husband, watching the news without her.

Ned told her that he loved every ounce of her. She was a little overweight, but not only did it not bother him, he saw it as positive. "Something to hold on to," he whispered in her ear. "Something to keep me warm at night."

She was sorry she wasn't there snuggled next to him on the couch, her eyes opened only a slit, ready to climb into bed. But she was at the sheriff's department, watching no one walk in the door and waiting to go home.

She left the desk for a few minutes to go to the bathroom and make a phone call to Ned. He told her he had just made popcorn. Then she came back to finish up her shift. She had told the sheriff she was leaving at eleven.

She had already worked three hours extra, and although she was glad she was getting overtime, it still wasn't worth it.

When she walked back to the front, a rolled-up napkin smeared with ketchup was sitting in the middle of the counter. She picked up the napkin to throw it away and it felt like part of a hot dog was still left inside it. She unrolled the napkin and stared at what she was holding in her hand. She couldn't believe it.

Without thinking, she flung it back on the counter. She couldn't even scream. She opened her mouth but the sound that came out was more like a whimper. She said, "No, no."

This was it. This was enough. She hated this kind of thing. She didn't even like watching scary movies.

The African American guy, Tyrone whatever his name, was walking in and looked over at her as she was whimpering. She pointed at the crumpled napkin.

"Look," she managed to say.

He gingerly rolled back the napkin and saw the bloody stump of a finger that was tucked inside. Debby actually thought he turned paler. She didn't know black people could do that, but he did. She swore he did. She stopped whimpering.

"How did this get here?" he asked.

"I don't know. I went to the bathroom."

"It happened right now?"

"Yes, in the last ten minutes."

"You didn't see anybody."

"No. The napkin was just sitting here on the counter when I came back."

"Would you get me a plastic bag to put it in? We don't want anyone else touching it."

The Tyrone guy seemed like he was holding his anger in. Debby didn't give a hoot. He could throw a tantrum as far as she was concerned. She was tired of working here. This was it for her. Ned didn't really like her working so much anyhow.

"I quit," Debby said.

Tyrone stared at her for a moment as if looking through her. Then he said, "Yeah, I bet you do."

He reached into his pocket and pulled out plastic gloves. That alone gave Debby the creeps. Imagine living with a man who walked around with plastic gloves in his pocket.

He gently unrolled the napkin and moved the finger to one side and looked at what was written in black ink.

Point this at one of your own.

Marie Lowman woke and found herself curled up in the lounge chair next to Andy's bed. Through sleep-heavy eyes, she looked up at the clock on the wall, which read eleven o'clock. The night air pressed against the window. She needed to go home. She hadn't seen her children in twenty-four hours. She hadn't changed her clothes in twice as long.

But the thought of leaving Andy tore at her heart. He hardly seemed to breathe in that white hospital bed. His hair was pushed back off his forehead, showing the tan line left by his Farmer's Cooperative cap.

She couldn't help herself. She put her finger in front of his nose and felt the gentle movement of air that meant he was still of the world. How long, she wondered, how long could he go on this way? If she thought of him being in a coma for weeks and then months and then years, she didn't know if she could bear it. How would she keep her family going without him? He supported them in so many ways.

A nurse walked in and said, "Just need to take his vitals."

Marie noticed how young the woman was. Maybe thirty, probably not. She had that clean-scrubbed look of a Wisconsin farmgirl: short bobbed blond hair, blue eyes, and pink skin. She wondered what it did to her to take care of people who were dying day after day.

Marie stood by and watched her go through the familiar routine: blood pressure, pulse, temperature. At first it had reassured her that they kept such a close watch on him, but when it all remained constant she wondered why they bothered.

"Do you expect it to change?"

"He could spike a fever. We need to watch for that."

"He's never sick," Marie told the nurse. She wanted to go on and explain what a strong man he was, but she knew the nurse didn't need to hear about it. Andy was only a patient to her.

When the nurse was done, Marie said, "I think I'm going to go home pretty soon. Just for a few hours."

The nurse nodded.

"You will keep an eye on him, won't you?"

"Yes, and if anything changes we will call you."

"It helps to know that."

The nurse was almost out the door when Marie asked her, "Do you think he'll wake up?"

The nurse thought for a moment. "They often do. I would hope so."

Her words were enough for now. She would be leaving Andy with someone who hoped he would wake up.

Marie felt tears rise up into her eyes, but she blinked them away. If she started she would never stop. She needed to hold them in check for a while longer. Until she got home, until she hugged her kids, until she was alone in bed.

She walked up to the bed and put her hand on Andy's forehead. Leaning over, she said his name. "I'm going home for a while. I'll be back." She stopped and then couldn't help herself. "Come back to me."

She took his hand and squeezed it. At first when she held his hand it felt like a small animal sleeping; then it stirred. She squeezed again. Again she felt his hand move.

"Andy," she said.

Nothing.

She leaned in closer to him. She raised her voice. "Andy, can you hear me?"

A moan came out of his mouth.

"Andy, it's Marie."

He coughed and his eyes flew open, then dropped shut again.

"Andy."

He lay still.

She sank down on the floor at the side of the bed, holding on to his hand. Whatever came she would not let him go. He was coming back if she had to pull him all the way.

Then she heard her name. She lifted up her head.

She heard Andy say, "Marie?"

Claire had called to talk to Meg, but Brenda Watkins, Meg's grandmother, told her that she was already fast asleep. "Do you want me to wake her up?"

"No, of course not. Just let her know I've called. She worries."

"We wore her out today."

Then Claire tried to call Rich, but there was no answer. It was after eleven o'clock and she wondered where he was. Maybe at a poker game. Maybe out for a beer. She wanted to hear his voice. He knew how to settle her.

After she had parked her car, she had walked by the

wild rosebush and saw that the roses were no longer blooming. They had all fallen and she hadn't even noticed. That was how fast things could change, if you didn't pay attention to them. She needed to give Rich some attention.

She hated nights like this, when she was so tired she hardly had enough energy to take her clothes off, but she knew the moment she got into bed, her mind would start to whir. She called it whirring and it sounded a lot like worrying, but it was faster and more disorienting. Drinking helped her fall asleep, but usually she woke up a few hours later and started up anyway. The one beer she had had with dinner was enough. A hot bath might relax her, she thought, and started to run a tub.

Just as she was ready to climb into the water, the phone rang. She had set it on the toilet right next to the bathtub.

"Hello," she answered.

"I hope you're not asleep," a male voice said, but it wasn't Rich. It was Tyrone.

"What's up?" She sat down on the toilet and grabbed at a towel. Without any clothes on, she felt odd talking to this man she hardly knew.

"We got a special delivery."

"What?"

"From the pesticide guy."

"Yeah, tell me." She didn't appreciate his fooling around.

"Well, you know how you were saying today that there weren't enough fingers?"

"Yes."

"Well, he must have agreed with you. He sent us another one."

"Does it look like it could be the father's?"

"Nope. It's a fresh finger."

"What do you mean, fresh?"

"It is covered with flesh. Someone lost it within the last day or so. That's what the medical examiner thought."

"I'm coming down."

"No, Stewy said you would want to, but we need you to be here early. Get some sleep."

"Any ideas whose finger?"

"Dr. Lord wasn't sure of the sex—probably middle-aged. Whoever it was had worked hard."

"That would match most of the people in the county."

"Uh-huh. See you tomorrow."

Claire let the towel drop and she looked down at her own fingers. What poor person was out there tonight without a digit? Would he or she still be alive—and be found in time?

CHAPTER 24

Earl pulled up in front of the hospital. It was after midnight, but he had decided, driving into town, that this had to be his first stop. Marie had probably gone home, but he needed to lay his eyes on his son. No matter what he looked like. That was where this journey home had to start.

A youngish woman sat at the information desk, but she was looking down at her lap. When Earl walked up closer, he saw that she was knitting. He stood quietly and watched her for a few moments. The needles moved in and out of the yarn like magic. A hot activity for this time of year, but it was air-conditioned in the hospital.

"What're you knitting?" he asked her.

"Oh." She jumped. "Sorry, I didn't know you were there."

"What're you knitting?"

"A sweater for my son. For Christmas. I always get a head start."

"He's a lucky son."

"Thanks." She smiled up at him. "What can I help you with?"

"I'm here to see my son, Andy Lowman."

Her face dropped slightly. She knew what had happened to his son. She felt sorry for him. "He's up on the second floor. It's not really visiting hours."

"I know, but I just drove up from Tucson. I'd like to see him for a moment."

"I guess that's all right." She gave him the room number.

As he stood in front of the elevator, he remembered all the events that had taken place in this hospital. His children had been born here. His mother had died here. He had lost his appendix at this hospital. The smell—why did all hospitals smell like that? A mixture of sorrow and ammonia. Not unpleasant, but sometimes a little too strong.

As he came up to the room, he could hear talking. He wondered if one of the nurses was in there. Then he stood in the door and saw Marie leaning over the bed. Andy was sitting up with his eyes open and he was talking.

"Andy," Lowman said.

They both turned and saw him. Marie's face was wet with tears. "He's back," she said, and Earl didn't know if she was talking about Andy or himself.

"Dad," Andy said.

"Is it okay if I'm here?" Earl asked.

Marie walked up to him and said, "You must be exhausted."

"I think we all are," he said as he hugged her.

"Come and take a chair." She pointed at the chair that was pulled up next to the bed.

"How long has he been awake?"

"A couple of hours. He's pretty groggy. Doesn't remember much of what happened. But doesn't look like he's going to slip away again. The nurses have come in and checked him over. Everything looks good. They're pretty sure they got all the pesticides out of his system."

"Hallelujah," Earl said quietly.

He sat down in the chair and looked at his son whom

he hadn't seen in ten years. His son was getting old. The wrinkles had set in around his eyes and down his cheeks. But he was wearing well. Looked strong.

"I'm sorry about everything, Andy."

The eyes fluttered shut, then jumped open again. Andy turned his head to see his father. "Don't go there, Dad."

But Earl couldn't stop himself. He knew it wasn't time to talk of such things, that it was only time to rejoice that his son was risen from the dead, but he needed to get it out and say it. He had promised himself he would. "I'm going to talk to the police tomorrow and tell them everything. I decided on my way up here that no matter what, I would tell them what happened."

His son nodded his head. "Mom would be glad."

The rich smell of deep summer night followed Rich as he walked up Claire's hill from town. The slight dip in temperature, probably from a high of eighty-five that day to about seventy-five right at present, caused dew to form, glazing grasses and lilac bushes. A silvery haze glowed around the streetlights as bugs flew in and out of it.

The light he was looking for was in Claire's house, and he found it. Her light was on in her bedroom. That meant she was still up. Before walking up the hill, Rich had decided that if her light was on, he would knock no matter what time it was. He needed to see her. They needed to talk.

After she had left the Fort, he had gone in and had two beers. He felt like such an idiot for the way he behaved. No wonder she was taking her time thinking about whether she wanted to hitch up with a guy like him.

He knocked on her porch door. Then he heard her coming down the stairs. The door opened and she was in his arms. She smelled like the last rose he had picked for her from her bush, sweet and spicy.

"I tried to call," she whispered. "You weren't home." There was no hesitation. She kissed him.

He apologized for his beery breath. "I've been at the Fort. Had a coupla beers."

"You want another one?" she asked, and led him into the house.

He tried to figure out what she was wearing. Her outfit looked like clothes he had left at her house—an old no-sleeved T-shirt that was very revealing and a pair of his boxer shorts.

"Cute pajamas," he told her.

"I needed you in bed with me. Didn't think I'd get you in the flesh."

She walked to the fridge and pulled out two bottles of Leinenkugel's and twisted off the tops. She sat on the edge of the table and he stood in front of her. They tapped beer bottles.

"How's it going?" he asked.

"Nuts. We've got a psycho man loose in the county. A chopped-off finger was just delivered to the sheriff's office. Fresh. That means there's someone in the county missing a digit. Who knows what he'll do next. He's probably lived here all his life and this anniversary of the Schuler killings has set him off." She tilted her beer bottle up and drank a good swallow. He could feel she was shaking.

"Are you cold?"

"Not really. Exhausted to the bone. Can't sleep. I needed you to come over. I'm glad you got my mental message."

"I wasn't sure you would want to see me."

She touched his nose. "Why ever not?"

"I wasn't sure what you wanted."

"Well, that'd make two of us." She leaned in and kissed him on the neck.

"I shouldn't have surprised you with the ring."

"Why not?"

"Well, I mean, we probably should have talked about it."

"I suppose, but it was fine the way you did it."

"You cried."

"I do that."

"Have you been thinking about it?" he asked. He knew he shouldn't ask any more, but he couldn't stop himself.

"In the few minuscule moments when I'm not trying to save our county from disaster, I have thought about it."

"You want to share your thoughts with me?"

"Are you sure this is the right time?"

"No, I'm sure it isn't, but it's driving me crazy not to know."

She nudged him with her knee. "I like driving you crazy."

"I know." He nudged her back.

"What do you think about getting married again?" she asked. She looked him straight in the eyes.

"I'd do it."

"Enthusiastic," she commented.

"Most of it I liked, but not the divorce part."

"We could skip that."

He nodded.

"And we could skip the getting married part."

He wasn't sure what to say.

She leaned in and kissed him hard, a kiss that reached way down into his groin. "Can't we try something else? Maybe we should try living together for a while. Forming a partnership. You cover my back; I'll cover yours."

"Cop talk for being there for each other?"

"Yeah. Hey, I am a cop. I get to talk like one."

"I'll cover your back anytime." He pulled her close to him and felt her wrap her legs around his waist.

"Take me to bed," she whispered in his ear, and he followed orders.

Claire fell asleep hard and woke up two hours later. Her head was smashed into Rich's back and he was snoring. The snoring wasn't what had awakened her. She felt deeply uneasy. She had dreamed about fingers, long, bony fingers coming into her room, climbing into bed with her, touching her while she was sleeping.

She straightened herself out in bed and tried to manage her breathing: deep and slow, deep and slow. *From the belly,* her psychiatrist had told her. *If you breathe from the belly it will calm you.* Unfortunately it seemed to invigorate her. She kept thinking about what she would do when she got up, all that she had to do, and finally she decided to get up and start doing it.

When she crawled out of bed it was about three-thirty. She wasn't supposed to show up at work until six, but she doubted they'd be anything but glad to see her come in a little early.

She started up her coffeemaker, putting in a little more than her usual ration of freshly ground beans. Then she dug a couple of caramel rolls from the bakery out of the freezer. She turned on the oven and put them on an old pie tin to heat up.

After grabbing the first cup of coffee that had streamed out into her carafe, she sat at the table and started to go through Charles Folger's scrapbook. She had been given all the same articles by Harold Peabody. But Folger had a couple from other papers, which were taken from the pieces that Harold had written. She checked every page, every article, but didn't come across any new information.

Finally Claire came to the photographs in the back of the book. They were so big he had left them loose. Obviously original prints—he must have had a contact with the photographer the sheriff had used. It was hard to look at the pictures of the dead children upstairs, sprawled out alongside their beds. The oldest brother stretched out on the hay in the barn, the cows looking on. The father by the front steps. But the photo that was the hardest for her to look at was the one of Bertha Schuler and the baby. And the table all set for the birthday party. The seven plates neatly placed around the edges of the wooden table, silverware laid out the way it should be, glasses up at the top of the plates.

Rich came down the stairs.

"Are you sure you want to be up?" she asked him.

He came up behind her and snuggled into her hair. "I smelled the coffee."

"Do you want me to set you a plate?"

"What's cooking?"

"Just caramel rolls."

"Perfect middle-of-the-night snack."

Claire leaned up into the cupboard and pulled down two dessert-sized plates. Then she stood still for a moment. The plates in the picture. How many plates?

She slammed the two plates down on the counter and grabbed the photograph. "Seven plates," she said.

Rich looked at the picture. "Yup, it looks like seven."

"But why would there be seven plates when only six people were eating at the table? See?" She pointed her finger at the high chair that was set up for Arlette.

"But there were seven Schulers," Rich said.

"The baby was too little to eat at the table. They wouldn't have set a real plate for her with silverware and a glass. She was only a year old. Someone else was there."

"At the Schulers'?"

"Rich, someone else had come to dinner. And whoever it was either murdered them or got away."

July 7, 1952

How long to wait? That was the question. How long to wait before he would venture out into the house? The clothes hung down in front of him. He grabbed on to them, clung to them as if they were real people. But he was afraid all the people were dead.

The gun had been fired six times in the house. The last time had been right outside this closet in the room where Schubert was. He had closed his eyes when the gun went off. He had stuffed his mouth with the hanging clothes.

He knew bad things had happened. His dad had always told him that these German people brought nothing but bad luck down on themselves, and now he believed that his dad knew what he was talking about.

In order to get out of the room, he would have to walk past Schubert. By peering through the clothes, he could see Schubert lying on the floor.

It wasn't the blood he minded so much—he saw blood on the farm when Dad cut off chickens' heads; he was used to seeing blood. It was the smell of death that would be coming out of Schubert. He would have to hold his nose when he walked by.

He decided he couldn't wait any longer. He needed to get out of there. It had been quiet for what had seemed a long time. He wanted to go home. He needed to tell his mom what had happened.

He hunched over and scuttled out of the room. In the hallway he stayed still for a moment, hearing his heart beat. Nothing. No noise. He walked by the girls' room, just glancing in to see the two of them heaped on the floor like a pile of clothes. Couldn't think about it.

He took his shoes off and carried them. Down the stairs he went as silently as he could. Just as he got to the bottom of the stairs, he heard someone out front; then the door to the kitchen banged open. He hid behind the door that led into the kitchen.

The man walked to the phone and called someone. He talked about murders. He said they were dead. He couldn't tell who the man was; he didn't recognize the voice.

Then the man went back outside.

The boy sneaked out from behind the door. And he saw Mr. Schuler talking to the man. The man was holding a gun. He and Mr. Schuler weren't yelling. They looked like they were talking about the weather. Then Mr. Schuler turned and walked away. He got about halfway across the barnyard when the man lifted up his rifle and pulled the trigger. Mr. Schuler stumbled forward; then he fell. The man shot him again.

The boy went and hid behind the door again. There was no safe way to get out of the house. The man was standing with the gun right out front. He felt like his legs were shaking so hard he would fall down. Then he heard the man come in the house, look around, and walk past him. The boy kept his eyes closed, praying the man wouldn't see him.

The man went up the stairs and the boy ran into the kitchen. The baby was under the table. The mom was next to the chair.

He ran out the door and that was when he saw the fingers. The cut-off fingers. He grabbed them and ran. He

ran past Mr. Schuler, lying facedown in the dirt. He ran
past Denny out in the barn. He ran up over the hill and
through the fields. He ran until he came to the hill above
his house.

His mom was down there and she would take care of
him.

But first he needed to put the fingers in a safe place.

He had a hiding place behind the barn where he
kept his favorite things. He went there and took out a
metal pipe tobacco container. It was red. His father had
given it to him. He put the fingers in the container and
closed it.

Then he ran to tell his mother what had happened.

CHAPTER 25

Claire found Tyrone sleeping in the conference room. The poor man was sitting in a chair, his head pitched forward on the table, cradled by his arms. It was five in the morning and the sun was coming in through the blinds, dappling his dark face. A cup of half-drunk coffee was next to his head. She needed to wake him and tell him what she had figured out.

Finding a last cup of coffee stewing in the coffee-maker, she poured it into his emptied cup. Then she walked back to the conference room and shook him.

He jumped and made a deep noise in his throat.

"Sorry," she said.

"Oh, God, I'm still here," he said, looking around.

She handed him the coffee. "Are you getting up or going back to your room to sleep?"

"The air conditioner in my room still isn't fixed. I figured I'd sleep better here than there. I'm getting up. I think I managed to get a few hours." He sniffed the coffee and mumbled, "This stuff smells singed." Then he drank it.

"What's going on with the finger?" Claire asked him.

"It's on ice."

"What?"

"Literally. Some specialist is coming to look at it. We've checked the hospitals, put out an APB, women's shelters, et cetera. No one has turned up with a finger cut off."

"God, that makes me sick. I wonder who the person is."

"I wonder how they are."

Claire sat down next to him. "Tyrone, I figured something out. I think there was another person at the Schulers' when they were murdered—someone who survived the massacre."

He closed his eyes and rolled his eyes around and then opened them wide. "Another person? Tell me."

So she told him what she had discovered.

He squeezed his mouth tight; then broke it open in a smile. "Takes a woman to count the plates."

"Well, in all fairness the plates were easier to see in the photograph that Folger had in his scrapbook than in the photos in the file."

"We've got to find this person."

Claire nodded.

"It could be our guy, the pesticide guy." Tyrone looked over at her. "Any ideas?"

"The person who comes to mind is Lowman, Earl Lowman. He always claimed that he went over to return something he had borrowed; but what if that was just a story; what if he was actually there when it happened? What if he was responsible?"

"We'll just have to ask him."

"I've been trying to get ahold of him."

"Well, he's in town."

"Lowman?"

"Yeah, he called late last night or early this morning from the hospital. He's arriving soon." Tyrone looked at his watch. "He said he'd be here around eight. He said he wants to tell us what happened that day. What really happened."

* * *

The sheriff's department was in the new building. They had been working on it when he had left the department twenty years ago. It perched up on the hill overlooking the town, although it didn't have much of a view. Earl Lowman sat in his car and blew on the cup of coffee he had picked up at the Burger King in town. A fast-food joint in Durand. Who woulda thought?

Marie and he had come home from the hospital about two in the morning. She had made up the couch for him to sleep on. The kids had awakened him when they were getting ready for school, but he managed to keep them quiet enough so they didn't wake up Marie. She had still been sleeping when he left. He had called the hospital and they said that Andy was eating his breakfast. He left a note for Marie so she would know right away that Andy was doing fine.

And now here he sat, about to do what it was starting to feel like he had come back to Durand to do. Tell the truth. How had he made such a mess of things? He had been so young. Would anyone understand? What could they do to him now? Throw him in jail for obstructing the law at best, sentence him to life for killing someone at worst. Take away his badge, when he had given it up years ago. Fine him. Whatever it was, he didn't mind. He had his son back and a family to get to know. If he had to go to jail, he'd just as soon it would be in Wisconsin, where they could come and see him.

He finished his coffee and wiped his face with his hands. It wouldn't get any easier for waiting. Getting out of his car, he checked his back pocket for his wallet. Then he walked into the sheriff's department.

When he gave his name, the young woman behind the counter called one of the deputies.

A dark-haired woman came out of a back room and

introduced herself. "I'm Claire Watkins, the investigator for the county. Can I get you something to drink?"

"No, thanks. Just finished my coffee."

She brought him into a large back room with a black man sitting at a long table. The man stood and shook his hand. "I'm Sean Tyrone, from DCI, Department of Criminal Investigation."

"You been sleeping in your suit?" Earl asked.

"It's been a long night."

"I hear you." Earl sat down at the table. "You want me to tell my story."

"You comfortable with us taping this?" Watkins asked.

"Sure. That's the way to do it."

She pressed a button on the tape player sitting on the table in front of him. "Should I ask you questions?"

"Let's start that way," he agreed.

"Could you state your full name?"

"Earl Anthony Lowman. Currently residing in Tucson, Arizona. I was a deputy sheriff for the Pepin County sheriff's department for thirty years."

"Can you tell us what happened at the Schuler farm on July the seventh, 1952?"

"In 1952 I was twenty-five years old. I had been working for the sheriff for maybe a year. I didn't know what I was doing." He stopped.

Watkins leaned toward him and Tyrone tapped a pencil on the table. They waited. They didn't care about his excuses. He might as well skip them.

"It was a hot day," he remembered. "Crisp and hot. Not too humid. I had borrowed a saw from Otto Schuler and decided to walk it over there. That was pretty unusual. No one walked much in those days. Guess they don't now either. I had on my uniform. I had just gotten home from work and hadn't changed yet. I was newly married and my wife was making dinner. I told her I'd be back in fifteen, twenty minutes.

"When I walked down the driveway to the Schuler place, no one was about, but that didn't surprise me. It was after five thirty and this was a farm family. They were probably inside eating. But then when I got to the door, I called out and nobody answered. The door was wide open. This wasn't unusual. No one locked their doors. But I was surprised I couldn't raise anyone. I called again. Then I stuck my head in the door."

Earl stopped for a moment. He could see it all. The scene came up in front of his eyes like he was there again. He had remembered it so many times it was part of his body. "Maybe I could use something to drink. Some water would be good."

Watkins went to the door and asked someone to bring in some bottles of water.

"Sorry about your son," Tyrone said.

"He's come around. He's doing better. I think he's going to be fine. He's a strong guy."

"That's great."

"Yeah, sometimes it breaks your way and sometimes it doesn't."

Watkins came back in with three bottles of water and handed them around. "So you were just walking into the kitchen."

"Yes. You know what I saw if you've seen the photographs from the crime scene."

"Let's hear you describe it."

"Well, first I saw Bertha Schuler. She was a lovely woman. Beautiful plain face, wonderful smile. Everyone fell in love with her. She was lying on the floor. Someone had shot a hole the size of a fist in her chest. Not too far from her was the baby. They were dead. There was no question of that. I called the sheriff's office. Told them what I found."

"Did you look around?"

"Not right away. I was sick, I was scared, I didn't know what to do. I wanted someone else to be there with me. I had never seen anything like what was in front of me and have never since." He took a sip of water.

"And then?" Tyrone nudged.

"I was outside, breathing the air and trying to figure out what to do, when Mr. Schuler walked out."

Tyrone's pencil dropped on the table. Claire set down her water bottle. They both said, "What?"

"He had a gun in his hands."

"Was it aimed at you?"

"No. I think by then he felt like he had done his work. He looked at me and said, 'I killed them.' 'All of them?' I asked. He said yes. I asked him why. He stood above me on the steps and said, 'I can't make it work. We shouldn't be here. Lindstrom is trying to take our land. I cannot fight him. Folger and Wahlund are threatening to run us out of town. It has been too hard and I wanted my family all to be safe. Now they will go to heaven and I don't have to worry.' He handed me the gun. 'You have come along in time, my friend. Will you please shoot me?' "

"He asked you to shoot him?"

"Yes."

"Did you?"

"Not at first. I tried to talk to him. But it became clear that his life was over. He had killed everything that had meant anything to him."

"Did he tell you why he cut off their fingers?"

"Yes, he said to keep them with him. He wanted to have part of them with him because he said he would not be going to heaven. He knew that."

"Then did you shoot him?"

Earl felt tears come to his eyes. This was the hard part to describe, but he would try. "He asked me so nicely. Calmly. He told me what a favor I would be doing him. He said he was going to go hang himself in the barn or shoot his own head off, but now I could save him that. I told him I couldn't. He looked at me sadly and then he turned and started to walk toward the barn. I had the gun in my hands. I turned and saw Bertha lying on the floor, her hand reaching out toward the baby. I watched Otto for a moment and then I shot him in the back."

"By this time the sheriff was coming?"

"Yeah, as soon as I shot Otto Schuler, I knew I couldn't tell anyone what I had done. They wouldn't understand. I hardly did. I threw the gun down into the cistern."

"What about the fingers?"

"When I came back, they were gone."

"What? The fingers were gone? What had happened to them?"

"I never figured that out. All I could think was that maybe an animal came and got them."

Watkins said, "Or maybe someone took them."

Earl looked at her. "Who?"

"I think someone else was at the farm, someone who had come for dinner, and they got away."

"Who could that have been?"

Watkins went over what he had said. "You said you had your uniform on and they saw you shoot Otto Schuler. Maybe they thought you had killed everyone. No wonder they wouldn't come forward if they thought a deputy had killed the family. Maybe they didn't feel safe telling the sheriff."

Tyrone jumped in. "Did you tell anyone what happened?"

"My wife. I finally had to tell my wife. She understood, or she said she did. When she was dying, she wanted me to tell the sheriff what I had done, but I wouldn't. My son learned about it and he turned against me. We fought over it after my wife died and didn't talk for many years. I'm ready to take what I deserve."

"Why should we believe this version?"

Earl knew they would ask him that. "I didn't have to come forward. I could have stayed living peacefully down in Tucson. You'll find the gun in the cistern. And you can ask my son."

Harold got to the newspaper office early. He hadn't slept well at all. Agnes shook him awake several times in the night, telling him he'd better start breathing again. She was on him all the time, claiming he had sleep apnea and that occasionally he quit breathing entirely in his sleep. "Doesn't bother me," he'd tell her.

He got to the office early, but he didn't feel very rested. He decided he'd have another cup of coffee. Agnes had him on a restricted diet of one cup of coffee in the morning. She thought that might help reduce his sleep apnea. But he missed guzzling away at coffee all morning. Another cup wouldn't hurt.

He went out to help himself to the pot that Sarah had started when she got in. She was going over some copy and looked up as he walked by. "What's going to happen today?" she asked.

"That's the sixty-four-thousand-dollar question." When he saw her puzzled face, he realized he was talking like an oldster, using expressions that she wasn't familiar with. But he *was* an oldster. "Water, the note said. He'll poison the water."

"I saw the deputies by the water tower."

"I know. I'm not sure that's where he'll go. I thought maybe the river, but I just don't think that would do much. Plus, it would all flow away. He wants to do something we won't forget."

When he looked up from talking to Sarah, he saw that the deputy Claire Watkins had walked in with an African American man in a suit. *Handsome guy. Wonder what he's doing here?* She introduced him as working for the Wisconsin crime department.

Claire asked Harold if they could go into his office and pick his brain.

"Best to do it in the office," Harold said. "Less messy that way."

When they all sat down, she told him about the pointing finger that had been dropped off at the sheriff's department. The coffee turned in his stomach. She told him about how she had counted the plates on the Schulers' table and had found one too many. He cursed himself for not ever noticing that. Then she told him that Earl Lowman was back in town.

"His son is recovering. He came out of his coma."

"Thank the Lord for small blessings."

"Lowman says that the killer was Otto Schuler," Claire told him, then continued, "and he said that he shot Schuler because Schuler asked him to. He's kept this secret all these years. Hard to believe."

"I'm supposed to say that," Harold reprimanded her. "Where does that leave us?"

"I think it leaves us with someone out there who wants to know all this and no way to get the information to them in time. Can you print a special edition of the paper?"

Harold thought about it for a moment, calculating what it would take. "We could do a one-sheeter that would hit the streets by late afternoon."

"Let's try it. We've decided to go public with everything. Lowman's role in the killings, the fact that we know someone else was at the dinner."

"We'll start writing it up immediately. Whatever you've got."

Claire looked at him. "Who do you think might have been the other diner at the Schulers' that night?"

Harold didn't have to think too long. "The person that immediately comes to mind is Bertha's sister, Louise Wahlund. But she's dead."

"I talked to Carl Wahlund already. Would he have known?"

"Maybe. I think the person to talk to is her daughter, Arlene. She lives close by her dad. I can give you the address. She and her mom were mighty tight. As I recall, she was born right around the Schuler murders. Maybe her mother told her something."

CHAPTER 26

—|—

"I don't think it could have been my mom," Arlene Rendquist told Claire. She had insisted that Claire and Tyrone sit down at her kitchen table for a cup of coffee. They had to have a piece of coffee cake that had just come out of the oven, she said. Claire blessed her. A cup of coffee and a piece of coffee cake would keep her going for another couple of hours.

After setting down steaming mugs of coffee in front of each of them, Arlene poured herself a cup of coffee and added a good slug of milk to it and then a heaping teaspoon of sugar. She saw Tyrone watching her production and she broke out into a big smile. "I like to make my coffee a full meal."

She cut them both big pieces of coffee cake and then a smaller piece for herself. "I'm watching my figure," she explained. Claire liked this woman who told you what she was doing and why she was doing it.

"But back to your question of who had dinner with the Schulers that night. My mom wasn't feeling too good, at least that's what I've been told. Having me was hard on her. In those days, women still gave birth at home, especially when they lived on a farm and the hospital was a good half hour away. But Mom was having such a hard time of it that Dad brought her in to the hos-

pital. I'm pretty sure she and I were still there on the day
that the Schulers were killed."

Claire took a bite of the coffee cake and found it to be
absolutely delicious, a slight taste of cinnamon. She had
to bring her mind back to her questions. "This is excellent coffee cake. Thanks again. What about your dad?
Might he have gone over there to eat—considering that
your mom was in the hospital?"

Arlene shook her head. "I don't know a lot about
what went on, but from what I can gather my dad and
Otto Schuler didn't get along. My dad didn't like Germans. He made a slight exception for his own wife, but
not always. I remember as a kid him yelling at her if she
tried to talk German to any of us. Makes me mad now
when I think about it. But the war was hard on everyone. They taught him to kill Germans, and it's hard to
not hate them for a while, I guess. Him and Chuck Folger were thick as thieves in those days."

"Did they do anything in particular to Mr. Schuler?"

"The way my mom told it to me when I was old
enough to understand, they hounded him. Bad-mouthed
him around town. Didn't help him out when he was har-
vesting. My poor mom. It must have made her feel awful
that her husband wouldn't help out her brother-in-law. I
know she loved her sister very much."

"Did your mom ever suspect your dad had anything
to do with the murders?"

Arlene picked up her spoon and stirred her coffee.
"She might have. My dad has always been quite close-
mouthed. Mom might not have been able to get anything out of him. And I'm sure she figured she needed
him. She had no skills, except as a farmwife; she had no
money, except what he gave her. The land they had inherited went right into the farm. I doubt she could have
taken that away from him if she had even thought of di-

vorcing him. Plus, they were Catholic. Divorce was un-
heard of. My mother found her happiness in her children. In the end, my parents tolerated each other."

"Was your dad happy to get the Schuler land?"

"Yes, a farmer's always glad to get more land. Because
it was contiguous with his own, it was easy for him to
handle. But he let the house just about fall down. I was
so happy when he decided to let someone live in that old
place. Another few years and it wouldn't have been
worth much."

Claire thought of the Daniels family living in the house
and farming some of the land. "What made him change
his mind?"

"My mom died. It made me think that he had done
it for her. Kept the place empty so she wouldn't have to
see another family grow up in it. Maybe he was more
thoughtful than I would have guessed."

Meg was glad to hear from her mom. This was the third
day of her visit with her grandparents and she was having a good time, but part of her was all the time thinking about her mother. Not exactly worrying, but a niggle
was always there. Like a little song that went on and on
in her head.

When she heard the phone ring, she stood up from the
game she was playing and waited to hear Grandma get
the phone, have a little conversation, and then holler,
"Meggy, it's for you."

Her grandparents called her Meggy and she let them.
She figured they were too old to change their ways, and
also she thought it was nice to have special names for
people. They were the only people who called her Meggy
and that worked for her. She would hate that name if
everyone called her it. It sounded like a name for a little

kid, and that was probably what she would always be
for her grandparents.

"Hi, Mom, where are you?"

"Hi, Meg. I'm at work."

"Figured. How's it going?"

Her mom didn't say anything for a moment, and Meg
knew she was working too hard. She could hear it in her
voice, the way her mom sounded tight and tense, her
words coming out in bursts.

"Not bad." Her mother tried to be cheerful. "I bet
you're having a great time."

"Not bad," Meg mimicked her mom. They could both
play this game. But she was having a good time. "We
went to the zoo yesterday."

"What did you see?"

"Everything. We even went on the elevated train and
saw all the animals out in the wild. I liked that the best.
We were enclosed in glass and the animals got to run
free. It seems more like the way it's supposed to be. I
even got a cupcake on the train. One of the kids was
having a birthday party and they had an extra cupcake."

"A birthday party?" her mom said, as if she were
waking up from a nap.

"Yeah, you know, a celebration when it's your birthday."

"That might be it, Meg. A birthday party. Another
kid."

Meg was getting worried. Her mom was rambling.
"Mom, what are you talking about?"

"I think I just figured something out."

"Good."

"Listen, sweetie. I gotta go. This is going to be over
soon, I hope. I'll talk to you tonight or tomorrow."

"Love you, Mom."
"Me, too. Bunches and bunches."

After noon, Deputy Watkins had called Harold and told him it couldn't have been Arlene's mother, as she had been in the hospital. She told him that she was thinking it might be a kid, and that made Harold remember a strange conversation he had had with an odd little boy not too long after the murders. He mentioned it to Claire and told her he'd call her back if he could remember the kid's name.

Harold remembered the conversation so well because he had told it to Agnes and then he had even written it down. He had thought of turning it into a piece for the paper, but it had seemed too dark, considering how recent the Schuler murders had been, so he had never done anything with it. He was pretty sure he had thrown the piece away in one of his cleansings that happened every few years.

The conversation had happened at the cemetery, when the Schulers were being buried. Harold was standing way toward the back and had started to walk away when he noticed a young boy staring in the opposite direction from the service. The boy, who must have been around six or seven, asked Harold if he knew that there were 236 gravestones in the cemetery.

Harold said, "No, how do you know that?"

The boy stared at him unblinking and then said, "I counted them. Do you know why they have gravestones?"

Harold had thought he knew, but he decided he was more interested in hearing the boy's thoughts on the subject. "Why?"

"So the bodies don't fly away. The gravestones pin them down like bugs."

Harold asked him if he had ever played with the Schuler kids.

The boy spit out, "Never. My dad says no. Krauts, he calls them. I'm no kraut lover."

The nasty words seemed so strange coming from a young child's mouth.

"They seemed like nice people to me."

"But they died."

"Yes, that was too bad."

"Maybe they'll come back," the boy had suggested.

"I don't think so."

"Do bones ever grow new bodies?"

Harold hadn't thought too much about the question. At the time, Harold had just assumed that the odd child was thinking about the buried bodies all around them. "Not that I know of."

What Harold couldn't remember was who the boy had been. On the way home from the cemetery, he told Agnes about the incident and had described the young boy, and she had known him. She might remember. He called her from his desk.

"Peabodys'," she answered the phone.

"Agnes, do you remember that strange little boy I talked to?"

"Hello, dear. Nice of you to call. Which strange little boy? There've been so many in your life."

"You know, after the Schuler funeral. I told you about our conversation. And you thought you knew who I was talking about."

"Remind me a bit."

"I asked him if he had played with the Schuler kids and he said never, that his dad didn't want him to be a kraut lover."

"Vaguely. What did he look like?"

This was where Harold ran into trouble. He could remember words much better than physical appearances. "He was a youngster, kinda skinny. Wearing shorts and a bow tie."

"Oh, yes. The bow tie. That would have been Paul Lindstrom."

"Why does the bow tie make you remember who it was?"

"I don't know. I just remember thinking how cute he looked in his little bow tie. His mother always kept him well dressed. She rather coddled him. The father was not a very nice man, but his mother took care of the boy."

"Paul Lindstrom. Yes, it would have been Paul Lindstrom. He still lives there in that same farmhouse that he grew up in, doesn't he?"

"I believe so. He and his wife. A pair of odd birds. They keep to themselves. Why? What has he done?"

CHAPTER 27

Claire left Tyrone and Lowman staring over the plat map, trying to see where there was a water supply the pesticide guy could pollute. She had told them she was going out to the Lindstroms', to call her if they came up with anything. This trip was probably a long shot. Harold Peabody had called her back, all excited about some conversation he remembered that he had had with Paul Lindstrom when Lindstrom was a little boy.

But it could pan out—Lindstrom was the right age to have played with the Schuler children, and he lived so close by. She had explained that she had already talked to the man once, but said she would go out and talk to him again. After that, she planned on driving around the farms that were close to the Schulers'. Maybe she'd see something.

When she drove up to the Lindstroms' it looked pretty quiet. She got out of her squad car and walked up to the house. She knocked on the screen door, but no one answered. She could hear voices coming from inside, so she knocked again. Nothing. She pushed the door open and yelled inside, "Hello? Anybody home?"

The voices didn't even pause. That was when Claire realized she was hearing a television. Maybe Mrs. Lindstrom had it on so loud that she couldn't hear her knocking. She walked farther into the house.

The messiness of the kitchen surprised her. It wasn't horridly messy, but dishes were strewn on the table and left in the sink. When she had been to the house before everything had been so spotless. Maybe Mrs. Lindstrom wasn't feeling so good.

She looked into the living room, but no one was there and the television was off. She could still hear the sound of a television, and when she walked back into the kitchen, she thought it was coming from the door by the pantry.

Claire opened the door and looked down a set of stairs. The sound was obviously coming from the basement.

"Hello?" she shouted down the stairs.

No one answered.

This was all making her uneasy. Something wasn't right here. It was lunchtime. Where were the Lindstroms? Why was the television on in the basement?

She patted her gun, then felt silly for doing it. Maybe they had gone into town and left the television running. She'd just check out the basement and leave them a note, asking them to call her when they returned.

Cautiously, she started down the basement stairs. And when she turned the corner at the bottom, she saw the television set. And then noticed there was someone sitting in a chair in front of it.

"Hello?" Claire said, but the person didn't turn at her voice.

When she got closer, she could tell it was Mrs. Lindstrom. Her wispy brown hair was out of the curlers and hung down to her shoulders. Her head was tipped forward. Claire walked around to see her. It looked like the woman was sleeping.

When Claire reached forward to shake her, she saw that Mrs. Lindstrom was tied into the chair she was sitting on. She was wearing the same housedress that she had been wearing when Claire had seen her last. One of her hands was clasped inside the other. This was all very bad.

Claire prayed the woman still had all her fingers.

"Mrs. Lindstrom?" Claire shook her shoulder.

Someone on the television talked about the problem of hemorrhoids and told you how to cure them.

The woman stirred and looked up at Claire. In a whisper she asked, "Where is he?"

"Who, your husband?"

"Yes, is he here?"

"I haven't seen him." Claire knelt down by her side and asked, "Are you all right? Did he hurt you?"

Mrs. Lindstrom uncurled her hands and reached out to Claire. "We've got to find him. He's acting so crazy."

Claire asked her, "What did he do?"

Mrs. Lindstrom raised her hand to her mouth, remembering. "He cut his finger off. After he tied me up down here, he took a hatchet and lopped it off. He did it right in front of me. He said he needed a witness, but didn't want me to tell anyone. He said he'd be back to untie me. What's wrong with him?"

Claire felt a deep shiver go through her whole body. With shaking fingers, she started untying the woman from the chair. "Why did he do that, Mrs. Lindstrom? Did he tell you what he intended to do?"

Mrs. Lindstrom shook her head and her face crumpled. She started to sob and spoke brokenly through her tears. "He's been a good man. I know that he has odd thoughts, but he's not mean. He said he had to find out the truth. He said maybe they needed another finger; maybe that would make it right. I didn't understand why he was doing it. I tried to stop him, but he left me here. He left me and he hasn't come back. He said he would go to the well."

"The well?"

"I'm afraid he's going to kill himself."

"I know what that is. I've been looking at it and looking at it, trying to remember what was there." Lowman snapped his finger down on the map. "That's a reverse well."

Tyrone looked down at where the man was pointing. He could see a circled X on Schuler's land that was near the edge of the Lindstrom property. "That mark right there?"

"Yes, that means a well, and as I recall that was a reverse well."

Tyrone had to admit his ignorance. "What is that?"

Lowman lifted his grizzled head. The man had been going over the whole map with Tyrone, explaining all he knew. "Just what it sounds like. Instead of bringing water up out of the ground it takes it into the ground."

"Why?"

"To drain the land. To make it fit for farming. Doubt it's used anymore."

"Could it be used?"

"I would expect so. Unless they filled it in. But if you wanted to poison a whole group of people, especially all those living right around the Schuler homestead, that would be a nifty way to do it. Just dump the pesticides down the well and it would go right into the aquifer."

Tyrone gave Lowman a look.

Lowman explained, "The water table. All these farms, as I mentioned to you before, are on wells. They all draw their water out of the same body of water under the ground. It's pretty far down there, because they're up on the bluff. They probably had to dig about three hundred feet to get to the water table, but it's there. And if the pesticides were dumped into it, it might poison a whole group of wells."

"Sounds like what we've been looking for."

Tyrone's cell phone rang. When he answered he heard Claire's voice. "Lindstrom. It's Lindstrom. That was his own finger he cut off. He tied up his wife and left her in the basement."

"Shit. Where is he?"

"Mrs. Lindstrom told me that she thought Paul had gone someplace not too far away. She said something about a well."

"Yeah, I think we've located it. I'll put Lowman on and he can give you directions. We'll meet you there."

"I hate to leave her, but I think I'd better try to stop him before it's too late."

Lowman got on the phone and told Claire where she would find the farm road that led to the reverse well. Then he handed the phone back to Tyrone.

"Listen," Claire told him. "This guy is crazy, but I don't think he's armed or even that dangerous. Let's try to bring him in peacefully. If he's even there. I'll meet you at the well."

Claire parked her car on the dirt road when she saw Lindstrom's truck up ahead. She sat in the car for a few moments and took deep breaths. Maybe this would go real easy. She could walk up on him and bring him in. She got out of her car and silently shut the door and started walking.

When she got to Lindstrom's truck, she looked around to see if she could tell where Paul had gone. Off to her right, she could see a path leading down through a ditch. At the end of it was an opening. It looked like a cellar door going down into the ground. A strange sound came out of the hole in the ground, a clicking and then a whine. Lindstrom must have started up the pump. The noise was good; it would cover up any sounds she might make approaching the well. She hoped she was in time to stop him from dumping any of the pesticides down into the water.

After making sure she had her gun, she moved forward, careful where she was putting her feet. When she was a few steps away, she stopped and readied herself. She hoped she would see him and the situation before he would see her standing above him.

Down in the pit a metal arm was rising and lowering. She saw it and then realized it was part of the pumping system. An old system. She stepped up to the edge of the well pit and didn't see Lindstrom down below.

She heard something behind her and then someone pushed her forward into the open pit of the well. Claire tried to grab for something and then remembered to protect her face. She hit the ground with a sickening force. Darkness swallowed her.

When she came to, she was sitting against the dirt wall with Lindstrom squatting in front of her, holding a gun in his hands—her gun—but it wasn't pointed at her. The gun was just dangling loose in his hands. She saw that he had a bandage covering his left hand.

Claire shook her head. Her shoulder hurt, her ribs ached, her head was spinning, and her ankle throbbed. She didn't think anything was broken, but she was banged up. She couldn't think about her aches and pains at that moment.

She held out her hand. "Don't do anything," she told Paul Lindstrom.

"Like what?" he asked, genuinely wanting to know.

"Make anything worse," she finished lamely.

"What are you doing here?" he asked.

"I just came out to talk to you about some new information we had on the Schulers."

"How did you find me?"

Time to lie, Claire thought. It wouldn't help the situation for him to know she knew what he had done to his wife. "I saw your truck go down this way so I just followed you."

He nodded. Seemed to buy it. "What new information?"

"Well, we have evidence that shows that someone else was at the Schulers' the day they were murdered."

He nodded again. She needed to get him talking. An outright question might do the trick. "Were you at the Schulers' when they all were killed?"

Lindstrom didn't say anything at first. She could tell he was thinking pretty hard because his eyes moved down to the ground. "I can't say."

Claire decided to step around that question. She felt that he had been programmed not to reveal that part of what had happened. She decided to just assume that he was there. "We know there was another plate set for dinner and it was Arlette's birthday. Were you invited to the party?"

At the word *party,* he lifted his head. "My dad told my mother to never let me play with the Schulers. He said they were bad people. But he was gone. He went to Milwaukee. I begged my mother. I wanted to go to the birthday party. I was good friends with Schubert and we never got to play together."

"Do you want to tell me what happened that day? What you saw happen at the farm?"

"I didn't see much at first. Just heard the gunshots go off. Then the man came upstairs and shot all the other children."

Claire let those words sink in. He had been there when they were murdered. "Where were you?"

"I hid in the closet."

"Good for you."

"I was used to hiding when my dad got mad."

"It saved your life." Claire pushed him to continue. "What did you see?"

"I didn't see who shot the children because I closed my eyes. When the noise was done I went downstairs, and that's when I saw the deputy kill Mr. Schuler. He shot him in the back."

"Did you take the fingers?"

He nodded.

"Why?"

Lindstrom shook his head as if it were too hard to say, too hard to explain his actions.

"You want the truth?" she asked him. "We have Earl Lowman at the sheriff's office. He was the deputy you saw at the Schulers'. He's told us everything that happened that day. Things you're not aware of. Do you want to talk to him?"

"It's too late," Lindstrom said, gesturing toward the bags of pesticide that were sitting next to the well shaft. "I'm through waiting. They all need to be punished."

"I think you need to hear what he has to tell you. I think it will make you feel better about what happened that day. You've been blaming someone who really didn't do everything you thought he did."

"Lowman?"

"You never knew who he was?"

"I didn't see his face. All I knew was that he was wearing a deputy's uniform. And that he killed them all."

"He didn't."

"Who did?"

Claire didn't know what he wanted to hear. She would

have told him almost anything to get him out of the well pit and headed back to town. "Who do you think killed them?"

Lindstrom shook his head as if he were weary from thinking about it. "I was afraid."

"Afraid of what?"

"Somehow I knew it was my dad's fault. Even though everyone said he was in Milwaukee, I thought maybe he had paid the deputy to kill them."

"Why?" Claire asked.

"Because he hated them so much. He did such mean things to them. He killed their animals. He poisoned their crops. I couldn't stop him. He wanted them to leave, to go away. He made their lives hell." Paul Lindstrom shook from the rage that he had held in for so many years. "My father made life hell for my mother and me."

Claire realized that Paul Lindstrom had actually seen the bigger truth all along. His father had probably had a huge hand in the murders of the Schuler family—driving Otto Schuler to do what he had done. "Well, I don't think your dad helped matters at all, but he didn't kill them or ask the deputy to do it. It was actually Otto Schuler who killed everyone in his family except himself."

"Schubert's father? But he was a nice man."

"He probably wasn't well and he was scared that he was going to lose his farm. He didn't think he could take care of his family anymore. We'll never know what caused him to kill his family, but I don't think he did it out of any meanness."

"Why did the deputy kill Mr. Schuler?"

"Because Mr. Schuler asked him to. He didn't want to live after what he had done. I'm not saying that what Deputy Lowman did was right, but he didn't come to the farm intending to do anything like that. You are the only witness. Would you be willing to testify about what Lowman has done?"

Lindstrom got up and appeared to be agitated. "I couldn't do that. I'm not supposed to talk about it."

There was something odd going on. Sometimes Paul Lindstrom acted like an old taciturn farmer and then sometimes he seemed more like a young boy. "Who told you that?"

"My mother. She made me promise."

"I think it would be okay. Everyone knows what happened now. You wouldn't be telling on anyone." Claire could see he was close to going along with her. She decided it was time to play mom with him. "Paul, I think you need to have someone look at your hand. Does it hurt?"

He looked at her and she could see tiredness and pain in his eyes. He nodded his head.

"Do you think you could help me up?" Claire put her hands down on the ground and tried to stand. Her ankle felt like it wouldn't hold her. She started to fall.

Lindstrom ran toward her, holding out the gun.

Then she heard a noise above her. When she looked up she saw Tyrone looking down at them. In an instant she knew what he was seeing: Lindstrom with a gun in his hands coming toward her.

She yelled to Tyrone to stop but at the same time the sound came out of her mouth, Tyrone shot his gun and the blast in the well pit was like a sonic boom. She felt it in her body as well as heard it ring in her ears.

Paul Lindstrom fell down on his knees. The gun flew out of his hands. Claire stepped in front of him so they couldn't shoot again. She bent over him and saw blood spurting out of his neck—and then he toppled to the dark soil.

CHAPTER 28

"I won't quit my job."

Rich put his Red Wing boots up on the railing of the porch overlooking what he liked to think of as his spread, his family's estate. "Good," he said finally, as he knew Claire was waiting for him to say something.

"Do you want me to?"

"Sometimes."

"I don't ask you to give up pheasant farming."

"No, you've never asked me to give up my birds."

"I know you don't like that I'm a deputy sheriff."

"That's not completely true. Sometimes I like it a lot. I don't like worrying about you."

Claire moved her cast-covered leg so that she could sit more comfortably in the wooden chair. "Would you get me a napkin?" she asked. "I appear to have dripped on my shirt."

They were eating chips and hot sauce. Claire had managed to get up the stairs with her crutches, but then sat in the chair she was in and didn't want to move again. She said her armpits were already sore from the crutches. The doctors had told her she'd be wearing the cast for a good month or so.

Rich brought her the napkin, then stood over her. "Have you told Meg about your broken leg yet?"

"Not really. She'll see it soon enough. I didn't want to ruin her vacation."

"So how is Paul Lindstrom doing?"

"He's going to be fine. He nearly bled out from that gunshot wound, but he's a tough guy. His wife went over to see him the other day. She seems to have forgiven him."

"What will they do to him?"

"Well, I would be surprised if a jury wouldn't see how mentally ill he is. I would think he'll be spending time in the psych ward."

"What about Lowman?"

"The county attorney is going over everything. I think he's looking at minimal time. I don't even think they're going to be charging him with much, maybe negligent homicide. He might serve a year or two."

They both sat quietly for a moment; then Claire said, slapping her cast, "You won't have to worry about me for the next month or so. They've got me tied to my desk. Oh, did I tell you I got a call from Ray Sorenson today?" She had told Rich about what he and his girlfriend had done in the storage area of the Farmer's Cooperative.

He nodded for her to continue.

"Looks like they're going to be having a retirement party for Chuck Folger, the agronomist. Ray sounded awfully glad he wouldn't be working with the man anymore."

"We have one more thing to talk about."

"We do?"

Rich took the box out of his pocket. "The ring. Even though we're not getting engaged to be married, I'd like to give it to you." He walked over to Claire and knelt next to her. "Would you like to wear my ring?"

"I would love to." She held out her hand and he slipped the small diamond on it.

They kissed and for a moment Rich was sure he smelled the sweet scent of roses in the air.

July 7, 1952

She made him get down on his knees on the floor of her bedroom and promise to never tell anyone else what he had told her. "They'll get us, Pauly, if you tell. They'll come and kill us, too."

"What about Dad?"

"Never tell your father anything. He would be so angry, who knows what he would do."

She cried and held him in her arms and rocked him and called him her baby. "You're all I've got, Pauly. You're the only person I've ever loved."

When she finally let him go, they ate dinner and he went upstairs to bed. But he couldn't stop thinking about what had happened, about the dead children laid out on the floors of their house. He had to do something. He had to try to save them.

After he heard his mother go to bed, he sneaked down the stairs and went outside. It was a warm summer night with a big full moon. Fireflies twinkled in the long grass and over the fields.

He walked around the barn and found his special hiding place. The red tobacco tin was right where he had left it. He knew what he had to do.

He went to the edge of the field and he made six holes.

Then he opened the lid of the container and put a finger in each hole and covered them over gently with dirt. Maybe bones grew people like seeds grew corn. All he could do was hope that they would grow into the people they had once been.

ACKNOWLEDGMENTS

I have owned a house in Pepin County for going on fourteen years, and I must acknowledge and thank all my neighbors and friends who have made my time there so satisfying. Also, thanks to Pepin County Sheriff's Department for their excellent job of safeguarding the citizenry.

Two writing groups must be mentioned for all the good advice they've given me. In Arizona: Elizabeth Gunn, Sheila Cottrell, Earl McGill, J. M. Hayes, and Margaret Falk. In Minnesota: thanks to Becky Bohan, Joan Petroff, Tom Rucker, Margaret Shryer, Jean Ward, and Deborah Woodworth.

Then there're my usual supporters: Ray DiPrima, Robin LaFortune, Dodie Logue, Mary Anne Svoboda, and the great man by my side, Pete Hautman.

NOTE: The two pesticides I mentioned throughout this book are not real, but are based on research I did on existing products.

If you enjoyed
Bone Harvest,
turn the page for
a sneak peek at
Mary Logue's upcoming novel,

Poison Heart.

Coming in hardcover at bookstores everywhere.
Published by Ballantine Books.

When Patty Jo Tilde heard her husband holler her name, she was inside the house, sitting at the kitchen table, looking at *People* magazine and wondering when Cher's face was going to split wide open from all the plastic surgery she'd had done. Patty Jo had considered a neck tuck. Nothing drastic. She figured she might lose ten years or so. She had turned sixty in May and wouldn't mind being able to pass for fifty.

Walter hollered again, and she could tell the sound was coming from the barn. She thought of ignoring him. Who knew what stupid thing he wanted to show her? When was he going to realize that she didn't need to see every little thing he discovered?

She stood up and walked to the screen door. It was warm out. The wind spun a dust devil in the farmyard.

"Hey," Walter yelled.

She wondered what he needed. After strolling out the door, she walked slowly toward the barn.

When she looked in through the large rolling door, she saw Walter seated on a hay bale, bent over like the old man he was, his hand to his head. She could hear his ragged breathing all the way across the barn. She didn't say anything, just stood and watched.

"Help," he hollered, and bent over as if he had been hit by some force. Then he lifted his head and saw her.

"Patty Jo," he whispered.

She didn't answer him. She had been waiting for this moment for months. She had married hoping it would not be for too long.

"Call." He pointed at his head. He knew what was happening. Walter had suffered a couple of small strokes in the last year. The doctor had told him the next one could be bad.

The stupid old man would take his shirt off when he worked. At eighty, his ribs curved in over his sad belly.

"You'll be fine, Walter. Just take some deep breaths. Told you not to work so hard in this heat."

"I need . . ." He paused and breathed. "Help."

Patty Jo walked over to the shirt and picked it up. Then she handed it to Walter. "Put your shirt on, Walter. I'll go call the doctor."

At her words, he slumped over farther. The shirt slipped from his fingers, then he fell to the barn floor.

Patty Jo stood over him and said, "Don't worry. I'll be right back. You take it easy. I just have to go call the ambulance."

She walked back to the house. She was pretty sure this was it, but she didn't want to take any chances. The doctor had told her that to make sure Walter survived the next stroke, he needed to get to the hospital within the first three hours.

Patty Jo stepped into the kitchen and looked at the clock over the sink. A little after noon. She could say she hadn't found him until close to supper.

She sat back down at the table and picked up the magazine. She heard no more shouts coming from the barn. The dust danced for another moment in the yard, then settled.